BROKEN CROSS
The Exiled Priest

Graham Baugh

 FriesenPress

One Printers Way
Altona, MB R0G 0B0
Canada

www.friesenpress.com

Copyright © 2021 by Graham Baugh
First Edition — 2021

Bobbi Beatty, Editor

This is a work of fiction. Names, characters, places, and incidents either are the product of the author's imagination or are used fictitiously. Any resemblance to actual persons, living or dead, events, or locales is entirely coincidental.

All rights reserved.

No part of this publication may be reproduced in any form, or by any means, electronic or mechanical, including photocopying, recording, or any information browsing, storage, or retrieval system, without permission in writing from FriesenPress.

ISBN
978-1-03-911453-1 (Hardcover)
978-1-03-911452-4 (Paperback)
978-1-03-911454-8 (eBook)

1. Fiction, Religious

Distributed to the trade by The Ingram Book Company

CHAPTER 1

Father Francis and His Church

"What are you doing to me?" Father Francis had been on his knees for an hour. His face was turned to heaven, his eyes full of tears of shame and anger. "Am I just a machine part you bolt on when you need it and then just throw it away when it's no longer useful? Or maybe I'm a computer that operates until it fulfills its function, and then you just turn it off and it finds itself in the city dump? What possible good is it to follow you when all I get is pain and suffering and abuse? I am choking on your will! I bring pain and suffering to everyone around me like Jonah did, and all I ever wanted was to do what I believed to be the right thing.

Where are you Justice? Where are you Compassion? Why do the stupid, insensitive, and intolerant get ahead in this ridiculous institution we've created? Blessed are the stupid, ignorant, and mean, is that the deal? Blessed are the poor in character? I am completely fed up with this. I would rather not follow you than constantly be the laughingstock of the Church." He slowly shook his head in disbelief, and his shoulders slumped with defeat. "I have followed your path since I was twelve years old. I took the path of ordination; I left my family for years when I yearned for my mother and father and to just be a kid. I missed being in a real family to join the Church family. What a joke! If this is supposed to be a family, then there is no more dysfunctional family on the face of the earth."

A deep sigh escaped. "Thanks to my dear brothers in the Church, I am forty-two years old and unemployed with no means of support. I've been thrown out of the Church and called a liar, a fraud, and a heretic. My reputation is in tatters, and I have nowhere to go. And to add insult to injury, you—my Heavenly Father—are behaving exactly like some earthly fathers, including my own. You're nowhere to be found—conveniently off on important business elsewhere. And you don't seem to understand me at all."

He felt anger and indignation blossoming from deep within him. "Forget it, I quit! Find some other sucker to do the work. Find some other dupe, someone bulletproof, to take the verbal bullets! Let the kings, princes, and fools of the Church rule. Why the hell should I care?! I'm finished. I'm done. I have nothing more to give and nothing more to say."

This was not the sort of prayer anyone would expect from a priest, let alone from a brilliant biblical scholar, theologian, and once-recognized academic pillar, but this was the prayer of Father Francis Bauer this very October morning during that early, post-waking hour when consciousness is still fully coalescing. He breathed his prayer aloud at that time when truthfulness is most likely and inhibitions and pretensions have yet to engage.

In the midst of his lament, the unbidden the words of Jesus echoed in his mind:

BROKEN CROSS

God blesses you when you are mocked and persecuted and lied about because you are my people. Be happy about it! For a great reward awaits you in heaven. And remember, the ancient prophets were persecuted too.

Those words pierced his heart. Rather than comfort him, they mocked him. When it is those who know us best that mock and persecute us and lie about us because we do what we honestly believe is right and good, then the words of Jesus create an impossible conundrum. That conundrum made the bile boil in Father Francis' gut. Hypocrisy is always a conundrum, but Church politics, persecution, and mockery condemn all believers to absurdity. As a result, the institution mankind created to showcase God and his kingdom to the world becomes a joke to be laughed at and ridiculed.

What a mess, he thought now as he stood, having ended his prayer, in the shower at the priests' hostel in Rome, the scalding water streaming down his face as his tears refused to do. These hostels were free for traveling priests, and traveling was the key word for Father Francis because he had no choice but to travel now. Had it not been for a loophole he had fallen through during the inquisition he had faced, he would not be a priest today. At least that much had survived the onslaught. He could no longer teach or preach or be a pastor, nor could he hold any office in the Church hierarchy, but he was still a priest. Father Francis was a one-of-a-kind, lowliest-position priest without privilege or portfolio, but he was still a priest.

From childhood, the Church had defined him as a priest. Never had he been anything else. He had always thought of himself as a priest. Now he was trapped in that definition.

His hostel privileges had been revoked, so after today, he would receive no more institutional sustenance. As he shaved, getting ready for the first day of his life in exile, he looked in the mirror at his trim, muscular physique. *At least my training, that the Church frowned upon of course, kept me fit.* He smiled absently at memories of good times with his trainer. Nothing else seemed to be working in his favor. He vigorously scratched his thick, slightly wavy, chestnut-brown hair that showed no signs of gray yet. Staring into the mirror, he wondered how he would eat, where he would sleep, how he would survive. As Jesus had said, he was just like the ancient prophets because it was God's wonderful people that seemed intent on destroying him. But so far, he had felt none of the promised blessing. He felt nothing but lousy: lonely, embarrassed, useless, worthless, unworthy of even life. His life was over, and he had no energy to begin again. He was destined to return home but without the fanfare of his leaving so many years ago.

Lord, why do you not just end my life if I am of no more use? I'm just taking up space on this planet now because I did what you wanted me to do. Yet I would do it again, exactly the same way, because I'm so sure of its rightness, he seethed, his thoughts turning dark in his fury and confusion.

Father Francis' combination of intelligence without arrogance, strength without dominance, and virility without apology was a source of magnetic charm. His air of innocence only compounded this charm. Men found him fascinating. Women found him alluring and adorable. It was precisely Father Francis' quiet charisma that lay at the center of his present predicament. He had been the star pupil of the Gregorian University in Rome at eighteen and had remained there for nine years absorbing the most intensive education the Roman Catholic Church had to offer. Allowed but one trip home to see his family every year, he had been cloistered and programmed in every minutia of life. When those long years had finally ended, he had graduated with the perfect Catholic education—including a relative fluency in six languages—and then over subsequent years, he had developed the perfect Catholic resume. At the height of his career, just before writing his infamous book, he had been appointed the official theologian of a future Vatican council.

Then he had written "The Book" that had become a gamechanger.

During his prayer this morning, he had naturally thought of the Bible story of Joseph in jail. Joseph's jail time was all part of God's plan, according to contemporary biblical interpretation, but the best theology no longer inspired this modern-day rejected and dejected priest.

They would have burned me at the stake if that was still acceptable, he groused to himself sardonically. *Luckily, execution via burning is frowned upon in the twenty-first century.*

His meteoric rise had reversed in a heartbeat when the pope became offended. This pope, determined to unwind all the good the last Vatican council had done and trash all the reforms that had been implemented, had brought the full weight of his authority to bear on the one he considered a rival, a threat. To this pope, who wanted all the power to himself, and his pet cardinals, Father Francis had become a nemesis. To this pope, Francis was a severe problem to be solved, and the pontiff had those at his command who would seek solutions—of all kinds.

Francis had had an inkling he was heading for trouble when his personal theology had begun to adjust and stray from traditional Catholic dogma. As he had studied the Bible and the history of Christianity from its roots and original writings, it had become clear to him the development of institutional churches had had everything to do with men and little, if anything, to do with God. Politics, and the compromises made necessary by political deal-making throughout the centuries, had gradually resulted in the current corporate structure and leadership of twenty-first century Christianity. Even the Protestant churches after the Reformation had developed similar structures. Was God directing all the compromises and political deals between popes, cardinals, monarchs, governments, and Protestant denominational leaders throughout history? The corruption and human casualties of the political deals would seem to indicate God was not a player. Hence, Father Francis had written a book explaining his findings. His book had triggered the beginning of the end for him—and not only as a priest.

The book, simply called, *Church*, was a comprehensive theology of the people of God researched extensively from the most credible sources that referred to the best scholarship Christianity had to offer. Alarmingly, after concluding his research, Father Francis had been unable to find any evidence to support an infallible pope with an all-powerful executive branch of Church government. Nor could he justify, based on the evidence, a professional clergy—particularly an all-male, celibate professional clergy—and a raft of other mainstream principles and policies in the twenty-first century Catholic Church. He had been forced to conclude these unwarranted institutional quirks were the result of wheeling and dealing over the millennia since Pentecost. Bit by bit, the human penchant for organizing, getting along, powerbroking, and acceding to powerbrokers had produced anomalies that could not be justified upon careful study of the Bible.

Francis' friends had warned him he would suffer consequences if his book was ever published, but ignoring the danger, he "did the right thing," and released the book for publication. It had been an instant bestseller, selling millions of copies in ten different languages. It was particularly popular among Catholics searching for answers to their visceral discomfort with their Church experience, but Protestant believers were also powerfully drawn to it because it gave them insight into their own angst and spiritual drift. Francis had suddenly become a Christian celebrity in Europe.

Father Francis' words produced an "aha" moment, for Catholics and Protestants alike. "So that's why I feel this way," they would say to themselves and then to others.

It was because a man of such charm and magnetism had made possible that "aha" moment for so many that had made it imperative the Church hierarchy diminish Father Francis in stature and ensure he never wrote another book. Sadly, he had neither thought of turning the Church upside down nor launching a second Reformation when he had authored the book. Unlike Martin Luther, who had been notoriously antagonistic to the Catholic Church and its hierarchy, Francis' only goal had been to work out his research on the Church on paper, mostly for himself. Publishing the book had just been a natural second step given the nature of his findings. Antagonism had been the last thing on his mind. He had wanted to be helpful. How naïve was that?

+ + +

"Can he just disappear?" interjected one prince of the Church in a secret, closed-door meeting in the dead of night the day after the troublesome Father Francis had been relieved of his duties. "It has been done before with dangerous ones, ones that strayed too far."

"There is plenty of historical precedent for that, but no, he is too well-known and loved by the commoners. These days nothing can be kept secret. If he disappears now, or anytime soon, it will create a scandal the likes of which would be beyond even our ability to control." Cardinal Carducci slouched insolently in his ornately carved chair. His reply was condescending and implied those present were lacking in political acumen, as he had meant it to. He presided over this small gathering as a sovereign would preside over his court. His black robe with scarlet ribbing was made of an exotic blend of silk and vicuna, exquisitely tailored to ooze power. Carducci had the ear of the supreme pontiff and was his closest confidante and ally. The cardinal had ruthlessly cultivated his political rise to the upper echelon of the Roman Catholic Church until he had become the second most powerful human being within it.

"Well, what are we going to do with him then?"

"We have to involve the pontiff. It is his power being eroded. He needs to decide." Carducci dismissed the others with a flick of his hand.

+ + +

As Francis packed his meager possessions in his hostel room, his father figure and mentor, the rumpled Cardinal Massey, arrived. Cardinal Massey was the one American cardinal left after his only American colleague had been forced to resign in disgrace over allegations of past sexual misconduct. Cardinal Massey was a moderate voice for humility and reform in a deafening, ultraconservative clamor for tradition and dominance. He was not viewed within leadership as powerful or particularly influential.

"I'm so sorry I couldn't protect you from them. I did my best, but I failed. You're a threat. I'm American, not Italian, and my words have little weight. They wanted your head and almost got it." He stepped closer to Francis and put a hand on his shoulder. "The Lord protected you from the worst of it, but you must get away from here," he said in a whisper.

"What do you mean get away from here? Rome has been my home since I was a boy." Fear welled up within him.

"There's no safe haven for you here. They weren't able to completely discredit you, and you still have enormous influence among ordinary folk, so you continue to threaten them. That makes Rome dangerous," Massey explained, his voice rising with urgency.

"Not safe?! Surely no one would try to hurt me!"

Massey stood still, his face like stone. "Don't assume anything. You must leave. Go to America where few know you. They won't expect you to go there. I have friends that will help you. Stay away from churches, whatever you do, and don't contact me unless absolutely necessary. I'll keep track of you. It may be safe someday for you to return, but it's not safe now. Here are some things that will help. Now, go quickly."

Cardinal Massey handed Francis a fat black leather portfolio before heading out the door, glancing furtively both ways before leaving. The door shutting behind him sounded to Francis like the door closing on his life.

+ + +

Once on the train to Zurich, Francis opened the leather case and found an envelope containing a cellphone and a hefty sum of money in several currencies. He counted enough to know his vow of poverty had to be suspended for the time being. He would be able to live for a long time on whatever road the Lord was leading him down. The Church may have forsaken him, but at least Cardinal Massey had not. Maybe his life wasn't over after all.

The enclosed note implored him to hurry away and not use the cellphone. But if it rang, he was to answer it. Exhausted by the events of the day, he absently stared out the window at the impossibly green pastoral landscape passing.

+ + +

The lazy rocking of the train to Zurich made him pensive. *What will I do? Where will I go from here? What adventures lay before me?* These were all questions that meandered through his consciousness.

The thought of adventures shocked him and snapped him out of his malaise with a start. An adventure was something he could get excited about. Adventure implied an interesting, even exciting, and perhaps hopeful future.

Where had "adventure" come from? he wondered even as his thoughts continued flowing. *I'm depressed and rightfully so. Life as I have known it is over ... or is it? My sense of adventure has always gotten me into trouble, so where does adventure fit into God's plan? Surely desiring adventure is just a selfish and spiritless emotion. Perhaps it's just a response to boredom? At the same time, how could that be true?* he thought with an inaudible chuckle. *My life is anything but boring, but the thrill of the unknown is still there. Maybe being thrilled by impending change, regardless of risk, is a genetic or spiritual flaw. But hey, flaw or not, it's me.*

Francis' thoughts settled on what America might be like. It would be new for him. *Was it really a place of adventure? Was this a chance for something new and different? Could I be happy in my new circumstances? Could I recover from humiliation and despair? Could I live outside the womb of the Church?*

With his head pressed against the cool window, Francis watched the hills and mountains flash by, and like the countryside, his imagination opened to a new panorama. Maybe he could still be a pastor, even if he had been discarded by the Church. Being pastoral did not depend on position. Rejection by leadership can't stop a willing heart. *Was this the Lord leading?* he wondered. Being pastoral was a state of being, wasn't it, not a profession or a calling. Humanity in every walk of life needed pastors unhindered by the dictates of stereotypes and paradigms. This could be a worthwhile adventure.

+ + +

Carducci sat in the presence of the aging pontiff. The surroundings were extravagantly plush. The walls were of rich, dark exotic woods from all over the world, the furniture massive and ornately carved, and the scarlet carpet deep and luxurious. The appointments and atmosphere of the papal rooms suggested extraordinary wealth and power. The pontiff was old, but he still possessed a personal authority that seeped into the room and was almost overwhelming even for Carducci, who was immune to most intimidation. Pope Paul was a man of subtle physical strength, even in his eighties. The muscles in his arms rippled with a vitality that belied his age. At this moment, the muscles of his face and jaw spoke of intense introspection. He was mulling over a problem with no easy solution.

Carducci's face was a mask of fury. He was purple with rage but trying not to show it.

"Who does he think he is, trying to set your people against you? He is a danger to us all. We need to do something about him." The cardinal spat out the words, the muscles of his face quivering under his loose skin. "He must not be allowed to erode your office and power," he fumed.

The pope knew this was not the time to interrupt the volcanic cardinal. It was obvious when he had said, "your office and power," Carducci really meant his own. If the pontiff said anything at this point, he would trigger an outburst neither man wanted. So, he patiently waited for the storm to pass, and the storm of rage slowly abated like a hurricane reaching landfall.

Once the cardinal's face had turned from purple to a ruddy reddish color, the pontiff spoke quietly but deliberately. "You say it was suggested we simply make him disappear. How tempting it is to sweep our problems under the proverbial carpet. However, we must keep our heads and not make any hasty decisions that would create a different and perhaps more disastrous problem." He paused to look the cardinal in the eye, quietly ensuring he impressed his decision on the still red-faced official. "No, I want you to keep an eye on Father Francis. Don't let him out of your sight. I assume you have the resources for that. For the time being, we will accept the status quo, but if this storm does not abate and his profile continues to rise, we may have to re-examine alternatives." He dismissed his second-in-command with a nod of his head toward the door.

+ + +

Carducci left the papal quarters steaming at being so easily dismissed. After all, he was head of the Congregation of the Doctrine of Faith and had power of his own. He immediately headed for an annex building at the edge of the maze of buildings making up Vatican City. The building's entrance hid at the end of a darkly lit and seldom-visited corridor. The man Carducci sought was unique among Vatican retainers in that he reported to Carducci alone. Carducci employed him to handle *delicate* assignments. No one but Carducci knew of the man's real purpose, and the cardinal kept no records that would reveal the nature of his operations. His man was well paid for his discretion and to do what he was told.

The cardinal looked around before entering the dark corridor, ensuring no one was about to see him. At the end of the passage, he furtively unlocked and pulled open a massive oak door and stepped into a cold, austere room with a single desk. The walls were bare brick, the ancient stone floor worn smooth by countless feet over the centuries. One man sat alone at a desk, empty save for a coffee cup and a pack of cigarettes. There was no clutter.

The man's name was Drago. A former Serbian secret service agent, he was now employed to use his considerable clandestine skills ostensibly for the benefit of God and the Roman Catholic Church, but more specifically, Cardinal Carducci.

Drago leaned insolently against the back of his desk chair, a foul-smelling French cigarette slowly smoldering at the corner of his mouth. He wore a wool sweater that stretched across his muscled chest, and his arms threatened to tear the seams of the poor garment every time he moved. Drago was a trained and practiced killer who had no remorse for taking the lives of his enemies. He had once been tasked by his superiors in the former Yugoslavia with those military and extra-military assignments requiring stealth and aggressive violence. In those cases, enemies had generally disappeared, but when terror was the goal, they had ended up as corpses in the streets.

Once things had sorted themselves out in that war-torn country, Drago had left to "pursue other interests" and perhaps avoid the clutches of the War Crimes Tribunal. So, he had come to Carducci highly recommended for his skills. Drago had no problem switching his allegiance to God from his former employers so long as the pay was right and regular.

"Mr. Cardinal, what can I do for you?" Drago drawled, his Italian obscured by a heavy Serbian accent and punctuated with a subtle sarcasm deriving from the obvious contradiction between the message of love the Church espoused and the operations he was regularly asked to conduct.

"I want you to follow a priest and report his whereabouts and activities to me every few days. He can't know you're there. Am I making myself clear?"

"One priest in the midst of so many. You all look alike to me," Drago retorted, sneering.

"Your quarry, our troublesome Father Francis Bauer, tends to stand out in a crowd."

"I wondered what you would do with him. He's causing trouble, no?"

"We are doing nothing with him. We just need to know his location at all times. Only that," ordered the cardinal impatiently.

He didn't like Drago and felt dirty every time he was forced to be in the same room with him. But his kind were useful and necessary in the world in which Cardinal Carducci moved. How could a man be so useful and at the same time be so distasteful? It was one of life's paradoxes, and paradoxes were not something to spend a lot of time thinking about.

"So, where is our little priest?"

Carducci responded, "He is planning to travel to Switzerland by train. His family is in Zurich. You can pick up his trail there."

+ + +

Francesco Carducci's family, like so many Italian families of his generation, were dedicated to the Catholic Church. The Church is an integral part of Italian culture, so living as they did in Rome, the Carducci family attended all major Catholic events and celebrations.

Francesco had been a good-natured, intelligent little boy. He had proved more emotionally sensitive than his father thought proper though, and no amount of criticism and punishment could resolve it. At twelve, Francesco had confirmed his faith in the age-old tradition of the Catholic Church. Some of Francesco's earliest memories were of standing in rapt attention, observing a man seemingly standing on a mountain high above great crowds of people. Even at a youthful age, Francesco had sensed the power of this man and had been in awe.

The Catholic Church had always been a big part of young Francesco's life; going to Mass was like breathing to the Carducci family. His mother had gone every morning, early, and then had come home to prepare the morning meal.

In his mid-teens, Francesco woke to the realization that he loved the pomp and circumstance of the Church. He had wanted his life to differ from the lives of other boys his age, and he had seen the Church as a way to be different. When other boys had been obsessed with football and girls, Francesco had set himself apart to reserve his purity for the Church. In his late teens, he had gone off to university to study philosophy, the required study for a priest candidate.

Francesco had not longed for a *normal* life as had many of his peers. This path of his had been of his choosing. He had not wanted to do the things his childhood friends had, and he had always loved being treated as special because of his devotion to his faith. Never had he tried to throw off the calling. In fact, his father had even paid a visit and tried to dissuade him once, but Francesco had not budged. He had vowed he would be the supreme pontiff one day. It had been essential nothing distract him from becoming a priest and eventually pope. So, while an Italian patriarch's word was ordinarily law, in this case, his father had made no headway.

It had been thanks to Francesco's emotional commitment to becoming a priest and his natural intelligence that he had exceeded expectations in his academics. His academic prowess had launched him with ease into the divinity graduate program: the second necessary academic step of his training. He had excelled in this phase as well, and ordination had quickly followed.

Once ordained in his mid-twenties, Francesco's first few assignments had left him cold. He had felt out of place and bored. He didn't really like people much, and rubbing shoulders with parishioners, as a pastor, had been awful for him. Finally, after several low-level assignments, he had been discovered by the bureaucracy.

He had always known the Catholic Church was a giant, fascinating bureaucracy with global reach. Finally finding his niche, Francesco had become a gifted Church politician and administrator as he had rocketed through the ranks, honing his skills as he went. Unfortunately, as his skills had advanced, his humanity had diminished. The sensitivity he had displayed as a child and youth were not valuable in a power-based hierarchy. Ruthlessness replaced sensitivity and cunning enhanced his natural intelligence. Francesco had learned early that the sensitive ones failed, and the simply intelligent ones were left behind.

The Vatican was a monarchy, and he became the consummate courtier. Empathy gave way to success and power. With each advancement, his focus on himself and his career grew. His life's focus became his influence over his environment. If he were honest, deep in the recesses of his mind, he knew his prevailing motivation was fear. He feared failure and humiliation, so he buried his fear under power and influence. Power, he knew, was the best antidote for fear. His mantra was, "Let no one control my destiny."

+ + +

Francis was lulled into musing by the gentle sway of the dining car and the faint *clickity clack* of the train's wheels. The subtle, monotonous sound triggered reminiscences he had rarely thought of in his adult life. His life had always been mapped out for him by others, and it had been so busy he had rarely had time to reflect as he did now.

> "Francis, hurry or you'll be late for school. You spend every morning daydreaming and don't get your chores done."
> "I'm sorry, Mutti. I wasn't paying attention to the time. I'll hurry."
> "Don't forget your books and your lunch."
> "I have them," said young Francis as he ran back to the kitchen to retrieve his lunch.
> "Remember you have to pick up your brother from school today. And remember your catechism class."
> "I will!"

Francis had been the only boy of his age who had actually enjoyed learning the catechism. He knew he had been chosen and called by God to be a priest, at least that is what his parents had believed. His parents had dedicated him, their firstborn son, to the Church. Under his mother's tutelage, he had become a disciple of Jesus Christ through whom he knew his Heavenly Father. There had been no question in his mind God was interested in his life and had a purpose for him to fulfill in the grand scheme of things. Back then, he had wanted what his parents had wanted, and that was for him to join the clergy. He would eventually attend the *Pontificia Università Gregoriana* and then the *Pontificio Seminario Romano Maggiore*. In the meantime, he had known he must learn as much as he could from the priests at school.

Resigned to the fact that Francis would be a priest, his earthly father had felt no need to focus on him. Why play football with him or take him on outings? To his way of thinking, Francis would soon be lost to him, and he had other children. Francis was his father's donation to the Church. Francis embodied an obligation fulfilled, so there was no need to teach or guide him. Francis had a heavenly father, so what did he need with another?

+ + +

"Francis, can I walk with you?" asked Chloe Romano, his best childhood friend but who had recently—and alarmingly—metamorphosed into an extraordinary young woman. He could not recall for sure, but he could not remember her being so pretty before.

"Of course, let's go." Francis had known Chloe all his life, and they had always been best friends even though Chloe was younger. Their relationship had always been familial, like brother and sister. They were three years apart in age, but that only enhanced the sibling-like qualities of their relationship. He liked it that way and could not see why Chloe felt it had to change.

She had changed out of the blue. Not only was she pretty now, but all of a sudden, she had breasts and hips. It had shocked him the first time he had noticed, and he had just stared. The staring had embarrassed Chloe, which in turn, had made her angry. Her embarrassment and anger had made him embarrassed too, and the whole event would remain disturbing into his young adult years. And what was that smell? She smelled like baking cookies or something. His childhood playmate had become intoxicating and disconcerting. And as they walked, he felt anew that sensation that coursed through him when their shoulders came together or when their thighs touched when they sat.

Francis had always known Chloe. She was truly the girl next door. They had played together as babies. The two mothers had found it easier to share maternal duties, so Francis and Chloe had effectively become siblings.

In Switzerland, families were typically of German, French, or Italian origin. Francis' family, the Bauers, spoke German at home. The Romanos spoke Italian, but everyone spoke everyone else's language. Only a few spoke Rumantsch, the Swiss dialect. Francis' mother often told a story about how a relative had once asked Francis when he was six or seven years old how he communicated with his friends. He had replied, "Everyone speaks German," when in truth, Francis and Chloe would transition seamlessly from German to French to Italian without missing a beat.

When Chloe had started school three years after Francis, they had arrived on her first day together, with their mothers. Their mothers had expected Francis to be her mentor and coach simply because before that day, they had always been inseparable, and after that day, they had only continued to be inseparable. At school, Chloe had proven to be popular. She was cute and gregarious, and teachers and fellow students alike fell under her charm. A leader in all her classes, she made everyone around her feel more confident and successful. She instigated class projects and outings and negotiated with teachers. She was a force of nature.

Francis' confused brain wondered, *Maybe this is what the priests keep warning about. They're always going on and on about the sins of the flesh and how young people in their teenage years are most vulnerable to their passions at this age. They make it sound like a disease of some sort.* Well, as a youth, his flesh was constantly burning, he felt too big for his skin, and he almost always felt a pressure in his insides. If that was the "passions," then he had them in a bad way. It did not feel wrong exactly, but the strangeness of it suggested that whatever it was, it could not be all good. He decided he would wait for an appropriate time to ask his mother about it. As the years passed though, he never did.

"I want to talk about what we talked about yesterday," said Chloe, insistent. "You've had time to think about it, and I want an answer."

"Oh, Chloe, I told you I can't be your boyfriend. I'm going to be a priest."

"I know you're going to be a priest, but you're not a priest yet," snorted Chloe impatiently.

"I know, but I just can't. Why do we have to change? Can't you just be my best friend?"

Chloe crossed her arms under her unnerving breasts and marched off in a huff, leaving Francis standing alone, baffled by all the changes Chloe represented. Even in his confusion, though, he knew he would be going to Rome soon, and nothing must divert his attention from his path, not even Chloe. His life's direction was decided, and nothing could change that.

+ + +

When it came to Francis, Chloe felt she was the elder, more mature one since he was so clueless. It was infuriating that he refused to see she loved him and wanted to be with him always. Why could he not wake up from his dream of being a priest and see her, really see her? She knew he loved her but not in the way she wanted to be loved. Her teenaged heart, she felt, would be broken forever if Francis left her behind. She felt deeply it was a tragedy inflicted upon her by the Church.

As she tried to reconcile her broken heart, Chloe's life ambition became to move to America. The teen magazines she was enthralled with convinced her America was the Promised Land, and her dreams would come true there. She had no plan, only dreams, and she knew intuitively her dreams and Francis' responsibilities were invariably incompatible, and she would follow her dreams alone.

+ + +

Francis endured his train ride home, and when he stepped off the train, he was met by his mother and father. As the oldest of their six children and the one they had dedicated to God from birth, he was their family priest, their gift to God, their pride and joy. Their affection and pride blanketed him as they clung to him on the platform. His mother held on to him for much longer than was comfortable for him, but he indulged her excesses because of his deep love and affection for her. His father stood aside waiting his turn before shaking Francis' hand formally, affection in his eyes but not in his demeanor.

Francis was tremendously relieved at escaping from Rome in one piece. He felt as if he had received a hundred emotional lashes, yet he was physically unscathed. The specter of some shadowy threat planted by Cardinal Massey had receded, but a twinge of fear coursed through him still as he recalled the warning. He had spent years studying the history of the Roman Catholic Church, and he knew the hierarchy could be provoked to viciousness when their authority was challenged, even inadvertently, so perhaps Cardinal Massey had been right to warn him. There were numerous examples from the past of well-meaning scholars who had been burned at the stake for their scholarship. He supposed he *had* stirred this primeval beast, which ordinarily was kept securely locked away and deeply buried under mountains of biblical rhetoric portraying only loving kindness. He felt relief and near panic simultaneously.

"My son," said his father. "How good it is to have you home. It has been a very long time since we last had a proper visit."

His father was in his early seventies, a devout Catholic, and an unswerving believer in the Church. It was going to be impossible for him to understand what had happened to Francis. He would not understand the inquisition, the judgment, the discipline, and the necessity for Francis to leave for parts unknown for an unspecified time. His father would be convinced he had failed. His mother, on the other hand, had no illusions about the Church. She knew of the agony Francis had endured when deciding whether or not to publish his book. He had confided in her, and she had agreed he had had no choice if he wished to stay true to God and to himself. She had known there would be conflict, and her son would be sorely tried and probably hurt, but in her heart, she had courage, conviction, and strength of steel in support of her convictions and her son. What she had not realized, though, was that he would be in danger.

"Hello, Mutti," Francis whispered.

"Welcome, my son," she said simply but with obvious emotion. She was a woman of few words but who had a spiritual and emotional depth Francis had always admired and tried to emulate. As Jesus had asked her to be, she was indeed wise as a serpent and innocent as a dove.

"I'm home for just a few days, Papa."

"Why only a few days?" queried his father.

"I'll explain when we get home."

His mother examined his face closely and apparently noticed the relief, anxiety, and fear. His father had turned to pick up one of his suitcases and did not see his expression—and probably wouldn't have noticed anyways. "We will talk later," concluded his mother with finality, reading him like a book.

+ + +

Francis' mother was as quiet as Francis as they drove to their flat in the center of the city. His father mentioned Francis looked tired and probably needed a rest from his busy life as a priest. She knew better but held her tongue, knowing it would be better to speak to her son alone when the time was right. She felt guilty about planning to hide her son's obvious trouble from her husband, but it would be best until she got the details. Her husband was a wonderful man but was often unable to see the subtlety of life and politics, particularly when it came to the Church.

It didn't help that he was distant from Francis too, and that often resulted in his being dismissive of Francis' problems and challenges. Her husband felt Francis had been dedicated to the Church; therefore, he had an easy life in the loving arms of God. If something went wrong, it must be Francis' fault. Francis had faced other challenges that he had discussed with his parents, but his father had not been receptive. She knew from past conversations it was simple for her husband: do what you're told, and everything will work out for the best. Yes, it was best she say nothing of Francis' troubles for now.

+ + +

Later in the evening after a gargantuan meal of all his favorite dishes, Francis and his mother sat over a cup of coffee in the kitchen. His father had retired to the local café for a visit with his friends. At this moment, Francis thought, he was probably bragging shamelessly about his famous son, who was such a successful priest and scholar and how he was so beloved by the Church. He would soon be a bishop, or a cardinal, his father would declare.

Francis knew his mother would soon begin a gentle interrogation, and he was not sure he was prepared to tell the whole truth. If he didn't, though, she would know, and her gentle questions would become a determined cross-examination, and the truth would come out one way or another. His fame and success did not impress her much.

"So, what's going on?" his mother asked gently but firmly, looking him directly in the eye.

"I guess you wouldn't believe me if I said everything was fine?"

Mutti's eyebrows rose, clearly answering his question.

CHAPTER 2

Drago

Drago methodically put his kit together, including his numerous passports in a variety of names and nationalities and his intelligence profile of Father Francis Bauer. From the file, he knew all he needed to know to keep tabs on this little priest. In his line of work, information was king, and he had enough information to begin the chase.

Although Drago spoke several languages, his heavy accent was sometimes a problem, but with all the emigration these days, Serbians were everywhere and held all sorts of passports, so he could still be invisible when the need arose. Early in his career in the intelligence community, he had had his features modified to be nondescript and eminently forgettable. He was highly trained to blend in, to draw no attention to himself. Drago was like a cougar moving undetected through its environment: silent, invisible, and deadly. He was the perfect stalker and predator.

When Drago finally ventured out of his apartment on Via Ottaviano, he boarded a train to Zurich just as Francis had. He was a bloodhound on the trail now; nothing would keep him from his quarry, and his quarry would never escape.

Drago's character had been forged in the heat of battle. Inside he was gun-barrel steel. He was cold and unbending. Designed for one purpose. His whole life had been a long series of battles since he was old enough to remember.

+ + +

"My little soldier, you are joining the battle against our enemies?"

"Yes, Papa. I am ready to fight," he said with all the enthusiasm and sincerity his twelve-and-a-half years could muster. He idolized his father. "Can I hold your gun, Papa?"

"Of course but be careful. Hold it like I showed you, and don't point it at anyone unless they're the enemy, and if it is an enemy, shoot to kill without hesitation. That is how we survive."

Drago took up his father's Kalashnikov and hoisted its four-kilogram weight to his shoulder with some difficulty. He pointed it out the window of the family apartment in a small town in eastern Croatia, aiming at nothing in particular but feeling very powerful and a part of the struggle of his people. His father continually emphasized the need for Serbs to band together against their enemies and that it was a struggle to the death.

In their town, all ethnic groups were involved in the fighting. The groups eyed each other suspiciously at the best of times, and hostilities erupted regularly. Young Drago was filled with pride and fear: he was proud his father was so strong and diligent in protecting his family and his people and fearful that this dangerous fight may end in his death or the deaths of those closest to him. *If my father is killed, who would protect me from our enemies?* he often worried. His father was a great fighter, but without him, Drago felt he would be helpless, and life would be hopeless. This inner struggle created a deep insecurity in Drago that would be burned into the deepest part of his being when he joined the battles himself and experienced the horrors of war firsthand.

When Drago turned fifteen, he was unceremoniously drafted into the militia. He quickly made a name for himself as a soldier loyal to Milosevic. Drago was a proud soldier in the image of his father. His first assignment was with a militia unit created to protect his own neighborhood. Each member of the unit lived there, and several were lifelong friends of Drago's, living within a stone's throw of his home. The military service these young men experienced was initially like a boy's club. The new conscripts were sent off to bootcamp in the mountains away from the prying eyes of the enemy to be trained in the basics of war. The training was not difficult, and the teenagers enjoyed each other's company and the community resulting from being welded into a cohesive military unit.

After basic training, they were issued weapons they would care for and use if conflict erupted in their neighborhood. Each boy carried his gun with him wherever he went and was responsible for maintaining it to high military standards. Deficiencies in performance or breaking the rules were dealt with quickly and harshly because lives were at stake. The club-like atmosphere of basic training gave way to the urgent, ruthless enterprise of civil war.

Drago's unit often was assigned to guard from the rooftops of his street. They were each given a building as their assigned position and were to watch through the day, and even some nights, for insurgency from other neighborhoods. Insurgents would have to run a gauntlet of snipers from above if they wished to take and hold ground in this part of the city.

One summer afternoon, Drago was dozing in the warmth of the afternoon sun when he heard shouting and the pounding of boots on pavement. He looked over the edge of his roof perch and saw a group of paramilitary personnel—not Serbs—rushing from house to house. They were obviously searching for someone on their kill list. Drago prepared to fire from his position when he realized none of his comrades were on the surrounding rooftops.

They must have left their positions early. He was alone. He felt certain that if he fired on the soldiers below, he would be seen and killed, so he waited to see what would happen. To his horror, part of the platoon stopped in front of his apartment building, and several men rushed up the stairs while others remained on guard outside. Drago was faced with an impossible choice. *How could he protect his family? What should he do? Maybe these men were after his father? Maybe they were after someone else in the building?* He didn't know what to do. The questions raced through his mind, but no solutions came to him.

Drago sat in shock as the soldiers exited his building with his bound father, mother, and little brother in tow. Drago's horror became overwhelming when he recognized them and realized the danger. He had no idea what would happen, and he had no idea what to do. The soldiers stopped in the middle of the street and summarily executed his family with a bullet into the back of each head. Drago felt indescribable anguish, agony, and revulsion. His stomach emptied itself. In that instant, he died inside as he watched everyone he most loved murdered.

His stomach and his soul now both empty, Drago came to his senses and opened fire, killing several of the enemy but revealing himself and drawing withering fire from below. He narrowly escaped the fusillade, coming out of it only slightly wounded by a ricocheting bullet. Drago experienced an enormous sense of guilt and self-loathing then at being alive while his family was dead. He had failed to protect them. He had a gun. Why hadn't he used it? To avoid insanity, Drago shut down inside. He chose the numbness of hate. The pain was too overwhelming to process. He had learned only he was trustworthy. Where had the others gone? His father's words echoed in his mind, *"You failed. Never fail again. You cannot trust."*

The numbness of hate, a powerful emotional defense mechanism, left him incapable of feeling his own pain and made him insensitive to the suffering of others. Once his superiors realized this highly perceptive and intelligent teenager had no inconvenient emotions, they began training him for the Serbian Special Forces: Black Ops. His initial training was as a sniper, and he earned the reputation of being one of the deadliest fighters on either side of the conflict. As the number of his confirmed kills rose, his training broadened to include all he needed to know to be a covert operative.

As the civil war in the former Yugoslavia wound down and the war crimes tribunal began its investigations and prosecutions, Drago felt no compelling need to stay in the Serbian military. There were rumors the investigations were narrowing in on some of his more notorious assignments, and Drago decided to take early retirement from the military and seek a more lucrative and sheltered position. Through a contact at the CIA, he heard someone in the Vatican was looking for a man of his stripe. Negotiations were held, a deal was struck, and here he was in a position once unimaginable to him: working as a covert operative for the Roman Catholic Church, not his Orthodox Church, but a church nonetheless. Life was full of surprises. Drago felt no affinity for his institutional employer, only an affinity for the money regularly deposited into his Swiss bank account. He was once a Serbian soldier, and now he was a Christian soldier. This thought made him chuckle sardonically.

On the train, Drago placed his Father Francis file on his lap and studied its contents intently. He had been ordered to follow, so he would follow, but he was ready for a change in assignment should the occasion arise.

He examined the face of Father Francis and noted a strange innocence there. It was as if Drago was looking at the face of a child. He scoffed at this. This man was unprepared for the world he lived in. He was too protected, too sheltered, a hothouse rose in a cold, cruel world. *Hothouse roses are good for nothing*, thought

Drago. They die too easily, and though they're beautiful to look at, they last only for a moment before they wither.

For a brief moment, Drago wondered what this man had done to piss off his superiors so thoroughly. Drago had sensed the rage in Carducci as he had given Drago his instructions. He had seen similar rage in superiors before. Drago did not understand the reason for the rage but recognized it at a visceral level. Carducci and his bosses would eventually want this innocent dead, and he would have to do it. *Oh well,* Drago thought. *Too bad for the little priest.*

+ + +

Zurich came into view in the train window just as the sun was setting. It was beautiful in the fading light, but Drago saw no beauty, just another city in which to ply his trade. As the train pulled into Zurich's Haupbahnhof Station, he made plans to check into a tiny guest house he knew of in the red-light district. Once he was settled, he would find Father Francis Bauer. He suspected the little priest was unaware of any surveillance so would never suspect Drago of following him. The Bauer family home would mark the beginning of Drago's assignment. This was going to be too easy.

Like last time, the guest house charged by the day, in cash, in advance. This suited Drago.

CHAPTER 3

Running Away

"I'm in serious trouble, Mutti," Francis admitted to his mother as he absently swirled the deep red liquid in his wine glass. "The Holy Father and Cardinal Carducci felt threatened, so they sent me to an informal inquisition. It was horrible. It lasted three solid days. They interrogated me on the details of my personal theology, my theological findings, my opinions, my understanding of Church law, my understanding of history, my relationships, everything. Eventually they judged my book to be of 'questionable doctrine.' The inquisition couldn't find heresy because my conclusions didn't stray from accepted biblical interpretation, but they tried." Francis had not realized how hard it would be to confess his situation to his mother.

"What does this mean for you then?" she asked, her heartbreak for her dear boy evident in her tone.

"I'm still a priest because they couldn't prove my questionable doctrine had resulted in any irreparable harm. In fact, the evidence suggested the book caused renewal in many places, but in the end, they decided that was no reason to sanction the book because they felt it threatened the absolute authority of the Church hierarchy and the supreme pontiff." Francis sighed deeply. "Cardinal Massey says I'm in danger and should flee and hide in America until the storm passes. He says Carducci is livid and in a nasty frame of mind. At the same time, I really can't believe I'm in danger."

"You listen to that man! He knows how things are done. If he says you're in danger, then you *are* in danger. It wouldn't be the first time they did away with an opponent. Remember the mysterious death of Pope John Paul I. No one knows to this day what really happened to him. So, you had better go quickly! If you're not safe in Rome, you're certainly not safe here," his mother stated emphatically, almost spilling her wine in her insistence.

Although everything in him wanted to hide right here where he felt safest, he knew she was right. With resignation he replied, "All right, I'll go hide. I'll leave tomorrow. It just makes me so angry that I must leave my work and my home!" Francis' grip on his glass tightened until his knuckles were white and the glass threatened to break. One look at his mother though, and the anger released in a rush, reluctant acceptance taking its place. "Cardinal Massey has given me the names of some people he trusts in America, and he gave me a British passport and some money. My first stop will be New York."

+ + +

Father Francis boarded the direct flight from Zurich to New York early the next morning. In the back of the taxi on the way to the airport, trying not to listen to the driver's nonstop monologue, he reflected on the awkward goodbye with his father, who could not understand why he was leaving and thought the whole notion of being in danger was absurd.

The conversation with his mother and father together had not gone well. Francis and his mother had not told his father in detail why Francis was leaving for America, giving him only the basics. His father had again affirmed his deep commitment to and faith in the leadership of the Roman Catholic Church, and his paradigm could not allow him to consider anything other than benevolent righteousness. He accepted the infallibility of the pope and rejected his wife's skepticism and apparent rebellion against authority. To him, his son must have done something terribly wrong to warrant punishment and exile. He had even suggested Francis should just repent and make it right with his superiors. It was as simple as that. He was the family's gift to the Church. He had made a mess of things with his rebelliousness. *"Make it right,"* his father had demanded.

"I'm sorry, Papa, but I can't just make this right. I believe in what I found in my research, and I believe what I said in my book. I honestly can't see where I went wrong, and I won't apologize when I didn't do anything wrong. Nor will I recant what I believe to be right. I am sorry for causing you pain though, Papa."

His father had replied sharply, *"If you were right, you wouldn't be in trouble."* And that had been the end of that.

+ + +

"Good morning, Mr. Smith. Your passport please," asked the attractive blond American Airlines agent at the Zurich Airport. He looked at her quizzically and then jumped as he realized she was asking for *his* passport, his falsified passport. He reprimanded himself for not remembering he was Mr. Francis Smith now, a British citizen. His English accent—a gift from his British tutor—supported his new persona: he was a British academic traveling to the United States on sabbatical.

With trepidation, Francis handed her his passport as if he was reaching into a flame. He hoped she wasn't looking too closely at his face when the blood suddenly drained out of it or at the tremor in his hand, for that matter, as he handed over the document. He felt like he was standing naked before her while at the same time breaking all the Ten Commandments at once.

"Thank you, Mr. Smith. How many bags will you be checking?" He had passed the test, but barely, it seemed to him.

Beside Francis was an immaculately dressed young man waiting for another agent to process his ticket. He wore a bold, stylish designer jacket displaying a Picasso-esque face on a bright yellow-and-black paisley patterned background and emblazoned with the Versace name in large letters across the chest. Under the jacket was a black t-shirt, also with the Versace logo.

His outfit must have cost a fortune, thought Francis. On his head, the man wore a stylish black knitted hat pulled down low over his forehead like so many of his contemporaries. The young man was thin as a willow but still well-proportioned for his height. Suddenly, he lost his balance, teetered, and fell into Francis, who instinctively reacted to steady him by grasping his forearm and firmly lifting him upright. Francis noticed the young man's face was gaunt under his cap, and his arm, under his long-sleeved flannel shirt, felt like skin-covered bone. The young man smiled and offered his thanks in English, his accent making it likely he was a New Yorker.

Francis made his way through the crowd to the gate assigned to his flight without incident and boarded the aircraft. He was still anxious and feeling vulnerable and guilty when he reached his window seat and began to settle in. As he sat down, he noticed the unsteady young man he had encountered earlier approaching. The man sat down heavily into his aisle seat next to Francis after struggling to put what appeared to be a light carry-on bag into the overhead compartment.

It was not Francis' habit to speak to people on airplanes, preferring solitude as he did, but something about this young man stirred him to introduce himself. "Hello, I am Francis. I guess we will be neighbors for a few hours," he said in his oily upper-class English accent.

"I'm Richie. Pleased to meet you," Richie said with little enthusiasm.

"Where are you traveling?"

"I'm going home to New York. I've lived in Paris for the past few years studying and then working in dance, but it's time to go home now."

As Richie settled into his seat, he took off his wool hat and put it with his coat under his seat. Francis noticed as Richie turned his head that he had several red marks on the right side of his face that had been hidden. As the young dancer turned to face front again, Francis was horrified to see that on Richie's temple, just above his hairline, was an open sore at least the size of a dime. From the wound, bloody ooze ran in a thin stream past his ear and down his cheek.

The sight caused Francis' stomach to flipflop, but he recovered and said, "You have something on your cheek."

Richie wiped the ooze away with his hand but left a long, viscous red smudge. "Damn, I hate this," he hissed under his breath.

Without thinking, Francis took a tissue from his pocket and reached across the seat separating them to wipe it away saying, "Let me help you."

Richie recoiled at Francis' near touch as if he had been slapped. "Be careful," he snapped, unceremoniously snatching the tissue from Francis' hand.

"I am terribly sorry for the intrusion," replied Francis, as shocked at his own invasion of this stranger's privacy as he was by Richie's alarmed, reflexive response.

"Please, just don't touch me."

The two sat in awkward silence for several minutes until finally Richie said, "I'm sorry for barking at you. I know you were only trying to help. I'm just not used to people touching me these days.

People like me suffer from a startle reflex when others try to touch them. It's weird. I startle even with people I know and love."

Another awkward silence ensued, during which Francis tried to make sense of what was going on. What had Richie meant by "people like me"? Was he mentally ill in addition to having a rather disgusting skin condition? Francis was wary of extending their conversation, so he settled down in his seat and closed his eyes.

Richie broke the silence. "As I said, I'm traveling to New York. Where are you headed? Are you stopping in New York?"

Francis paused for a long moment because he had not really thought through how he would answer this simple question. He hadn't even thought of what he was going to do or where he was going. "Well, um, I guess I'm traveling to New York as well."

"You guess? It sounds like you don't really know," Richie said with a chuckle.

"As a matter of fact, I just made up my mind." After a pause, Francis added, "That probably sounds strange."

"It doesn't sound strange, but it does sound funny. What is it you do?"

This was a day of shocks for Francis because he had not prepared an answer for this ordinary question either. "Actually, I'm not doing much at the moment. I'm an academic. I'm just traveling," he stammered, hoping he did not sound too evasive or like an idiot. This being a fugitive was going to take some planning and much thought, so he did not constantly sound like a criminal.

"From your accent, you're not American. Your accent is British, but you speak very formally without contractions and idioms, so you're not British. English must not even be your second language, I'm guessing."

"It is true, I am not British, but I learned English from a British teacher. I guess English is my fourth language in terms of vocabulary and fluency, so I do not speak as well as I should," explained

Francis. "I speak much more personably in German, Italian, and French. My Spanish is about on par with English."

"Wow. Where are you staying in New York?" inquired Richie, changing the subject.

"Well, as you gathered, I am not well prepared, and frankly I do not really know where I am going to stay. I left Zurich in a rather hurry and haven't caught up to myself yet." Francis caught himself once again being a lousy fugitive. Why had he told a perfect stranger he was traveling from Zurich? *Good grief,* he thought, *I can't keep anything secret. I had better start learning.* His lapses in judgment were going to be problematic. It was just that by nature and temperament, Francis was transparent, and one of his personal core values was honesty. He just was who he was with everyone, and he was pitiful at being duplicitous or devious. How could he live a life not his own and still be honest? That would be a challenge.

"Listen, why don't you stay with me? I have a big apartment in Manhattan left to me by my parents, and I'm all alone with plenty of room. Hotels are incredibly expensive in New York, and I'd be glad of the company," Richie offered spontaneously.

"Richie, you have yourself a house guest," Francis responded equally spontaneously. He immediately regretted being so hasty and reckless but felt stuck with the decision, so he said nothing more.

+ + +

From his vantage point two rows behind and across the aisle, Drago listened to the exchange between Richie and Francis with fascination. *This little priest truly is a pussy,* he thought savagely. *I have never seen such a weakling. I hate weaklings. This priest is so easy to hate.* Drago's rage grew to a crescendo as he watched the scene. His only thought was of an irrational desire to kill, to rid the earth of such pathetic weakness. If all human beings were as powerful and steel hard as he, then it would be an orderly, predictable place. Weakness was a disease, and it was Drago's job to snuff it out.

CHAPTER 4

New York

The plane landed at JFK Airport in New York without incident. In fact, the flight was relaxing, and Francis enjoyed an easy, friendly conversation with Richie. Richie proved to be bright, well read, and articulate, although his exaggerated artistic streak was something Francis found a bit odd. But he found he liked Richie. There was something else different about Ritchie that Francis could not put his finger on too, but overall, Francis felt he had made a friend when he desperately needed one.

Customs and immigration was another horror show, his anxiety and guilt bubbling up all over the place to the point that Francis thought for sure the immigration officer would suspect fraud. But Francis' poker face must have been better than he thought because his documentation was accepted without question, and the passport passed the computer verification test. Cardinal Massey must indeed have excellent connections to create such a document.

Once out of immigration, Francis was approached by a man who obviously wanted to carry his luggage on his trolley. He was just a young man, and as he stepped up to Francis, he said, "*Yo dawg, y'all want sum hep wit jo bags, man?*"

BROKEN CROSS

Francis stood dumbfounded long enough for the porter to get annoyed. The next thing Francis heard was, "*Sup dood? Y'all harda hearin', yo?*"

Francis was shocked not everyone in America spoke English. In fact, he didn't recognize this language at all, so he said, "No," thinking he had a fifty percent chance of saying the right thing, assuming it had been a question he had heard. He must have said the right thing because the young porter swept past him impatiently and approached the next person leaving customs.

Richie hailed a cab and gave the driver his address. The ride from the airport to Manhattan was harrowing. The cab driver drove at breakneck speed, weaving dangerously in and out of traffic as if his life depended on beating every car into the city. Francis held onto the overhead handle and tightened his stomach muscles to lessen the fear and motion sickness. He felt like he was in a fighter jet flown by a pilot with serious mental health issues.

The driver, while racing along, never stopped talking. His thick accent made it somewhat difficult to understand, but Francis got the gist of the story. It involved the driver always carrying a gun under his front seat, and only the week before, two men had tried to rob him, but before they had come at him, he had grabbed his gun and shot them both. One had died on the spot, and one was in critical condition in the hospital with a life-threatening head wound. The driver proudly boasted he had rid the world of two parasites on humanity, and the police had agreed with him. The driver bragged that he was facing no charges and said he was ready to do some more housecleaning if the circumstance arose.

The paradigm of life and death this man presented intrigued Francis in a morbid way. It was both fascinating and surreal at the same time. The comparison that immediately popped into his mind was sixteenth-century Europe. In 1483, a man was born who would create chaos in the Catholic Church. His name was Martin Luther. He became a monk in 1505, and as a professor of theology at the University of Wittenberg in 1517, he took issue with how his archbishop raised money. The archbishop was essentially selling forgiveness of sins to believers. Luther's objection and subsequent theological writings resulted in an existential threat to the Catholic Church, so the Church reacted to this existential threat with violence. Eradicating the threat supported the continuation of business as usual. Since the Church and the government were entwined in several European countries in the sixteenth and seventeenth centuries, Luther's objections started a series of wars and persecutions that cost multitudes their lives. The leaders of these wars and persecutions, both Catholic and Protestant, saw each other as threats requiring housecleaning.

This kind of violence was almost unknown to or forgotten by people in twenty-first century Western countries. But Francis wondered whether the outward veneer of civilization, if scratched, might reveal the same diminished value of human life exhibited by this taxi driver. What would it take for our espoused social justice system to break, and what would it take for Church followers to participate?

This New York cabby was displaying self-interest on an extreme level: if you threaten my personal well-being, I will kill you without thought or remorse. Francis' own situation flashed into perspective because it was that same philosophy forcing him to run and hide. *Human insecurity in a variety of settings seems to elicit remarkably similar responses,* Francis thought.

The best thing about the taxi ride was that it was soon over, and they pulled up in front of an elegant apartment building decked out with shining glass windows and doors and even a uniformed doorman.

When exiting the cab, Francis looked around at the scene, having never visited New York. Towering buildings demanded his immediate attention, but then he noticed a man emerging from a taxi nearby. He was a large brute of a man, and their eyes met briefly. Strangely, Francis sensed a vague recognition, but not knowing why, he soon forgot the feeling and the man.

"Welcome home, Mr. Mossman," the doorman said coolly as he heaved the luggage from the trunk of the taxi.

"Thanks, Jonathan. I'm glad to be home. You're well?"

"Yes, Mr. Mossman. Thank you, sir."

"Jonathan, this is Francis. He'll be staying with me for a while."

Jonathan acknowledged Francis with a chilly nod of his head, giving him a look Francis could not read. It was as if this man did not approve of Francis even though he had no idea who Francis was. He found it confusing and not a little disconcerting because, as a priest, he was not used to making bad first impressions. Typically, first impressions were positive to clergy even if many people had strange preconceptions of what it is to be one. People often attributed radical honesty and piety to clergy without realizing they are only human.

Jonathan helped them put their luggage in the elevator, and when they reached the top, the door opened, revealing a penthouse with an elegant foyer elaborately decorated with rosewood paneling and original oil paintings. Expensive antique furniture filled the apartment. The first piece in the foyer Francis noticed was a beautiful bureau, elegantly carved with shapes and faces accented and bordered with inlays of light-colored wood that contrasted with the dark sepia of the rest of the wood. Francis had seen similar furniture in the Vatican.

"Is this your flat?" asked Francis.

"In America, we call them apartments, and yes, it is mine—and my sister's. When my mother and father were killed in a car accident two years ago, they left their estate to my sister, Rebecca, and me. The estate included this place as well as houses in Florida, California, and Colorado. We sold the Florida and California homes."

"You were very fortunate," said Francis.

"I'm not fortunate. I'd rather have my parents back," responded Ritchie.

"Of course." Francis was finding Richie somewhat mercurial. He was often pleasant but just as often touchy.

"I'll show you your room, and then we should find something to eat."

As Richie led him down the hall to his bedroom, Francis could not help but be impressed at the opulence of the surroundings. They walked on what looked like an authentic Persian runner that seemed to go on forever. He had never personally experienced this kind of wealth other than the institutional variety at the Vatican that had always made him feel on edge, insecure, and diminished in some way. *So, this is how the other half lives,* he mused.

His private thoughts were interrupted by an unbidden question that did not seem to fit the circumstances. "You are valuable. Wealth is not a sign of value," the voice continued. "Where does your value come from?" That was a question Francis was struggling with because of the Church's rejection of him. The rejection had made him realize he had always measured his personal value to a great extent by the standards set by the Church. The Church measured value in different ways for different people. A priest was valued by his position, for his devotion to the mission of the Church, and for his skill in furthering the interests and influence of the Church. In a parish, this would typically mean obeying his superiors, particularly his bishop, and working tirelessly to serve the bishop's vision. The piety a priest projects was valued and often emulated by his parishioners, but his superiors simply expected him to be like them.

In the Church hierarchy, as Francis well knew, subservience was valued over individual human beings. From his study of the Bible, though, Francis was convinced God valued only human beings, one person at a time. His love only extended to human beings, not to their undertakings and organizations. Human value was intrinsic because God loved them. Priest or parishioner, saint or sinner, God loved all of them equally. Being a priest, Francis knew, did not make God love him more. Being a rejected, runaway priest did not make God love him less. Being pious and presenting holy behavior did not increase God's love. Nothing he or anyone else could or could not do would change God's love for them. It just *was*. Was the Church a human undertaking or a God undertaking? If the Church did not value what God valued, could it be a godly undertaking?

Where had that come from? thought Francis. His thoughts had whirled around and down the path of considering his own intrinsic value and the value of others to God in an instant, and the questions remaining to be answered hovered in his mind as he continued along the hallway to his bedroom. *It's strange the way my mind works these days. I wonder if Protestants ask the same questions? From what I've read, they do.* Francis shook the thoughts loose as he and Richie slowed to a stop before an exquisitely detailed door.

+ + +

Cardinal Carducci was seated across from Pope Paul in the sitting room of the papal quarters. They had finished with the agenda for the meeting when the Holy Father brought up the subject of Father Francis Bauer, the renegade author and priest as His Eminence called him.

"What has been done about our troublesome priest?" asked the pontiff quietly.

"I am having him watched," replied Carducci noncommittally.

"I assume you're pursuing a path to resolution?" replied the pontiff, refusing to let the subject go, but at the same time, clearly wishing not to be drawn into the "solution."

"The goal is to have him publicly recant the book," Carducci replied delicately, understanding his activities would be disavowed if they went badly for the Church and that he would personally pay the price of failure.

"Good, I want this concluded as soon as possible. Is that understood?"

"Understood," Carducci responded, a hint of bitterness in his voice. He craved the power this man had, which ensured the plausible deniability of any resolution of the matter of Father Francis Bauer.

+ + +

Drago had watched as the target and the gay boy had climbed into a cab together. He had hailed a cab and followed theirs on the pretense he was traveling with them and did not want to be separated. Since Francis had no idea who he was, Drago could be brazen in his surveillance and not risk being exposed, but his training still insisted on professional stealth.

The two cabs arrived together at Richie's apartment building. Drago waited a few seconds before getting out, pretending to fumble with his wallet before paying the cabbie. When Francis and Richie were well out of their cab and about to carry their luggage into the building, he exited his cab. But just as he was taking the handle of his suitcase from the cab driver, Francis glanced back at him. Their eyes met. There was no recognition, or even interest, in Francis' eyes, but it was a rookie error by a veteran intelligence officer. Drago cursed under his breath. *How could I let that happen?* he reprimanded himself. Now he would have to be much more careful.

+ + +

Francis' assigned bedroom was enormous. A massive, king-sized sleigh bed dominated the room, and on the far side of the bed was a sitting area with its own fireplace and magnificent leather furniture. The walls were painted a deep burgundy, and the curtains were made of heavy velvet in a pattern that matched the bedcover. Accents of soft cream made the large room seem cozy and warm.

What a fabulous place, observed Francis. How fortunate he was to have met Ritchie. Where would he be right now without the chance encounter?

"Well, here's your room. I hope you'll find it comfortable."

"I know I will, Richie. It is wonderful. Thank you so much for everything. You are so kind to have invited me to be your guest." For a moment, it struck Francis how bizarre it was for him to be here.

Richie turned to leave but stopped mid-stride, and turning to Francis, said, "I'm very glad you're here, Francis. I've been needing someone to talk to, and I sense you might be a good listener, like a priest or something," Richie said with a laugh. He turned once again to the door and added, "When you're ready to go out, meet me in the living room, and we'll have a glass of wine before we go."

Francis unpacked his suitcases and freshened up after Richie had left. Then, retracing his steps back to the living room, Francis passed a room with an open door. His curiosity got the better of him, and he stuck his head through the door to look around. Judging from the size of the room and the even more luxurious décor, he decided it must be the master suite. The floor was covered with an enormous Persian handwoven carpet the color of turquoise jewelry with elaborate borders and designs in complementary colors. It was exquisite and undoubtedly worth a fortune. Strangely, this room looked clean but untouched. There were clothes in the partially open closet, and even a woman's suit hung on a special suit hanger at the end of the bed as if the suit's owner would step out of the dressing room and put it on any minute. It reminded Francis of the dining room, frozen in time, like Dickens' *Great Expectations*. He wondered if two years ago this room might have had life.

When Francis found his way back to the living room, Richie had not yet arrived. Francis had no idea in which direction Richie's room lay, so he contented himself with examining the living room and its contents. The living room, he saw through the floor-to-ceiling glass doors, was attached to a large corner balcony with a collection of comfortable outdoor furniture that matched the overall interior color scheme. Beyond the balcony, Francis could see the southeast section of Manhattan in the direction of the Hudson River. The view of the lights of New York was spectacular at this time of the evening. *What a place,* he thought. He felt like he was in a dream. Just yesterday, he was despairing about having to leave his family and flee from an ethereal threat hovering over him, an apparition in which he had not allowed himself to wholly believe. And now here he was, basking in luxury. Weird.

Francis considered how he had gotten here. Meeting Richie had been predicated only by seat selection on an airplane. It had been pure chance, but life was filled with chance meetings. The unusual element had been Richie extending his hospitality to a perfect stranger. Why would he have done that, and why had he, Francis, accepted hospitality from a perfect stranger?

"Have you settled in?" asked Richie, shaking Francis from his reverie.

"Yes, thank you. I feel very fortunate you saved me from my lack of foresight."

"I have never invited a fellow passenger to stay before, but I'm glad I did in your case. I just have to attend to a couple matters, and then I'll find us some wine."

As Francis stepped out on the balcony, he considered once again the oddity of being in the home of a stranger and yet feeling quite comfortable. *How do relationships develop between strangers?*

he wondered He thought back to his experiences as a parish pastor. The people of his parishes had tended to keep him at arms-length, perhaps fearing he would learn something he wouldn't approve of or discover some secret. All his relationships, with the exception of his family and Cardinal Massey, tended to be professional. They were either working relationships with colleagues or professional relationships with parishioners. Either way, they had all resulted in him giving to others without a corresponding offer from them. He had often felt left with a relational and emotional deficit he had to make up on his own.

Working relationships and professional relationships did not satisfy the longing in his soul for kinship and closeness. *Could strangers achieve kinship and closeness?* He didn't know. If the relationships he'd had as a priest were the standard, the answer was no. Arriving in a new parish, he was always the stranger. Parishioners would invite him into their homes out of duty or obligation, but he was not part of the family. The Church had taught them he was God's representative. Having God's man in their home required them, so they thought, to be guarded and solicitous. He was always a familiar stranger with frightening Church baggage.

However, he wasn't a priest now.

Turning from the view of the city back to the living room, he noticed an elegant Louis XV table along one wall of the room covered with framed photos. The most prominent photo was of Richie's family. An older couple was obviously Richie's parents, and the fourth person in the picture after Richie was a strikingly beautiful young woman about Richie's age. It must be Richie's sister, Rebecca. Her emerald eyes glowed with humor and warmth. Francis drew in a ragged breath as he realized he was drawn to the image of this woman in a decidedly unpriestly fashion. He wondered whether being chased out of the womb of the Church with his cassock torn from his back would foster the unhealthy freedom his life as a priest had deeply buried. As a priest, just wearing the collar and cassock fostered a sense of accountability other people may not feel. However, the Apostle Paul had said that, "It was for freedom that Christ has set us free." It might be that Francis would discover what that meant in the days to come.

+ + +

"That's my family," said Richie, breaking Francis' musings to hand him a glass of wine. "I guess you noticed Rebecca?"

"She is hard to miss," Francis said with a chuckle.

"That's very true."

"What is she like?" asked Francis, betraying an interest in her beyond what he had intended.

"We're twins. When we were growing up, we were very close. We went everywhere together and did everything together. We had the same friends and had a great relationship."

"You said 'had a great relationship.' Is that in the past?"

"Unfortunately, it's part of a long, sad story. You see, when we were in college, Rebecca met a guy, an evangelical Christian. He wooed her and she eventually got involved with his church group. She said she had become a completed Jew, or a Jewish Baptist, or something like that. She told me that since she was Jewish and had become Christian, people said she had become complete from the combination of her two traditions. You know our last name is Mossman." He waved a hand in emphasis and at Francis' nod, went on. "Anyway, now she's a Christian and takes it all so very seriously. She and Daniel set me up to hear their pastor speak one Sunday. He spoke about homosexuality. After that, Rebecca and I parted ways. We haven't seen each other since our parent's funeral."

Truly perplexed, Francis asked, "How could that have happened if you were close as children?"

"Well, you see, one day I realized I was different from other people. I realized I'm gay, and Rebecca's Church had taught her I was 'an abomination to God and was going to burn in Hell.' Her pastors told her to have nothing to do with me because I wouldn't change and fit into their mold. They thought it might be catching, I guess," Richie explained, laughing wryly.

"Oh my, I do not really know what to say to that. Except Jesus certainly never wrote people off for any reason. He was very hard on the Pharisees for their self-righteousness, and he delighted in associating primarily with people who didn't fit an acceptable social mold. His friends were tax collectors, fishermen, and prostitutes. In God's economy, each individual has the same intrinsic value, so I have no doubt our Heavenly Father loves you unconditionally."

This trite response gave Francis pause. He had developed a ready inventory of pat answers to life's questions. *This one sounds stupid in its simplicity in light of Richie's confession and his obvious pain at having lost his sister*, Francis thought, chastising himself.

"You sound like a believer yourself, Francis," said Richie with a suspicious tinge to his voice.

"That I am, Richie."

"Well then, Francis, there's something else you have to know."

As he waited for Richie to speak, Francis tried to further digest what he had just learned. That was what it was about Richie he had not been able put his finger on. Richie's manner was slightly effeminate. He did not exaggerate that aspect of himself, but he did not try to hide it either. Richie was comfortable with himself and his sexuality; it was just a natural part of who he was. It was something he acknowledged and accepted about himself. Francis had never met anyone openly gay. Certainly, he knew of priests who'd had indiscretions with members of their sex, but often they weren't really gay, rather, expressing their sexuality in a manner that did not, to them at least, offend their vows of celibacy.

"I'm not only gay, but I have AIDS and I'm dying."

CHAPTER 5

The Twins

It was as an eighteen-year-old freshman at Harvard, her father's alma mater, Ellen Mossman had met her future husband. At the time, Richard was, at twenty-one, the experienced older man. A colorful figure, he was a dashing young law student destined for greatness, or so the gossip predicted. He was third generation Harvard and had his career and success in life scoped out for him. In short, she found him irresistible when he first showed interest in her. Their romance lasted until he graduated, and they married the same summer.

Richard was from a wealthy New York Jewish family with interests in shipping and aircraft leasing. His stint at Harvard Law had been part of his grooming to take over the family business. Becoming a lawyer was the first step because, according to his father, "These days, everyone needs a lawyer in the family."

Ellen's own family was from old money, and she had always known plenty, but it had not spoiled her. She still had compassion for those less fortunate and knew how fortunate she was. Marrying a Jew had really not been an issue. Neither Richard nor his family were religious; they saw themselves as Jews ethnically but had no affinity for the religion.

Three years after their marriage, Ellen gave birth to the twins, Rebecca and Richard Junior. It was not only a joyous occasion, with both families so proud of their grandchildren, but also a sad one because as a result of complications, Ellen would never have more children.

The twins were lavished with every conceivable affection and advantage. The only advantage Ellen could not give them was an abundance of friends. Since the twins went to private school and the Mossman's lived in Manhattan, their school friends were out of reach after school. Several girls Rebecca's age lived within walking distance of their apartment but no boys. The fact that Richie had to play with his sister and her friends most of the time did not seem to bother him at all, so Ellen did not worry about it. The twins were twins and behaved like twins should behave. They finished each other's sentences and had a special relationship that defied intrusion. Vaguely, Ellen had noticed that from birth, Richie was ... what? She would have said delicate if asked. Even as a toddler, he had not liked rough games and later avoided games and sports that involved physical contact.

The one thing he had been desperate to do was dance. The twins both loved to perform. They constantly performed plays and presentations and dance numbers and often involved their girlfriends in the performances. But Ritchie wanted to learn how to dance "properly," he said. He wanted to learn ballet. His father, of course, was put off by his passion, saying it was sissy. Richie did not care; he just wanted to dance.

Eventually, his mother acceded to his wishes to put a stop to the nagging, and he and Rebecca both began ballet lessons. The ballet teacher, Miss Revere, was thrilled to have Richie in her school. Boys in ballet were a rare commodity, and to put on a proper recital, you needed boys. As a result, she prioritized keeping

Richie in the class. When Rebecca lost interest, Miss Revere was terrified Richie would quit too. The loss of Rebecca wasn't much of a problem, but the potential loss of her boy was potentially detrimental to her. To induce Richie to stay, she offered him extra classes and private lessons. He accepted all the challenges and attention with great delight; it was a dream come true. While he was dancing, he was happy, and the attention he received from Miss Revere as her star male pupil made the experience even more exciting and satisfying.

"Richie, straighten your leg, dear. You want to look crisp not sloppy. Did you do your stretching? If you want to be Baryshnikov, you have to work on your flexibility. Excellent, excellent, that's proper form. Now try the next routine."

By the time Richie was a teen, he had worked harder than any other student in Miss Revere's dance school. He was intent on winning a spot at The Juilliard School in New York. Only the best would get in, and he would be the best. His dedication left little time for a personal life, but his passion for dance never abated, and if possible, was only been enhanced by his growing ambition to become a professional. Juilliard was the steppingstone to fame and fortune. For a young man from a wealthy family, fame and fortune were more important than one would expect, particularly when one's father's approval was hard to come by.

"Why do you drive yourself so hard? You have no time for friends or even for me, your most beloved sister. Look at the bruises on your feet. Good grief, they're swollen all the time. They must kill," Rebecca had observed once, a concerned pout on her face.

"I know, I know, I've heard it all before. Stop nagging. I'll schedule us some time."

"That's great! Kindly schedule me into your busy life. Do you have to try to be a jerk, or does it just come naturally?" Rebecca barked, slamming his bedroom door behind her.

Richie rushed to open the door and shouted, "I'm sorry! Wait. *Waaait!* Please don't huff off," he implored. "I'm sorry, I'm sorry, I'm sorry. Let's do something tomorrow. I'll phone Miss Revere and tell her I can't make it. Let's go to a movie, just the two of us."

Rebecca stopped and sighed, then turned around and returned to Richie's room to sit on his bed, now in a much better frame of mind, her anger abated. "Excellent! We can go to a matinee and then get something to eat."

"Deal. Now let me get dressed."

+ + +

"I'm worried about Richie," said his father one day while he and Ellen lay reading in bed before going to sleep that night. "He doesn't seem normal for a seventeen-year-old boy."

"Why would you say that?" queried Ellen, a little put out.

"All he wants to do is dance, for heaven's sake. What healthy boy wants to dance? He should be playing baseball or football or basketball. He's tall and strong, so why can't he play sports?"

"Stop worrying. Julliard is full of young men who want to dance. Richie has big dreams and he's ambitious. He wants Julliard and he's determined to get in. He doesn't have time for anything else. Don't worry, it'll all work out."

"What about girlfriends? He's never had a girlfriend. That's not normal," Richard fumed, sounding desperate.

"He has plenty of girlfriends. In fact, girls love him," Ellen pointed out, defending her son.

"True, he hangs out with girls, but there are no girlfriends, if you catch my drift."

Ellen didn't want to admit it to Richard, but she wasn't so sure it would work itself out either, and Richard would just have to get used to it when the time came.

+ + +

After the matinee, Richie and Rebecca stopped for an early dinner.

"Richie, Sarah likes you," Rebecca announced over hamburgers.

"What do you mean?" Richie asked as he froze with his mouth agape, just about to take a bite of his burger.

"What do you mean, 'What do I mean'? She likes you."

"How do you know?"

"She told me."

"Why would she tell you?"

"Because, you idiot, she's not going to tell you, and I'm her best friend. We're seventeen. That's the way it's supposed to work. Don't you know anything?" Rebecca, both incredulous and exasperated, leaned back and sighed.

"What do you want me to do about it?"

"Ask her out. She thinks you're great, and you'd make a lovely couple," Rebecca offered in her most affected voice.

"Shut up with the lovely couple thing. Rebecca, I'm not interested in girls," Richie confessed with a worried look on his face.

"I know, you're too busy for girls, and you're going to Juilliard, but Sarah is different. We've known her since we were little. She's smart and pretty and …" The embarrassment and vulnerability on Richie's face brought her up short.

"That's not what I mean," responded Richie.

"What do you mean then?"

"I think I'm gay."

"What?! What do you know about being gay?"

"Actually, I don't know much, but I think I am."

"How do you know?"

"I don't know for sure, but when you talk about being in love with Bobby or John or Jerry, which, I think, was all last week, I can relate to what you're saying in a way I probably shouldn't if I was like everyone else. Do you know Jeffery, in my dance class?"

"Yeah. What about him?" asked Rebecca hesitantly.

"He's gay. Did you know that?"

"I sort of figured by the way he walks and talks. He's more girly than the girls in your class."

"I know, but I like him."

"You like *him*?!"

"I do," admitted Richie.

"That's pretty scary, Richie. What if you are gay? That's going to be terrible for all of us. What will Dad say?"

"I know. I'm scared," Richie answered, a slight tremble in his voice betraying his anxiety. "But I can't help it. It's just who I am, I think. I've been like this as long as I can remember."

"Why haven't you mentioned it before now?" Rebecca implored.

"I don't know. I always felt confused and couldn't put what I wanted to say into words. And I was worried you wouldn't understand and wouldn't want me around."

"Well, that's not going to happen," concluded Rebecca vehemently.

+ + +

After their burgers, the twins were walking home when they were approached by five men, young but older than them. The siblings had never seen any of them before. The swagger of the group walking side by side taking up the whole sidewalk and their loud, crude language told Rebecca and Richie they were drunk. The five stopped when they came to the twins, and as Rebecca tried to pass, they blocked her way.

"What's your name, girl?" the apparent leader slurred.

"Get out of my way," said Rebecca firmly.

"What are you doing with sissy boy?" demanded the young thug.

"Get out of our way, and leave us alone," said Richie anxiously, not liking how this encounter was going.

"So, you're going to be the tough little queer, are you?!" shouted the leader while his buddies gathered around the twins.

An opening appeared between two members of the group as their attention focused on Richie. Rebecca darted through. But she immediately stopped when she realized Richie wasn't with her. She turned with alarm and shouted, "Leave my brother alone!"

"So, he's your sissy brother," said the instigator. "I thought he was your sister, the way he walks. I think we should teach this queer to stay off our turf. What do you say, boys?" With that, he lunged forward and tackled Richie, driving him to the ground and grinding his face into the pavement.

The others swarmed around Richie and began kicking and punching him until his face was a mass of blood and gore and his limp body rested half on the sidewalk and half on the road. It happened so fast Rebecca had little time to think or respond. She began screaming for help, but passersby refused to intervene, rushing past in an apparent effort to put distance between themselves and the one-sided altercation as quickly as possible. Left to her own devices, she spun around, looking for the nearest phone booth to call 911.

When the beating ended in just seconds, the group ran from the scene whooping and laughing at how they had taught that queer a lesson he would not soon forget. Rebecca heard one young man congratulate another on a particularly vicious kick he had delivered to Richie's groin.

Rebecca rushed to Richie's side, tears streaming down her face as she bent over Richie's battered body before running back to the phone booth to call her father at home. Her mind reeled as she tried to reconcile the violence against her brother, who had never hurt another human being in his life. How had they known? Where had they gotten that idea? Even Richie hadn't been certain until recently. *I should have stood up to them,* she thought in vicious self-recrimination. *But it happened so fast I didn't know what to do,* another voice countered in her own defense. All the while these thoughts whirled through her mind, she was on her knees beside her brother, terrified he would die before the ambulance came, saying over and over, "I'm sorry, I'm sorry, please forgive me."

+ + +

By the time the ambulance came, Richie was beginning to regain consciousness. He asked Rebecca what happened and how badly he was hurt.

Rebecca didn't know how to answer, so she took one of the paramedics aside and asked, "How badly is he hurt?"

The paramedic responded vaguely, "He'll be assessed further when we get him to the hospital. A doctor will give you a report in due course." Rebecca noticed the worried look on her otherwise poker face and that worry transmitted to Rebecca and magnified.

Rebecca was at the point of emotional explosion when the ambulance finally reached the hospital, and the first person she saw when the back doors opened was her mother.

Rebecca burst into tears, sobbing uncontrollably, but she managed to whisper to her mother, "They beat him because he's gay. How did they even know?"

Ellen, already in shock, blurted, "What did you say?"

Rebecca mumbled, hardly knowing what she was saying so deep was her confusion and shock, "They beat him because he's gay."

Ellen took Rebecca by the shoulders and gave her a little shake to get her attention. When Ellen finally had it, she looked her daughter square in the eye and firmly said, "Listen to me. You keep that to yourself. Do you understand?"

Snapped out of her daze at the fierceness of her mother's voice and demeanor, Rebecca nodded her understanding mutely.

Richie was whisked away from Ellen and Rebecca by the efficiency of the system, leaving them in a panic to know what was going on. It was a confusing and frustrating time for the whole family for several hours after that as they waited for word of Richie's condition from the emergency room staff. When Richard arrived, he stormed about and threatened everyone but was met with exasperating calm and patience as the staff continued their practiced stonewalling. Finally, after two hours of pacing and fuming and worrying and weeping, the resident in charge of Richie's case found them in the waiting room.

"Richie is going to be fine," reported the resident with infuriating impassivity as if he was talking about a piece of furniture that had recently been broken. "He suffered a concussion, cuts and abrasions to his face and scalp, massive bruising to his torso and groin area, and several broken ribs, but that is the extent of the damage. We'll keep him for a few days to make sure nothing else shows up, but I don't think anything will. He was lucky there was no internal bleeding or organ damage. His spleen is a bit bruised, but that should heal quickly. Do you have any questions?"

The numbness all three felt did not lend itself to asking questions, so the resident turned on his heel and was about to leave when Richard asked, "Can we see him?"

"Of course, follow me," the doctor said officiously as he led them through the double doors across the hall into the inner sanctum of the emergency room. At the far end of the room, they immediately saw Richie and ran to him.

Rebecca was devastated at the sight of his face. It was at least twice its normal size and covered with livid bruises and scrapes. Hot tears leaked out of the corner of her eyes even after she told herself not to cry, for Richie's sake. He had sutured cuts above his right eye, in the middle of his forehead, and on the bridge of his nose. The skin on his face was stretched unnaturally tight by swelling, and he looked so young and helpless. Too, his eyes revealed something new. There was a knowing that showed through the pain where once there had been innocence. Richie had lost his innocence at the hands of five drunks, and he would never get it back. Richie had come face to face with evil on the streets of Manhattan and had become fully acquainted with it.

+ + +

Richie's physical recovery was slow but steady, and he was released from the hospital four days after the assault. His face had lost its overblown expression, the blackness of the bruising was turning a sickly green and yellow, and he had innumerable aches and pains, but overall, he was on the mend. Psychologically, he was still torn. He felt an overwhelming fear when the doors of the hospital opened, and he was pushed through in his wheelchair. The world had become a dangerous place with unknown assailants around every corner and in every shadow. The violent violation of his body had left physical wounds, but he had also been left with psychological and spiritual wounds that would take much longer to heal.

+ + +

A year later, Richie and Rebecca moved to Boston together to attend Harvard. Their parents had both graduated from Harvard, so their attendance there was a foregone conclusion. Richie's heart was still in a career in dance, but he had reluctantly agreed to pursue a degree before studying dance at Julliard. Richie majored in English while Rebecca studied economics. Rebecca's ambition was to follow her father into legal practice.

Richard had sorely disappointed his father by never actually taking over the family business. He had become instantly enamored with the law once he had entered Harvard Law School and spent his career in practice as a partner in a small but highly profitable boutique litigation firm specializing in medical malpractice. He was the lawyer in the family, but other family members had taken over the running of the family business.

Rebecca wanted nothing more than to follow in her father's footsteps, but during her freshman year, Rebecca met Daniel Blain, a handsome young man that had the distinction of being the most persistent suitor she had ever had. He noticed her in one of the campus restaurants and began a campaign to learn her identity. After discovering they had common acquaintances, he made his approach valiantly and courageously through Rebecca's roommate, who he had enlisted to his team.

His subterfuge and circumspection proved to be a delight to Rebecca once introductions were made. She was flattered at having a secret admirer and touched by Daniel's obvious affection for her, which had developed without the benefit of his even knowing her. Rebecca soon discovered Daniel was a Southern Baptist, pronounced "Suth'n Babdis'd," from Atlanta, Georgia, pronounced "Adlana Jo-jia."

It was a case of love at first sight for Daniel. Not so for Rebecca. After numerous advances and many rejections, Rebecca finally agreed to go out with Daniel, not on a date mind you, just out. Their first outing was to dinner and a movie. The outing went well until Daniel asked Rebecca about her religious convictions. She cut off the conversation by informing him her beliefs were personal to her and no business of his. He immediately dropped the subject in case he was sinking his proverbial ship, but not before there was a large hole in the hull with water gushing in. Later, Rebecca raved at her roommate for introducing her to a 'Bible thumper,' and for several months, she would have nothing to do with Daniel.

Daniel was undeterred by one terse rejection after another and was finally rewarded with another chance. The second outing, which by this time was definitely not a date, went much better than the first as a result of Daniel's newly minted discretion on the topic of religion. Daniel took Rebecca to a lakeside restaurant where they dined by candlelight on a water's-edge, open-air patio. Rebecca was at first uncomfortable with the romantic surroundings, afraid the surroundings alone would give Daniel weird ideas about a future together. The scene was so soothing and relaxing, though, that Rebecca found herself enjoying the outing and participated fully in an animated conversation full of easy laughter and good-natured kidding. Rebecca's roommate heard later that they had had a "very nice time on their *date*."

+ + +

Near the end of Richie's first year, he got the call from Julliard. The admissions officer was clear this was his opportunity to attend the school. There would be no other offers. He took the opportunity without further consideration. This was his dream, and this was the way to his dream, so what good would it do to go through a tortuous decision-making process? He was going to do it and damn the torpedoes. After accepting his spot in the dance school, he phoned his mother to tell her the news.

"Hi, Mom. Guess what?"

"You're going to get all 'A's' this term," teased Ellen.

"Not exactly. I accepted a place at Julliard starting in September."

"I see," his mother replied tartly. "I'm very happy for you, but you agreed to finish your degree first."

"I know, Mom, but they said I wouldn't get another chance because I would be too old if I wait any longer. It was now or never, and I had to choose, so I went for it. Can you please talk to Dad for me?"

"I'll talk to your father, but you know he'll be disappointed. He was hoping you'd give up dance for business."

"I know, Mom, but I hope he can find it in him to support me in *my* dream for me instead of *his* dream for me."

"Your father loves you dearly, and I'm sure he'll be fair. I'll talk to him this afternoon, and then you and I can talk more later. I love you, my son, and really, I am proud of you for getting in. It took a great deal of effort and dedication on your part. I don't think I could have done anything like that."

Richie heard the supportive words but detected a decided lack of joy in her statement.

"Thanks, Mom, that means a lot. I love you. Talk later." Richie hung up the phone, having accomplished his mission but not feeling very proud of himself. He was breaking his commitment to his father to finish out his degree at Harvard, and that did leave him feeling a little guilty. He truly hoped this wouldn't tear them apart.

+ + +

Richie's dream was coming true finally, but all was not a bed of roses. Daniel and Rebecca had invited him to a special event at their church the next Sunday. Daniel had finally won over Rebecca's strenuous avoidance of all things religious, and she claimed she was now "saved" and baptized. She was born again, she said; she had given her heart to Jesus Christ at a service at Daniel's church, and she wanted Richie to check it out.

He had agreed to go, but he was a little worried. He had seen a change in Rebecca since her conversion, and it wasn't all good in Richie's estimation. She was still loving and kind, but she had always been loving and kind. Perhaps it was that she seemed a bit more compassionate, but again, that wasn't a dramatic change. She seemed slightly happier, and definitely more comfortable with herself and her future, and she said that was because she was now in God's hands, and he was a good and benevolent God.

All of that was good, he guessed, but along with the good, she seemed to have developed a dislike for alternative points of view. She said she was now learning the truth, and the truth was the truth for everyone, not just her. Richie tried to point out that perhaps there was a range of opinion that was still true, but she recoiled at that. She had accepted the truth that she had been taught at her church without much consideration. Pastor Davies was a godly leader, and he knew what was true and what was not, Rebecca insisted.

Sunday morning came and Rebecca and Richie drove together to First Baptist Church. They would meet Daniel there, and Rebecca and Daniel would introduce Richie to all their friends. They had even invited Richie out for lunch after the service.

The building Rebecca drove up to was ornate and elaborate. It had imitation Greek pillars and an impressive steeple on the roof. Richie's first impression was of a buzz of activity. The parking lot was bustling, and attendants were busily directing traffic, efficiently moving cars around the lot and people in the direction of the building. Climbing out of their car, they were met by a fresh-faced young woman who greeted them warmly and asked if they needed assistance finding their way. Rebecca said she was a regular, and the greeter gave her a warm smile and moved on to the next car full of people, greeting them just as warmly. Richie got the same feeling from the greeter as he did when he received a pleasant form letter: nice but impersonal.

As they made their way up the front steps, Richie was glad he was mostly secure in himself because otherwise this would be intimidating. Everyone else seemed to know where they were going and what they were doing. Richie knew neither of these things but trusted his sister not to lead him astray.

The foyer was full of people and was also bustling with activity. It was hard even to get to the doors of the auditorium, but eventually they managed. Once inside, they found seats close to the front because the back seats had already filled. Richie found the vocabulary odd as he listened intently to what Rebecca and Daniel were saying to each other. They called the auditorium a "sanctuary." The use of that word suggested a protected, or secluded, place. Richie wondered what it was these people were hiding from or afraid of that they needed sanctuary. They called their gathering a "service," and Richie wondered who was serving whom and why they would use such an odd word to describe what they did on Sunday. In any other setting, this would be a concert, performance, or production.

The words used by Rebecca to describe her experience came back to him. She had said she had been "saved" now. *Why did she need saving?* he wondered. *And what did the saving do for her or to her?* She had been "baptized." Who could tell what that meant? These people were fluently speaking a different language, and they assumed he knew what the words meant.

Finally, the room filled, and a musical group mounted the stage. The music was professionally produced and harmonious; the sound coming through the concert sound system was warm and rich. The arrangements were engaging and layered, designed to produce an emotional response in the audience. The lyrics were foreign to him, but overall, they were pleasant, and the musicians performed admirably in Richie's estimation. Again, the words to the songs might as well have been in Greek because Richie had no context for understanding the concepts associated with them. Most of the music spoke to what God had done or was going to do for these folks and how they loved him for that. From what Richie could gather, God was making them healthy, wealthy, and wise, and they were really happy. Richie wondered how that concept played out in the Third World where Christians presumably had little hope of being healthy or wealthy, though he knew they could undoubtedly be wise. One thing in particular that surprised Richie was the man leading the singing looked at his watch from time to time, giving the impression the program was finely tuned, and his part of the performance had to conclude on time.

Once the singing finished, a man who looked to be in his late fifties rose from the front row and bounded onto the stage with great enthusiasm. He wore what looked like an expensive and well-tailored light-gray suit that set off the silver in his hair, creating a distinguished look. His voice boomed into his remote microphone as he welcomed the audience by saying, "We are so incredibly happy you came to worship the Lord this morning. Isn't it great to be in the presence of the Lord? Who would rather be on the golf course this morning? Or at the Patriot's game?" The audience tittered in response to his greeting, and no one lifted their hand. Richie's biggest question at this greeting was who "we" was. Was it this man and his colleagues, or he and God perhaps?

Rebecca nudged Richie with her elbow, and with misty eyes, informed Richie this man was Pastor Davies, the man she couldn't stop talking about. He was the man she said had led her to the Lord through one of his sermons. She had felt he was speaking directly to her when he had admonished the crowd to accept Jesus Christ as their Lord and Savior.

After he had welcomed the crowd good-naturedly, Pastor Davies launched into an appeal for money. His talk touched on what he said were Bible sayings. Richie had never read the Bible, so it was difficult for him to follow what was being said, but he got the impression it must cost a lot of money to put on this performance every week, and Pastor Davies wanted everyone to help pay for it. After outlining in detail how people could give online, he called some people forward, each carrying some kind of platter, much like you would serve a turkey on.

Pastor Davies then asked everyone to pray with him. In his prayer, he said to the Lord, "Lord, we thank these generous people for their giving this morning. Bless them with abundance and favor as you have promised, in relation to their generosity. Let this money be used for your purposes." Richie wondered again who "we" was.

The men and women with the platters passed them down each row of seats, and people put money into them as the platters came their way. When the platter came to Richie, Rebecca told him he didn't need to give because he was a visitor, so he passed it on to her. Once the platters had been passed to everyone, they were taken away, and Pastor Davies began to tell the audience about events at the church during the week. There seemed to be events almost every night for various age groups. It was impressive and all so well-orchestrated. He wondered how many people worked here and could see what Pastor Davies said must be true: to keep all this going must cost a fortune.

Eventually, the pastor's voice changed tenor and became deeper and more serious. He placed a black leather-bound book and some notes on his podium and began speaking with much less humor and much more severity. The crowd changed as well. As a group, they sat up straight or sat forward in their seats in rapt attention. They obviously wanted to hear everything this man had to say. Not only that, but they seemed to have a deep affection for the man. Richie vaguely wondered how so many people could actually know the man.

Dramatically, Pastor Davies went on to pray for God to direct him when he spoke to "these people," that "He would place every word in his mouth," and that "they would listen carefully and understand completely what was said." He said the topic of his speech was dear to the heart of God and important to the whole of America. This intrigued Richie because the lead-up to the speech was so dramatic and theatrical that it created a powerful air of authority. In fact, the way he introduced his topic suggested he was purporting to speak for God. From his seat, Richie had to look up at the man, which only added to the power of the situation. Richie saw it as a rather cheap theatrical trick, but he realized those around him, including his sister, were awed by what they were experiencing and nodding their agreement. Then the bomb dropped. It was atomic.

"The title of my sermon this morning is, *Homosexuality: God's View*. Homosexuality is a scourge on humanity, and that scourge is becoming rampant in America. I tell you, the Bible is so crystal clear about men and women lusting after their own kind that good Christian folks should have no doubt about this issue. I can't understand why there is any debate at all, and if a Christian participates in the debate, he either lacks spiritual depth or has not spent enough time studying the Word of God. Homosexuality is being thrust upon the people of God by godless, self-seeking gays and lesbians out to destroy the Church, seduce boys and girls into their ungodly lifestyle, and diminish the quality of life of God-fearing people all across this country. If a Christian condones homosexuality, he is in open rebellion to the Word of God and is condemning himself to the same fate God has ordained for all sinners."

Richie sat alarmed at what he had just heard. He felt the steel jaws of a trap snap shut around his chest. In disbelief, Richie now knew his sister had set him up. The person he trusted most. His invitation to this particular meeting on this particular day had been no accident. It had been a carefully orchestrated attempt by Rebecca and Daniel to show him the "truth" about himself and what God thought of him. Richie was revolted and angered by their deception and duplicity. How could Rebecca do this to him? They must have known what this guy would say.

Pastor Davies continued. "Open your Bibles to the Book of Leviticus, Chapter 18. In this chapter, God tells us what he thinks of gays and lesbians. In verse twenty-two, God says, 'You shall not lie with a male as one lies with a female; it is an abomination!'" the man shouted. "How clear does it have to be that men and women who are attracted to their own kind are an abomination to God? It is an abomination to God and defiles our nation. God says homosexuality is sin, and we cannot condone it by allowing these people anywhere near us. They cannot be allowed into our churches, and as Apostle Paul says in 1 Corinthians 5:5, we must 'deliver such a one to Satan for destruction of his flesh so that his spirit may be saved on the day of the Lord.' And Hebrews tells us, 'Marriage is to be held in honor among all, and the marriage bed is to be undefiled; for fornicators and adulterers God will judge.' We must turn our backs on these fornicators that defile our churches and nation with their presence as they defiled Sodom and Gomorrah. God himself rained fire and brimstone down on Sodom and Gomorrah for their sin, and he is raining AIDS down on present-day sodomites as judgment for their sin."

The sermon went on and on, describing God's clear hatred for gays and anyone who would have a relationship with them. He said the only salvation for a gay was to repent and "get the sin out"; otherwise, they were condemned to hell. The pastor's message was clear to Richie: God hates you and I hate you. Richie glanced over at Rebecca, the horror and revulsion communicated through his eyes and the special, unspoken bond between the twins.

When the sermon finally wound down, the pastor gave a brief dismissal, and then people gravitated toward the exits. Daniel bid Richie and Rebecca farewell at the front door, saying he had responsibilities at the church that afternoon and wouldn't be able to join them for lunch. He looked smugly at Rebecca, and as he turned to go, Richie saw him wink and smile with satisfaction.

Richie kept his cool in public, but once he and Rebecca were alone in Rebecca's car, he erupted. "How could you do that to me? What did I ever do to deserve that from you?"

"Richie, I just wanted you to hear the truth."

"What truth did you want me to hear? That I'm going to hell because of how I was born, or that I'm condemned even though I've never done any of those things that man said? I have never fornicated, whatever that means. I'm a virgin. How could I be damned when I'm a virgin, for crying out loud? You know me. You know I didn't ask to be gay. How can you believe the stuff that man said about your own brother?"

Rebecca sighed and pulled out of the church parking lot and into the street before she answered. "Richie, Pastor Davies is trying to reach you and people like you. I believe Pastor Davies knows God and speaks for him. If he says homosexuality is a sin, then you need to recognize that and change. You have to do what he said, get the sin out of your life."

"Okay, tell me how to get the sin out of my life. Your pastor guy didn't explain that. And if he's trying to reach me, he's not going about it very well. If he really wanted to reach me, maybe he ought to start by not yelling at me and calling me a scourge on humanity and a sinner who's going to hell. He's a harsh, mean asshole." Richie wanted nothing more to do with Pastor Davies or the God for whom he supposedly spoke.

Rebecca sighed, deeper this time, and stared sadly out the windshield. "Richie, I don't know how to get the sin out, but I do know that what he said was true, and you need to change to be acceptable to God, and if you don't change, I can't be around you."

Richie was taken aback. He was speechless for a long moment before he leaned forward and clasped his hands tightly between his knees. "Hold on a minute, we're family. Are you saying you'll cut me off, just so you line up with what that guy says?" *What had happened to his loving twin sister?*

"Don't call him, 'that guy.' He's a great man of God, and he is God's man for our congregation. I'm going to do what he says."

"I can't believe I'm hearing this from you, but if you've made up your mind, I suppose there's nothing I can do to change it." Richie paused to choke back the tears that threatened behind his eyes. "Okay, you don't want to see me anymore, so stop the car and let me out. We can start this right now."

Rebecca silently did as he bid and continued to say nothing even after Richie had stepped out of the car.

"Have a nice life!" Richie yelled after he'd slammed the door shut.

That was the last time Richie spoke to Rebecca. Then he left Boston for New York, and their paths did not cross again until their parents' funeral three years later. Even then, Rebecca still held true to the belief that she must turn her brother over to Satan and have nothing to do with him, just as Pastor Davies had instructed.

+ + +

Pastor Davies sat behind the vast desk in his office after the service feeling distinctly satisfied. *Influence*, he thought. *Influence is the currency of the Church. I had influence today. I spoke well, and my topic was perfect given recent headlines. Homosexuality is an abomination and must be eradicated from Christianity, and I boosted that cause today. This message was essential to show that I am worthy to be the pastor of this church and worthy of advancement.*

Pastor Davies' reverie continued as he thought back over his career in ministry. *My father and grandfather were clergy in this denomination and were great men in their own right. Their reputations and interventions launched me into the clergy and afforded me opportunities. Like royal families, we look after our own. We're really the royalty of the Church, when you think about it. We are the ones that understand ministry, after all.*

He leaned back in his leather desk chair and steepled his fingers under his chin. *I have twelve hundred souls in my flock, but I know I'm destined for more. The senior position at Broad Street Church is opening up soon, and I'm the obvious candidate. Just think, preaching to ten thousand people every Sunday plus a national television spot. That's my shot at the big time. That's what it's all about.*

CHAPTER 6

Detached Lives

As they comfortably sipped their wine on the balcony overlooking the city, Francis asked, "When did your parents die?" As soon as he asked the question, he wondered whether the subject was off limits to Richie.

"Two years ago, this summer. They were driving back to New York from Aspen, and a semi hit them head on. The driver fell asleep and crossed over to their side of the road."

"That must have been a terrible shock. How did you process it?" asked Francis. He had never had someone close to him die and was genuinely curious.

"I haven't really processed it at all. Every time I have a memory of either of them, the pain is so intense I force it out of my mind. That makes me a bit weird at times," Richie confessed.

"What do you mean, 'weird'?" Francis asked gently.

"Sometimes I'll wake up at night after hearing my mother's voice, or as I'm walking down the street, I'm sure I see my father. It's as if they aren't really dead, just avoiding me. And I'm really angry with them for leaving me, particularly when I need them now more than ever." He let out a quiet snort. "Being angry seems weird to me. How can I be mad at dead people I loved so dearly? But I am, and I can't seem to get over that."

"Anger is a natural part of grieving," Francis responded. "Broken relationships always seem like betrayal, even if one didn't have a choice."

"When Rebecca rejected me, I was devastated, and I still am. She indirectly convinced me I was worthless. I was always afraid that eventually my parents would reject me too. I never told them I was gay, but somehow it came out when I was in the hospital. No one ever said anything about it, but then they died, and you're right, it feels like betrayal. I don't even know what to do with it. Now here I am, afraid to die, and my family isn't here with me."

Francis sat in silence, wondering if there was anything he could say or do to help Richie mourn his parents. What was there to say? It truly was terribly sad. *My being here at such at vulnerable time for Richie is perhaps enough,* he thought. So he chose to say nothing. His heart was breaking for Richie, but he really had no experience with the things Richie had gone through. He silently cried out to God: "Lord, let me feel what Richie is feeling right now."

Immediately, Francis felt, empathetically, tremendous sorrow, loneliness, and fear, all mixed together. The effect threatened to make him double over. It pierced him like an arrow, and he could hardly breathe.

From deep within himself, he implored of the Lord, "How can people like Richie live with such pain and sorrow? Why is there so much suffering on earth? It seems we constantly find ourselves in situations that cause our hearts to break. The rejection Richie is feeling is hurting him to the core of his being. What do you want me to do? You put me in Richie's life for some purpose. What do you want me to do?"

Just then Richie pulled himself together and said, "Enough of that. I will not be maudlin tonight. Let's go out and celebrate our friendship. I feel like I've always known you. Thank you for being here, Francis."

Francis' reply did not equate to the stance of the Catholic Church on homosexuality, but it did equate to his own feelings. "It is my distinct pleasure to be here, and I am grateful too for your friendship. And before we go, let me say again that your value as a human being comes from the fact that you are loved by God, not from how you behave or what your personal makeup includes."

"Thank you for saying that, Francis. I appreciate your compassion and your obvious faith. You keep telling me God is loving, accepting, and kind, and I really want to believe you."

+ + +

Drago's lodging was comfortable and close to his target. So, he was lounging in front of his window across the street from the apartment building, watching, when Francis and the boy left and walked toward the center of Manhattan. Drago grabbed his phone and keys on his way out of his room and slowly followed, keeping his pace random and not looking directly at the pair. This surveillance was so easy he feared he would get sloppy as he had when they had arrived from the airport.

His instructions were simple: keep an eye on Father Francis. He had reported by email to Cardinal Carducci when he had arrived at his hotel. He had not received a reply and had not expected one. When the time came, Carducci would tell him what he wanted done. In the meantime, Drago would know where the priest was at all times. As he followed, Drago wondered exactly what the priest had done to cause such rage among the higher-ups. He seemed like an ordinary priest, nothing special. He knew the priest had written some book, but he knew nothing definitive about why it had made such a negative impact, and he didn't really care.

+ + +

Francis and Richie walked two blocks from the apartment building and stopped at a club. The man who welcomed them at the door had a bleach-blond bouffant hairdo piled high on his head, obviously cemented in place with several layers of product. He wore a colorful Hawaiian shirt unbuttoned to reveal a muscular, hairless chest and abdomen. He greeted Richie as if he was a long-lost brother, gushing all over him in a high, squeaky, effeminate voice. Richie introduced him as Maurice and told Francis they had known each other for several years. After greeting Francis with an appraising stare, Maurice clucked knowingly over Richie's appearance, commiserating over his apparent weight loss and ill health. Francis got the feeling the signs of Richie's illness were commonplace to Maurice.

Maurice led them to their table with an exaggerated wiggle of his bottom at every step. He reminded Francis of a dancer on stage using exaggerated movements to communicate with a large audience. Maurice may not have had a large audience, but that did not seem to hinder his performance. Francis had little experience with the gay community, and though Maurice's behavior made him uncomfortable, it also intrigued him, piquing his curiosity. He was clearly immersed in a different culture with different body language and a different set of social conventions.

At this realization, Francis became self-conscious and afraid of the signals he may be sending into this new environment inadvertently. Without thinking, he walked more stiffly and glanced from side to side, trying to discern the reaction of other patrons of the restaurant. When he caught himself giving this comical performance he thought, *Give yourself a shake. Be exactly who you are, no more, no less.* At this, he relaxed and became Father Francis again, even if he was in an unusual and unfamiliar environment. One could be a representative of Christ anywhere. The culture might change, but the spirit remained the same. His Heavenly Father was the Heavenly Father of all human beings, no matter what form their sexuality took. This was an opportunity for discovery and ministry, and Francis decided he would make the best of it and follow Christ where he was leading.

As this decision formed in his mind, his heart was filled anew with affection for Richie and for those he passed on the way to their table. He was not in danger from these people any more than he was from anyone else. He may be an object of sexual inquisitiveness in this room but no more so than he was in other situations. And, while he knew he was a heterosexual male, his sexuality had been submitted to a relational vow to Christ. That did not negate it or even change it. The stares from these men did not make him less of a man or less surrendered relationally to Christ. There was absolutely nothing to fear and certainly nothing to be angry about. Just like him, these were God's creatures that He loved dearly.

As they arrived at their table, Maurice flamboyantly threw his arms in the air and gave a rudimentary curtsy, saying loudly, "Here you are, girls." Francis could not help himself. He laughed out loud at the comic ridiculousness of this man's behavior. He choked down his mirth, however, when he realized no one else was laughing. He quickly sat down, trying to overcome the grin that had erupted all over his face. Tears came to his eyes as he made a valiant but unsuccessful attempt to stifle the snorts coming out of his nose. At this, he was rewarded with a grin from Richie.

"So, what do you think?" asked Richie, goading Francis.

"It's very ... um, nice," replied Francis in a strangled voice. He managed to control his outward appearance only until Maurice had made his way back to his rostrum at the front door.

Richie could not contain himself any longer and laughed out loud at Francis' discomfort while Francis nearly choked on his own laughter. Maurice gave them a wink and a wiggle in return.

After several minutes and a glass of water, Francis was finally able to talk normally. He asked Richie, "Why did you bring me here?"

"I just wanted to introduce you to my world."

"Why is this your world? You have a choice of what world you belong to, do you not?" puzzled Francis.

Richie sighed and grew serious. "I was chased out of my world—my family—and I had to land somewhere. Rebecca is my only living family, and she refuses to even see me. I've been barred from her world now that they've handed me over to Satan, "for my own good." And I've never really had any close friends other than her, so once she threw me out of her life, I landed where I was accepted. In this world, I don't have to pretend, and I don't have to prove myself. My personal character and behavior are all that's important. I am who I am, and I'm accepted for that without interrogation or suspicion. These people have become my family because my real family wouldn't accept me," retorted Richie passionately.

At this, Francis considered his own experience. At an early age, he had adopted the Roman Catholic Church as his family and had in turn been adopted by the Church corporate. Adoption meant that for the better part of his life, he had existed within the Church—living, eating, studying, and socializing—primarily with his fellow priests, and to a lesser extent, with parishioners during his pastoral assignments. He had felt comfortable, nurtured, and safe in the Church. While he had at times chafed at being pampered and stifled, that was part of the life he had chosen. As he looked around him now, all he could see was oddity, yet his Church family in many ways displayed oddity too. He had been chased from his world too. Where would he land?

"Tell me about dancing in Paris," asked Francis, changing the subject.

Richie's countenance lit up like a Christmas tree at the mention of dancing.

BROKEN CROSS

+ + +

Rebecca leaned back into an overstuffed leather chair in front of a cheerless fire at her log chalet in Aspen. She had been living in Aspen for more than a year, trying desperately to heal after her divorce from Daniel and the death of her parents. She lived alone, too depressed to socialize with neighbors and far too depressed to join the transient and shallow Aspen jet set, even though she had the resources to do it. Her depression made her listless, fearful of people, and disoriented. She did not want to see anyone, and friends and acquaintances were even scarier than strangers. If she saw someone she knew, she was immediately and irrationally tempted to run or cross the street to avoid contact. She was a recluse, despondent and suffering, without anyone with whom to share her thoughts and feelings.

Reminiscing, she realized that from Daniel's point of view, their romance had been nothing short of spectacular despite her initial reluctance. He had been oh-so attentive and obviously smitten with her. She was his find, and he would conquer her as if she was Mount Everest. The courtship had been planned and executed with surgical precision, and Rebecca had been swept off her feet and down the aisle before she had known what was happening. Back then, she had been happier than she had ever been. Her childhood had been great but being in love had been something special. Her newfound faith had only added to her sense of well-being and joy. She and Daniel had gotten married in their last year at Harvard, right on schedule, and she had felt strongly that her life was finally coming together. Just as they had planned, Daniel had graduated with a business degree from Harvard and joined his father's financial services business in Atlanta.

The move to Atlanta had been a shock Rebecca had not anticipated. After all, she was only moving to another part of America. What could be so hard about that? For Rebecca, though, it seemed everything had been hard about that. Being a "Northern girl," she had not been accepted by the Southern belles as she had expected. Not unreasonably, she had anticipated being married to Daniel would have given her an automatic entrée into Atlanta society. Instead, it had turned out that even in their large Southern Baptist church, Rebecca could not break into the existing social order.

People had been outwardly friendly, affectionate, and cheerful, but she had never been invited into any close relationships. In fact, in many ways, their exuberant affection in public, calling her "honey" and "darling" and "sweetie" from their first meeting, had made the subtle rejection thereafter even harder to take. As Rebecca had soon discovered, the social order was based on family ties, and the families were self-contained and rigid when it came to accepting strangers into their midst. Even Daniel's family had been cool to her. Daniel had married a Yankee, so her mother- and sisters-in-law had built a reserve between them and her that had felt a lot like disapproval. The women in Daniel's family had clearly been disappointed at his choice of spouse.

Rebecca had phoned her parents every day or so but never mentioned her struggles with her new life. She had been afraid they would think she had made a mistake. Even in the face of probing questions from her intuitive mother, she had kept silent about her misgivings and her loneliness.

Daniel's father, unlike the female element, had accepted Rebecca generously and warmly, showering her with enthusiastic affection. In fact, whenever he had grabbed her and hugged her, Rebecca had had the uncomfortable feeling he was enjoying it in a way he probably shouldn't. She had often felt like he was taking something from her when he was supposed to be giving something to her. However, he was a founding member of Shiloh Baptist and a member of the deacon board, and her Christian training told her she was to trust his piety and propriety because he was in leadership. So, as she had done many times in her Christian life, she had put her instincts on the back burner and chosen to believe the best of a person with spiritual authority over her.

Daniel's first months with the firm had revealed he had a knack for the business, and he had begun almost immediately to make substantial amounts of money. The money had a price tag though because he'd had to spend long hours and most evenings either at the office or entertaining clients in restaurants and on golf courses. Daniel was following his father's lead and insisted he and Rebecca move quickly to buy a large house near his parents.

"I want the house, Becky. It's close to Mom and Dad, and it's a great deal. Dad says so. He always says if you're going to stretch financially, stretch on the old homestead. It'll be great. We'll fix it up nice, and it'll be a fabulous place to raise kids. Come on, Becky, get excited."

"I'm worried about taking on so much debt," Rebecca had replied seriously. "Two million dollars of debt seems like a huge amount of money to me. How will we ever pay it back?"

"Don't worry, hon; I intend make tons of money. It won't be a problem at all."

Daniel continued to maintain it was a steal. The mortgage had been initially daunting, but they had lived a frugal lifestyle Rebecca had engineered, and they had dedicated themselves to paying it down. Rebecca had offered many times to find employment to help with the expenses, but Daniel had categorically refused. A woman's place was in the home. His mother had never worked and look how his family had turned out. It was the natural order of things to Daniel.

Faced with appearing rebellious, Rebecca had contented herself with making her house the home she had always dreamed of. She had read widely on interior design and carefully planned and implemented her creation. Her creativity had come to the fore as the house that had begun as a large, plain barn-like structure was transformed into a home with a cozy, stylish atmosphere that included a bright, warm sunroom where she and Daniel had breakfast if he did not have to leave early to attend some meeting, a comfortable den for Daniel, a cheerful living room where they could entertain, and several plush but homey bedrooms.

She had even decorated one of the smaller bedrooms as a nursery where the inevitable first child would begin their life.

Rebecca's loneliness had abated while she worked on her renovation projects, so she had thrown herself into her homemaking with abandon and often worked well into the evening while waiting for Daniel to come home.

Once the interior had been finished, she had started on the garden, which was overgrown and ugly. Its one redeeming feature was the classic sixty-foot magnolia tree in the front yard. It was an emblem of the South and Rebecca loved it. She had begun by investing in the right gardening tools and then meticulously researching horticulture in the Atlanta area. As she had done inside, she carefully laid out the environments and spaces she wished to create and then had begun to build and cultivate.

The garden had soon matched the elegance of the interior of the house. She was finished. After she had paced and asked herself what to do next, she had decided it was time to start a family, and when the subject had come up, Daniel had been all in favor. He had felt it was their duty to God to have a large family and bring the children up to share their parent's faith and to serve God. Daniel had frowned on Rebecca's decision to take birth control when they had first married and was glad when she stopped. His parents had been pressuring them to have their first child, and the pressure would ease as soon as Rebecca became pregnant.

When they had been newlyweds, their sex life had been exciting and new. Every day had been a new experience, and they had enjoyed each other immensely. Unfortunately, as Daniel's work had begun to play a larger and larger part in their lives, their home life had ended up suffering, and sex often became rushed and somehow unsatisfactory. They had promised each other that in the future, things would change. They had been sure things would be better when things settled down at work and Daniel was able to take more time off.

Things had not changed though, and work had just never seemed to abate as Daniel strove to meet his father's expectations and the requirements of their increasingly expensive lifestyle. "We have a mortgage now," Daniel would often comment, "and this is no time to let up." Once that mortgage was paid down, they could relax. Paying off a mortgage was a painfully slow process, Rebecca had discovered, and her life with Daniel had begun to seem routine and ordinary. She had a degree and often thought of having a career just for her.

When they had been formally trying for a baby, sex had become even more purposeful and less spontaneous and pleasurable. The last vestige of romance had, in Rebecca's subconscious, become part of the routine. After six months of trying, they had begun to worry.

"What do you think could be wrong?" Daniel had asked. "We try and try, and nothing happens. Are we doing everything right?"

"What's right or wrong?" Rebecca had retorted, annoyed he had seemed to be blaming her in some bizarre way. "We should just relax and let things unfold as they should," she had said, snuggling close to him and trying her hardest to be supportive and responsive.

"I just can't get it out of my mind that we're failing at what should come naturally. Maybe God is punishing us for something. Do we have sin in our lives that could be making you barren?"

Rebecca had put some distance between them then. "Barren? What do you mean barren? We've only been trying to get pregnant for six months. Even your mother says it can take longer than that," she had replied, shocked.

"I told you not to take birth control. Maybe you messed yourself up inside with that stuff. I was afraid something like this would happen." Daniel had run his hands through his hair then. "Everybody knows we're trying to have a family. What are the people at church going to say? They're going to think I don't have what it takes to get my wife pregnant, for heaven's sakes. I have to go for a walk and think this through." He had jumped out of bed and all but run out of the house in a frenzy, leaving a bewildered Rebecca trying to make sense of his unbelievable behavior.

"What would the people at church think?" What kind of question had that been? *Who cared what people at church thought? Let them think whatever they want,* she had thought. *What difference was that to us?* The whole thing was ridiculous, as far as she had been concerned, but Daniel had taken it as a blow to his masculinity, and he had taken it very hard indeed.

Daniel had returned much later, waking Rebecca when he had fumbled with his keys trying to open the front door. She had finally gone down and opened the deadbolt herself. When she had opened the door, Daniel had been leaning heavily against the brick wall beside the door, obviously drunk.

"What have you been up to?" Rebecca had demanded.

"Jush lee mee 'lone," had been his response. "Ge' ouda my way," he had said, pushing past her and almost falling into the foyer. When she had tried to help him up the stairs, he had pushed her hand away and climbed up one unsteady step at a time, holding onto one banister with both hands.

Rebecca had stood dumbfounded at the bottom of the stairs, gazing at the stranger staggering toward her bedroom. She had followed tentatively, not knowing what to do. Seeing Daniel had fallen face down on the carpet at the foot of their bed, she had shaken her head and tried to pull him to his feet, but he had been a dead weight.

He had mumbled again for her to leave him alone and tried to get to his feet. When he had finally managed to stagger up, he had looked at Rebecca with a wild look in his eye and shouted, "You're a bish. You're trying to roon my life."

Rebecca had not taken it personally at first, assuming it had been the liquor talking, but then he had come at her, driving her up against the wall, crushing her chest until she could barely breathe. Her slim 115 pounds had been no match for his brawny 210.

"You're jus' trine t'embarash me, you bish." With that, he had swung with his right fist and hit her squarely on the left ear, knocking her to the ground. Blood had spurted from her ruined ear as she lay unconscious on the floor.

At the sight of his beautiful, delicate, young wife stretched out before him bleeding, Daniel had sobered up enough to realize what he had done. As she had come to, he had furiously raked his fingers through his hair as he bent over her prostrate form and begged over and over, "I'm sorry. I'm sorry. Please forgive me." He hadn't, however, called an ambulance.

CHAPTER 7

Different Paths

Rebecca had spent two days in bed recovering from the blow administered by her loving Christian husband. When she had felt up to it and her ear had stopped ringing, she had visited their pastor. She had been distraught and upset. Daniel had just pretended everything was fine, so she had been afraid to bring the matter up for discussion and needed perspective from someone she trusted.

Just as she had trusted Pastor Davies in Boston, she trusted Pastor McCallum, lead pastor of Shiloh Baptist Church, so she had made her appointment with Rose, Pastor McCallum's cheerful assistant. When the time for the appointment arrived, Rose had ushered her into Pastor McCallum's office. The furniture had been a heavy dark wood, probably oak, Rebecca had thought. Pastor McCallum had sat behind a huge desk, and behind him had been a wall of books. Rebecca had noted several titles he had recommended to the congregation. Her impression of his office had been that it should have belonged to a powerful executive. Pastor McCallum had not stood when she had entered but had invited her to sit in one of the chairs across the desk from him with a wave.

After exchanging pleasantries about the weather and church services, Pastor McCallum had asked, "Now, what can I do for you, Mrs. Blain?"

Hesitantly, Rebecca had said, "I need to talk to you about something that happened."

Suddenly serious, Pastor McCallum had motioned for her to proceed.

"I don't know how to explain it without coming right out and saying it," she had stammered. "Daniel got drunk and hit me a couple days ago, and I don't know what to do," she had said, pleading.

"Wow, that's not what I expected you to say. I'm sorry to hear that. How did it happen?" Pastor McCallum had reflexively pushed his chair away from her and sat up straighter, wariness animating a face turned ever so slightly away. His body language had been of someone sitting on a splinter.

Rebecca explained what had happened. She had promised herself she wouldn't cry, but she had ended up weeping anyway as she told her story. She had felt foolish, vulnerable, and weak at being the stereotypical woman in distress, but she had also felt she was in a safe place with a man she trusted, and her emotions had just burst out like a dam breached by a flood. When she had finished telling her story, she had wiped her eyes, blown her nose one last time, and looked up at Pastor McCallum expectantly.

"Well now, young lady, that is quite a story," Pastor McCallum had said blandly. "I'm sorry this has happened, but I'm not sure what you want from me."

Rebecca had choked back her emotion and steadied her shaky voice, noticing his taut body language, his hesitant response, and the flush in his cheeks. A light sheen of sweat on his forehead evinced fear.

"I don't know what I want," Rebecca had said cautiously. "I guess I just wanted to tell you what happened and get some advice. You know Daniel and his family, so I thought you would be the one to talk to since you're our pastor and might have experience with things like this."

"Yes, I know the Blain family well. Daniel's father is on the board of the church, as you know, and the family has been supportive of me throughout the many years of my ministry here at Shiloh."

"I know. I know all that, but what should I do?"

"What do you mean by 'do'?" the pastor had replied, again looking wary and uncomfortable.

"I mean, what should I do about Daniel knocking me unconscious while drunk as a skunk?" Rebecca had asked with growing incredulity.

"Well, the answer to that question is quite simple. You support your husband."

"Excuse me?"

"The Bible tells us a woman must submit to her husband, so you must submit," had said Pastor McCallum, piously peaking his hands as if preparing to pray.

"So, you're saying I have to submit to being punched?"

"Well, those are your words, not mine."

"They are my words, but you're telling me I have to submit to Daniel after I just told you he beat me up, so what am I to conclude from that?"

"Now, Rebecca," Pastor McCallum had said gently, placatingly. "I know sometimes men get carried away physically with their wives, especially when their wives make them angry, but this is an isolated incident, and I'm sure you don't want to embarrass your husband or his family. Daniel has probably seen similar events in his own home and simply reacted the way his father has from time to time."

"What ....?" Rebecca's voice had trailed off and she had gripped her purse so tightly her knuckles went white as Pastor McCallum had continued.

"If your story were to circulate throughout the congregation, the Blain family would suffer grave humiliation and loss of status in the church and community. Their business would probably suffer. We have to be careful about that, don't we? But your secret is safe with me. I'll call Daniel and suggest he take an anger management course. That will help him in the future and smooth over this unfortunate incident."

Rebecca had been unable to hide her shock. "Are you saying I should pretend this didn't happen and just accept it as a part of life?"

"Again, Rebecca, those are your words. What I'm suggesting is that a man is the head of his home, and even though he may make mistakes and take things too far occasionally, it's his wife's responsibility to support him and submit to his authority."

"No, Pastor McCallum, I can't accept it's my role to endure physical abuse from my husband. That's not submission, that's insanity. My parents never struck me when I was growing up, and I don't need to tolerate it from my husband," Rebecca had said firmly.

"That sounds like rebellion, Rebecca," Pastor McCallum had warned. "It would be best if we ended this meeting now. Go home and carefully consider what I've said. You must consider the ramifications of your position on this matter. A lot of what will happen in the future depends on what you decide."

Pastor McCallum had dismissed her, making her feel like a little girl who had just had a meeting with the school principal. She hadn't gotten the strap, but she had felt as if she had, emotionally. Her head had reeled with what he had said and the implications. So, it ran in Daniel's family. *Great!* She just hadn't been able to believe Pastor McCallum had been so nonchalant about it. *Was this the way all Christian husbands treated their wives? How common was it?* she had wondered. Judging by the fact that Pastor McCallum had not been shocked by her story and he knew one of his board members occasionally "got carried away" with his wife, it had certainly looked like it wasn't uncommon at all.

When she had gotten home, Daniel had been there waiting for her, arms crossed as he stood in the kitchen.

"Hi, honey, where have you been? I noticed there's no supper on the table."

"I went to see Pastor McCallum."

"About what?" Daniel had asked rather less than cheerfully.

"I went to talk to him about what happened the other night."

"You what?! That was private between you and me! I told you I was sorry, and that should be the end of it. Just don't make me mad, and it will never happen again. You're my wife. You don't get to tell other people our private business. What were you thinking?" He had taken a step closer to her then, but she had refused to back down.

"I was thinking I needed some perspective about getting beat up by my husband. That's what I was thinking," Rebecca had responded, her chin out and her hands on her hips. She had had about enough of this nonsense.

Daniel had balled his fists by his side. "Now you're making me mad. I told you not to do that. Just leave the subject alone and it'll be over."

"Oh, really. Mr. High and Mighty thinks I should just leave it alone. Well, I don't think so. I'm going to talk to your mother about this and see what *she* says."

"You will not talk to my mother about this," Daniel had said menacingly.

"Not only am I going to, but I'm going to call her right now, this very minute."

As she had turned to pick up the phone, Daniel had grabbed her blouse, spun her around, and backhanded her across the face. He held her up, backhanded her again, and shook her violently, shouting, "You should do what your told!"

Her head had spun when he had finally let her go, and she had fallen to her knees in a daze. Her nose had dripped blood, and she had felt the welts exploding on her cheek. She had not cried though. She had been past tears, her mind made up.

When her head had cleared, she went up to their bedroom and packed a suitcase, leaving the house with Daniel's words echoing after her. "You'll be back! You'll come crawling back to me when you realize what you're missing!"

She had gotten in her car and begun to drive. Her destination had always been Aspen, where she knew she could find sanctuary. She had wished her parents were there; she had needed them then more than ever.

+ + +

Richie talked animatedly about his dance career. He spent more than an hour telling Francis every detail of his time at Julliard, his first opportunity with a New York dance company, and his eventual move to Paris.

The hour flew by for Francis. He was caught up in Richie's passion and enthusiasm for ballet. Richie's story was a fascinating mixture of highs and lows. His professional life was full of honor, acclaim, and success while his personal life was characterized by rejection, loss, and suffering. He told Francis of his life with his partner, Michel, who he had met while in Paris. Michel had also been a dancer, and they had had so much in common that they had ended up together. Michel had died of AIDS a year earlier but not before he had infected Richie. Richie had stayed in Paris during Michel's illness, nursing him, and finally visiting him daily in the hospice. Richie's own symptoms had shown up shortly after Michel had died, and he had been fighting them ever since. When he could no longer dance, he had decided to return home to wait for the inevitable.

"I know I'm dying. It won't be long now," said Richie distractedly, sitting back and staring at the drink in his hand.

"How do you know that?" asked Francis.

"I can feel it inside me. There's a dark shadow in the center of my being. It's trying to kill me. I try to be cheerful and have a good attitude, but deep down, all that's left is death. It makes me so sad. My life has been too short." He shook himself out of his morbid reverie and looked up. "Hey, I've been doing all the talking. I want to hear your story. It might cheer me up. Besides, I've been waiting for the mysterious Francis to reveal himself."

Francis wasn't sure where to start, so he took a deep breath and rested his elbows on the table before deciding to just dive in. "You mentioned several times I talk and act like a priest. Well, I am a priest. I am a priest, but a disgraced priest, running away from the Church."

"I knew it!" an excited Richie sat upright and exclaimed. "Not the running part, but you act just like I would have hoped a man of God would act. I've never really known a priest before. Aren't you afraid to be around me?" he blurted out.

"Why should I be afraid?" Francis raised an eyebrow, genuinely curious.

"I'm gay and have AIDS. Isn't that reason enough?"

"I only see a sensitive, intelligent young man. The rest doesn't seem important to me."

"Huh. That's a first." Richie paused to let that sink in before continuing. "So, tell me the whole story. I don't want you to leave anything out. What did you do to become a disgrace?" Richie asked with a twinkle in his eye, leaning forward like a child waiting for a special story from his father.

BROKEN CROSS

Francis found he wanted to tell Richie the whole story. He had only told his mother, and his pent-up pain, frustration, and confusion encouraged him to be open where Cardinal Massey had told him to be guarded.

So, he told Richie the whole story. He told him about his decision at an early age to become a priest, about his education in the Church, and about his work as a teacher, theologian, and pastor. When he mentioned he was a theologian, Richie interrupted to ask what a theologian was. That surprised Francis because he took it for granted that everyone knew the word. He went on to tell him about his book, how he had decided to publish the book over the objections of some of his colleagues, and then about the inquisition.

"You mean like the Spanish Inquisition?" Richie asked. "I thought that ended in the Middle Ages."

"Yes, much like that. The Church is still much the same institution that has survived throughout the ages. It's been modernized but still organized to protect the Church from heresy."

"So, your boss thought your book was heresy?" asked Richie, feeling proud of this bad-assed priest he had befriended.

"Well, they never actually called it that, but they feared the message. They were afraid it would shake the confidence of members of the Church in the authority of the pope and priesthood."

"You mean they were afraid they would lose power and control?" suggested Richie, taking a sip of his drink.

"I guess when it comes right down to it, that's exactly what they were afraid of."

"Is institutional power and control over Christians prevalent in the Bible?" asked Richie innocently.

"Actually, the Bible doesn't have much good to say about institutions because institutions are man-made while the true Church is a spiritual community made up of all those who follow Christ and—one could argue—those who don't know him yet.

The spiritual community doesn't require a command-and-control structure to thrive, but institutions need them in one form or another to stay cohesive and well-funded. The Bible has a lot to say about relationship with God and relationship with other people, but it doesn't teach that the Church ought to be a cohesive, powerful, controlling institution, if that's what you mean. In fact, Jesus was adamant he did not come to create an earthly kingdom or monarchy. He, in effect, rejected being the founder and head of an earthly, political institution in favor of being the head of a heavenly, spiritual community resident in the hearts of believers." Francis sat back, satisfied with his spontaneous reply. He had not known how he was going to respond to that question, but now that he had said it, he knew in his heart it was right.

"Well, my limited experience wasn't with the Catholic Church, but it seems to me that what I saw was all about power and control. And from what I heard from Rebecca, the pastors favored submission and alignment to spiritual authority and vision. Although Rebecca would never say this, I thought they exerted tremendous control over the opinion and behavior of their people, and over her. They may or may not recognize it as that, but the more they want their people to follow their lead, the more power they need to accomplish that, and the more power they're given, the more they want, I suppose. Is that what you're saying?"

"Wow. You're asking me a question I'm wrestling with right now in my own life. My father believes that if I had just submitted to my superiors, everything would have been fine. While it is true that if I had submitted, I would not have been disgraced, but I would have had to ignore what I believe and what I think is right. Writing and then publishing my book was the hardest thing I've ever done, and the consequences have been dire for me, but if I had to do it all over again, I would do the same thing."

Francis took a much-needed gulp of his drink before continuing. "The bottom line is that I'm struggling with what a healthy gathering of believers looks like, and I'm really struggling with what the corporate institutional Church, with all its power and politics, has to do with the Kingdom of God on earth. What I do know, though, is that God loves me, that he arranged for Jesus to be his expression on earth, and that Jesus died for me. I'm his and Jesus has saved me from my lack of relationship with the Heavenly Father."

Richie sighed and shook his head. "I wish I felt the assurance you feel. I'm having trouble with the idea of dying without knowing what's next. I'm very afraid. Terrified in fact!"

"Let me assure you of one thing. God loves you beyond anything you can imagine, and if you allow your mind to focus on even the potential of him, he will respond because acknowledging him and directing our attention toward him is the essence of prayer. He sent his son, Jesus, to die for all of us, not just some of us."

Richie lapsed into deep thought and was quiet for several minutes, but the silence was not uncomfortable; rather, it was comforting. Francis was not sure how Richie was processing what he had said, but the new and improved Father Francis hoped this pastoral moment would not be fruitless. He chuckled to himself because he had been so worried his ministry was over. He may not be a priest acceptable to the Roman Catholic Church, but he could still be a pastor with a flock he could touch from day to day. It would not be very sexy, but he determined it would be an exciting, satisfying adventure nonetheless. Who did he have to impress? The important and powerful people were thoroughly unimpressed already, so what did he have to lose? He was being forced to live this chapter of his life in the space between God and the Church, and he was becoming at peace with that.

Richie returned from his musing with a calm, confident look on his face. "The pastor at Rebecca's church said that to be saved, I had to repeat a prayer after him. I had a hard time just repeating words with the idea that that was all there was to it. What do you think?"

"Well, I think a relationship with God is the essence of redemption. God's hope is for every human being to have that relationship. Introductions to God can come in a variety of forms, but there is nothing magical about certain words or phrases. If you are aware of your need and consciously reach out, God will find you, and you will find him. Jesus was God displaying himself to humanity in concrete fashion, so if you look to Jesus, you will find God. What Jesus said and did creates the foundation, and he is the guide for our relationship with the Heavenly Father."

"The way you describe it doesn't seem so scary. Do I have to be different than I am to be acceptable to God like Rebecca's pastor said?" asked Richie.

It was Francis' turn to lean forward. "No, Richie! In fact, you must not try to be acceptable to God because he loves you exactly the way you are, and any attempts on your part to be acceptable will be counterproductive. Trying to be acceptable to God is a trap that has enslaved men and women throughout the ages. He wants nothing from you now. There's nothing you can give him that would be more valuable than just reaching out. By acknowledging Him and your need of Him, you're giving Him everything he wants."

"You know, I've always wanted to know God, but I've felt, from what I was told, that that wasn't an option for me because I'm gay. But now I hear you say God loves me and wants me to relate to him. And that feels right to me, so I feel better about myself knowing I don't have to try to change. I can't change because I didn't choose to be who I am. Who would choose to be gay? Who would choose ridicule, rejection, and hatred? This is just me. If I could have just changed, it would have made my life a lot easier, let me tell you."

As Richie was speaking, sweat had begun to bead on his forehead, and he grabbed the table to avoid falling over. In the process, he spilled his drink and sent the glass over the edge with a crash.

"What's wrong?" demanded Francis.

"I feel very weak suddenly. I think I'm all right, though," he said, but his face was ghostly pale, and his strength was obviously leaving him by the second. "Well, maybe I'm not all right after all. My head is spinning a bit. Maybe it would be best if we go."

"All right. Let me help you."

"I'll be fine. Could you get our coats? I'll say goodbye to Maurice. He'll understand."

+ + +

All the while Richie and Francis were talking in the club, Drago was perched across the street like a vulture in the desert waiting for something to die. His hunched shoulders and long thin nose added to the caricature. He smoked cigarette after cigarette and cursed the frigid wind blowing down the street. When Francis and the boy came out of the club, Drago snapped to attention. He immediately noticed the boy was stumbling and needed Francis' support as they walked.

Francis and Richie walked in silence back to the flat. Richie's countenance showed he was suffering considerable pain, and he was sweating profusely. Francis was worried as he increasingly had to lend his support to keep Richie walking in a straight line.

"Should we not find you medical attention?" asked Francis.

"Maybe tomorrow. Please, just help me home, then I'll be all right. It's probably just the flu, but it hits me hard. My immune system isn't what it used to be," Richie said with a fleeting smile.

Once Francis and Richie were up the elevator, Francis helped Richie to undress. When Richie took off his shirt, Francis gasped at what he saw. Over much of Richie's neck and torso was a kaleidoscope of raised, livid red and purple skin lesions of diverse sizes and shapes.

"What are those bumps?" blurted Francis, verbally betraying his shock.

"Oh, that's what you're looking at," replied Richie. "Those are called Kaposi's sarcoma. They're a type of cancer people with AIDS get. They look worse than they are. They don't hurt, but they can spread to other parts of my body: my mouth, my feet, lungs, liver, and digestive tract, and if they do, they cause all sorts of nasty problems. They go well with the seeping lesions on my scalp, don't they?" Richie said, trying and failing to sound cheerful. "The little guys that cause those are called *herpes zoster*. In people without AIDS, those little fellows cause chicken pox and shingles. My sores are the shingles variety, and they hurt like hell and ooze all the time, as you saw on the plane. I'm becoming a veritable retirement home for microbes. There are all sorts of critters trying to kill me," Richie said, falling into bed finally exhausted. "I need to sleep now. I'm sorry, Francis."

Richie immediately dropped off into a fitful sleep as Francis turned to leave.

Francis realized now he was out of his depth. How does one care for someone with AIDS? What precautions were necessary so one doesn't get infected? He knew nothing. And then the big questions dropped into his mind. *What am I doing here? Why me? I hardly know this young man, yet I've become his primary caregiver. Am I the one to take on this role?* These questions were disconcerting, but he had to admit his belief that nothing happens by accident would suggest he was in the right place at the right time for both Richie's benefit and his own.

He wondered, though, whether Rebecca should be made aware of this situation. He took a deep breath and pulled himself out of his thoughts. *Well, he didn't need to decide anything tonight.* He was starving. They had not stayed for their meals, so he explored the kitchen and found to his relief it was fully stocked. He barbecued a steak on the balcony and prepared a salad, then after discovering an excellent selection of wines, he chose a wonderful Merlot to go with his steak. He felt a little guilty making himself so much at home, but he had to eat, and it looked like he would be around for quite some time while Richie recovered.

What are my plans? Francis asked himself. *I have to have plans. I can't just float along without a plan. I feel so irresponsible and unfocused.* As he chewed over these thoughts, his mind naturally settled on the life of Jesus as recorded in the Gospels. Jesus had lived a life of ministry. His adult life had in many ways seemed dictated by the needs he had faced from day to day. He had not been an institutional man, but instead a man of the people. Jesus had not wandered, exactly, but his path and objectives had not been easily understood by observers either. He had always implied he was "about his Father's business," and that was about as specific as he got, except when he had talked vaguely of his death and resurrection. *What he had meant by this phrase is key,* thought Francis, *key to how we must live our lives.* Should we live our lives like Jesus lived his? It's clear we must believe what Jesus believed to have sound theology, and what Jesus believed about how to invest his time on earth should then logically apply to us.

If Jesus had purposefully ministered in a noninstitutional setting as he moved from place to place, did that give clergy guidance as to our roles in ministering to our world? Jesus could have established his ministry in the temple, waiting for people to come to him, but he hadn't done that. He had gone to the people, not in a global but a personal sense. He had interacted with those few that directly crossed his path. Had he been guided in this? From the accounts, it was easy to conclude he was.

If that was true, thought Francis, *then it would seem my aimlessness may not be aimless at all, but part of God's divine plan. And if that was true, then my goal is clearly before me. I must minister to those who cross my path. Today, that is Richie. Ministry to God's creatures rather than ministry to institutional Christianity. A liberating thought if I have ever had one. Tomorrow may involve others, but tomorrow will take care of itself as long as I continue to be willing to lend myself to ministry to those close by.*

Modern churches offer ministry within their walls, but in reality, that had not been Jesus' model, Francis realized with a start. If he followed Jesus' model, he could pursue effective, meaningful ministry for God's creation in spite of being rejected and disowned by the Church. It had been real ministry discussing spiritual concepts with Richie in his strange and disturbing world.

Thinking back over his own life, it was clear to Francis that his path had been so orchestrated and intricately interwoven with the goals and objectives of the Church that he had had no time uncommitted. How did that fit with the Jesus model?

If Jesus' model was correct, there was no need for the current harvest-and-ministry machines. Our modern model is a mechanistic model of Christianity where people are the fuel and cogs in the infrastructure that is the focus. Instead, why not build a relational model where people are the only focus? Enjoying this line of thought, Francis continued to ruminate late into the night.

+ + +

Drago watched as the priest helped the young gay boy out of the club and along the sidewalk to their apartment building. The behavior of this priest was curious. He had just met this boy, and yet he treated him as if he was important to him. The boy was obviously dying. Why would the priest care, or even get involved? He should just leave him to die and get on with his business. It was very curious. It reminded him of the times when he had carried fallen comrades to safety. His response had been automatic because they were fellow soldiers, but afterwards, he could not understand his own willingness to put himself at risk for them. Why should he have risked his own life for another? It logically made no sense, but Drago had chalked it up to the fog of war, not altruism. *We needed all the fighters we could get,* he thought. *I was just preserving a resource.*

+ + +

The next morning found Richie feeling more like himself again. He had color back in his cheeks and had an appetite for breakfast. Francis' relief was palpable. Last night, he had been afraid for Richie's life, and today Richie seemed as well as he could be given the circumstances. Francis was just starting to experience the rollercoaster ride of this horrible disease.

At breakfast, Richie broke out his bag of medication. After he had put all his bottles on the table, it looked like he could open his own pharmacy. Richie meticulously extracted the antivirals, the antibiotics, the antifungals, the anti-inflammatories, the supplements, and the analgesics. He had separate containers for morning, afternoon, and evening. It was these medications that were keeping Richie alive. In the parts of the world that did not have access to these expensive drugs, AIDS patients were alive one day and dead the next. They died of any number of diseases a healthy person would barely notice.

For the next three weeks, Francis and Richie spent the days seeing the sites in the Big Apple. Richie was intent on "doing the tourist thing" with Francis, and Francis was treated to all New York could offer. While acting like tourists, they talked and talked. As a priest, Francis had often found himself reluctant to be truly transparent and open with people. He was always honest but rarely open. His colleagues could be prone to judging weaknesses or faults as they sought and projected a lifestyle of holiness, righteousness, and strength. Being truly honest and transparent in an environment charged with projected piety was seldom rewarding.

On the other hand, besides his family, the rest of humanity was supposed to be his sheep, which he needed to shepherd. These relationships were professional relationships. There was distance between the shepherd and the sheep. The sheep looked to the shepherd for spiritual guidance and leadership. They confessed their faults and sins to him, and as a result, they stood apart from him. He was, by definition, a holy man and was in danger of being soiled by everyday life and everyday people. He knew too much about them for comfortable friendship.

Richie was different. Francis wasn't Richie's priest. He was just Richie's friend. Richie had no preconceived notions of what a priest ought to be like. He just saw Francis for exactly who he was, no better, no worse. In this relational environment, Francis found he was free to share his thoughts, his hopes, and his dreams. They became true friends without artificial barriers or distance between them, like brothers.

+ + +

Drago watched the friendship develop over the weeks and felt nothing but contempt for both men. The little fairy boy was not even a real man, and the priest, in befriending him, revealed he was grossly weak and pitiable. Drago despised people that did not know how the world really worked. Didn't they know the world was run by men like him? To rule, you had to be hard and ruthless, not soft and meek. There was no room for friendship in Drago's world. He had been friendly with a few of his fellow soldiers, yet one he had even sacrificed in battle to further the cause. The man had foolishly allowed himself to be separated from the platoon and could not be recovered without excessive loss of resources.

Many others had simply disappeared into the meatgrinder of civil war. Better not to have friends than to have dead friends.

Drago had expected a call from his boss during the weeks he had been watching the pair and was not disappointed. "Allo," said Drago into his cell one evening.

"Report."

"The priest is with the boy he met on the flight to New York. They live in the boy's flat, leave most mornings, and visit various tourist locations."

"We must make the priest disavow his book. Sales of the book are climbing, not dwindling. I am considering options to put pressure on the priest. Be ready."

"I am ready," confirmed Drago.

+ + +

After the call, Carducci contemplated what to do next. He was not hopeful that he could make the priest recant his conclusions, but perhaps some official pressure might help. Perhaps, he mused, if the Church made a strong public denunciation of the errors contained in the book, people would be turned off, and the priest's ideas would simply die on the vine. Using the power of the Church was, however, a double-edged sword. Wielding power is a blunt instrument that can be effective as a bludgeon but can go badly and backfire with equal and opposite force.

CHAPTER 8

Crisis

Richie was much worse now. He had a raging fever, was dripping perspiration, and had begun to cough incessantly. His face was drawn and gray, and he was not always lucid. Francis now knew enough about AIDS to realize Richie needed to be in hospital where he could be cared for properly. As he was questioning Richie about his insurance and which hospital he should be taken to, Richie surprised him by saying weakly, "Call Rebecca. Her number is in that book over there on the table. She's in Aspen. I need her. She'll come."

After finding Richie's insurance information, Francis arranged for an ambulance and phoned the Mossman family doctor. He left a message with the answering service, emphasizing that it was an emergency. His third call was to Rebecca.

"Hello, Rebecca. My name is Francis Bauer, and I'm calling on behalf of your brother, Richie." Francis could almost hear Rebecca's mind whirring trying to figure out the context of his call. "I'm a friend of Richie's. We met on a flight from Frankfurt to New York, and I've been staying with him." He paused, unsure of what to say and how much to say. "I'm calling because Richie is dreadfully ill and has asked for you to come to him. He told me to tell you he needs you and assured me that if I called, you would come," added Francis hopefully.

"Richie and I haven't spoken in a couple years. The last I heard he was in Paris. Besides, he's never been sick a day in his life. What could be wrong with him?" In her confusion, Rebecca spoke rather curtly, which alarmed Francis.

"Rebecca, I cannot presume to understand his condition. It would be best if you discuss it with his doctor when you get here. I've arranged for an ambulance, and it will take him to Mount Sinai Hospital. I hope that's what I should have done. I found his insurance information, and I can look after arrangements until you arrive."

"Mr. Bauer, I'll leave immediately. I should be able to get there later this evening. I'll come straight to Mount Sinai." As the urgency came to life, so did Rebecca. "Mr. Bauer, thank you for being with Richie and for calling. I'm on my way."

"It is my pleasure, Rebecca. I am very fond of Richie. We have become close friends over the past month, and I certainly want to help any way I can. And please, call me Francis, Rebecca. I've heard so much about you I feel as if I know you. I'm looking forward to meeting you in person." Francis felt badly that he would not be meeting Rebecca at JFK airport, but Richie needed him. Besides, he thought it would be better if she heard about Richie's condition from a professional rather than from him. He must feign ignorance until the proverbial cat was out of the bag.

+ + +

Rebecca wondered whether this was one of Richie's gay friends, but this man sounded different than the others. All at once, she was flooded with waves of emotion and almost broke down, but she caught herself. She had feared for Richie when Francis had said the word, "ambulance." On top of all that, she felt guilty at having treated Richie so badly. She should never have let Daniel talk her into shunning him. What had she been thinking? It had all seemed so logical at the time. Her loneliness flooded back, and she could not hold in her sorrow a second longer. She finally remembered to hang up the phone and then just wept and wept.

Once she had pulled herself together and the tidal wave was over, she was impatient to get moving, so she ran around the lodge, frantically throwing things in a bag.

+ + +

The trip to Mount Sinai in the ambulance was uneventful, and when they arrived at the emergency room, Richie's doctor, Dr. Swanson, was there waiting. He was a tall, attractive man in his sixties dressed in a tuxedo. Obviously, he had just left some gala. Dr. Swanson had been the Mossman family doctor since the twins were born and had, in fact, delivered them. He was a family friend. When he first saw Richie, his shock was obvious. He took Richie's hand after the paramedics had crashed the gurney through the double glass doors. Recognition of Richie's condition came swiftly, and he directed the paramedics to take Richie directly to the intensive care unit, commanding them to adhere strictly to the infectious diseases protocol. While the paramedics loaded the gurney onto the elevator, Dr. Swanson turned to Francis. "Who are you?"

Francis told him he was a friend of Richie's and a house guest at the Mossman Manhattan apartment.

"Good you were there," the doctor grunted. "What did Richie tell you about his condition?"

"He told me he has AIDS and he's dying."

"That last part may well be true. Do you know what medications he's taking?

"No, I'm sorry, I don't. I didn't think to bring them."

"Follow me and we'll catch up to him."

They arrived at the ICU just as Richie was being wheeled in. Dr. Swanson left Francis in the waiting room and went to scrub before entering Richie's room. Francis could see Richie through the window into the unit. They had him on a heart monitor, and they were piping oxygen into him. Richie appeared to be conscious, and every minute or so, his body heaved as a wracking cough shook his body. His breathing was evidently difficult because every few breaths he would gulp air in through his mouth. Dr. Swanson was soon bending over him, carefully listening to his heart and lungs and presumably getting an update from him on his condition. Nurses took blood samples at the same time the doctor gave his orders to the charge nurse.

After what seemed like hours, Dr. Swanson came out to the waiting area. "Have you called Rebecca?" he asked.

"Yes, doctor. I called her before the ambulance arrived. She's on her way from Aspen."

"Good, she had better hurry. Richie has an advanced case of pulmonary tuberculosis and now a secondary bacterial pneumonia. They're both opportunistic infections common in AIDS patients. Both are attacking his lungs, so his condition is grave. As soon as you see Rebecca, please have the charge nurse page me. I want to talk to her before she sees Richie. Does she know he has AIDS?"

"I'm afraid she doesn't. I didn't feel it was my place to tell her about Richie's condition."

"That was wise. It's my job to tell her. Richie and Becky's parents were dear friends of mine. Their loss was a tragedy and now this."

+ + +

Lord, my life is totally out of control, Rebecca thought, breathing deeply after settling into her seat on the plane. *I feel as if you've kicked me away from you, and I'm no longer acceptable to you. My marriage has failed, and I feel like it's my fault even though I can't think of anything I did wrong. I decided to leave Daniel because of the violence. Surely you don't want me to be in a relationship like that, but you say you hate divorce.*

Oh, I just don't know what you want from me, and Daniel is already married again, she thought as the flight attendant started down the aisle with the drink cart. *Nothing makes sense anymore, Lord. Everything seems like a paradox, an insoluble paradox, and frankly, you're not much help. Can't you just tell me how to respond to these conflicting situations?* she asked silently, stifling a sob.

My pastor tells me I have to break my relationship with my brother because he's gay, so I do that, and I lose my best friend and alienate my parents. I marry a Christian man like the Church teaches, and he turns out to be a violent, abusive jerk. Pastor McCallum tells me I have to stay married to Daniel and pray for him to change. But I just couldn't stay in the relationship, right or wrong. I was afraid and it wasn't in me to live like that. Surely, you wouldn't want me to.

She mentally ticked off the next items on her list of personal tragedy. *Then my parents die in a car accident while I'm driving to see them with the bruises of the last beating still on my face. And now my brother is dreadfully sick. If you're in control of all these events, how can this be fair? What do want from me? My life is being crushed out of me, and you feel light years away with your back turned to me. Lord, I am yours, and I have tried to follow and serve you. Save me. And Lord, don't let Richie die,* mutely pleaded Rebecca, her face in her hands, not caring what those around her thought.

+ + +

Richie was terribly uncomfortable and having trouble breathing, but his mind was clear. *It looks like my time is up*, he thought. *My lungs aren't working well at all, and this cough! If I could only catch my breath, I would be all right.* Yet another terrible cough interrupted his thoughts.

God, I know I've never really spoken to you before. My experience with people who call themselves Christians led me to believe you're horrible and nasty, but that's not what Francis believes. He says he knows you love me exactly as I am, and you want the best for me. He sincerely believes that. It looks like I'm going to die, and I want things to be right with you, so if you're there, I'm ready to meet you. One thing I would ask though. Keep me alive until I see Becky. I want to tell her how much I love her before I go.

Richie's rudimentary prayer exhausted him, and he drifted off once again, but before he fell completely asleep, he felt a peace he could not explain. The universe seemed to suddenly make more sense—unlike only a few minutes before—and he felt a new warmth and love in the midst of his discomfort. *Weird*, he thought.

+ + +

Francis was anxious about meeting Rebecca for the first time. It wasn't who she was that made him anxious but the situation she was facing. She did not know the extent of Richie's illness and would undoubtedly be upset when she learned the details. *How do I comfort a stranger?* he wondered. His question became critical the next instant as Rebecca ran through the sliding glass doors into the ICU, dragging a wheeled suitcase behind her that careened off the doors as they tried to shut. Francis recognized her instantly from the pictures in the apartment. The pictures, though, had not done her justice. Her eyes were red from exhaustion and emotion, but they did not detract from her overall appearance. She was incredibly attractive. As Francis approached, she was stepping up to the nurses' station, about to ask after Richie.

"Rebecca, I'm Francis Bauer. We spoke on the phone."

"Oh, Mr. Bauer, thank you for all you've done for Richie," she said, shaking his hand with a firm grip for someone so petite, then giving him a brief, perfunctory hug that broke the ice between them. "What can you tell me?"

"Actually, Dr. Swanson would like to brief you. I'll arrange for him to be paged." He turned to the nurse, but she had heard him and was already on the phone to the operator.

Over the speakers they heard, "Dr. Swanson, to the ICU. Dr. Swanson, please meet your party in ICU."

"Dr. Swanson assured me he would be here quickly," Francis assured Rebecca.

The awkwardness of waiting quietly lasted only thirty seconds. Dr. Swanson came striding purposefully down the wide hallway. "Becky," he called with a mixture of delight and sorrow. "I am so glad you've arrived. Come and sit down. We need to talk."

"Rebecca, I'll leave you and Dr. Swanson alone."

"No, Mr. Bauer, please stay with us." Rebecca looked at him pleadingly, so stay he did.

The three went and sat in the bare, featureless waiting room outside the ICU. Francis and Rebecca sat side by side, and Dr. Swanson sat directly across from them, leaning in close to them, having pulled a chair over to be nearer. His voice was soothing but firm as he spoke to Rebecca. "Richie is very ill, Becky. He has pneumonia, which is complicating tuberculosis."

"How did he get TB? Nobody gets tuberculosis anymore, do they?"

"Becky, Richie has AIDS. People with AIDS get TB," revealed Dr. Swanson as gently as he knew how.

Dr. Swanson's words dropped like a bomb on Rebecca. Her eyes went wide and then blank as she began to faint. She slumped forward and was about to fall from her chair until Francis quickly put his arm around her shoulders and held her firmly in place. Dr. Swanson jumped up and ran to get a glass of water.

Her head lolled to the side and rested on Francis' shoulder. As Francis looked at her beautiful face, so angelic with her eyes closed and her hair fallen across her cheek, he felt an enormous wave of affection and concern for this young woman. She was a maiden in distress, and he was her knight in shining armor, there to protect and to love. It was a feeling he had never experienced before. *Oh my, how very trite and ludicrous,* thought Francis. *Where had this come from? I don't even know this woman, yet I have these strong feelings for her. Is it sympathy or ... I don't know what this is? And how inappropriately timed....*

As he gazed at her face, he realized his hand was touching the side of her breast. At this realization, he felt blood flood into his groin. There was no doubt what that was. *Even in the middle of a crisis, my body has a mind of its own. I am so ridiculous.* His mouth went immediately dry, and he felt his face grow hot, uncomfortably hot. A crimson blush grew on his face, and his neck and scalp felt damp with perspiration. His head swam and he too thought he might faint, but he shook his head and got control of himself. *Good grief,* he thought. *You'd think I'd never seen a woman before. And this is so uncomfortable and wonderful and confusing and terrifying all at once. My goodness, I had better take a step back from this.*

When Dr. Swanson returned, he looked at Francis with a strangely annoyed look on his face as if to say, "Isn't one enough?"

Rebecca stirred as the doctor gently stroked and patted her cheek. When she had revived, she began to cry, hot tears streaming down her cheeks and into the corners of her mouth. She pulled a tissue from her purse and dabbed the tears away, but her grief and shock overcame her sensibilities, so she put her face into her hands and wept. She mumbled as she wept, "It's my fault. I wasn't there for him. I'm so sorry ..." Her words, her tears, expressed all the guilt, the grief, and the impending loss that was hers.

After long moments, during which the two men sat silent letting her release her demons, Rebecca had exhausted her emotions and was calm, not peacefully calm but the calm of resignation. "I want to see Richie now," she said in a near whisper, rising to her feet, her back straight and her head held high. "If my brother is dying, at least I can be strong for him."

Dr. Swanson led Rebecca toward Richie's room, leaving Francis feeling foolish and out of place. Francis did not know what to do next. Should he leave or follow or stay in the waiting room? As if on cue, Dr. Swanson turned and waved him forward. Relieved, he complied, hoping he could be of some assistance or comfort but worrying he was out of place and perhaps in the way.

+ + +

When Francis finally reached Richie's room, having scrubbed and gowned with the help of an ICU nurse, Rebecca was already in a chair with her cheek resting on his pillow and her face close to his talking quietly. Richie stirred, opened his eyes, and smiled weakly.

"I knew you'd come. Thanks, Becky," Richie managed weakly.

Rebecca's emotion flooded to the surface as she poured out all the words in her heart. "I love you, Richie, and I'm so sorry for shutting you out. I don't know what I was thinking. I'm so ashamed. I should have found you a long time ago. I needed you."

"Don't worry. I love you too, and I'm glad you're here now, best friend. Have you met Francis?"

"Yes," Rebecca responded. "We met a few minutes ago."

"He has become a great friend, Becky. Stay close to him. He's a good man." Richie's head nodded with fatigue and he said, "I have to go to sleep now. Go with Francis and get something to eat and some sleep. I'll still be here when you get back," Richie said with a sly grin obviously designed to try to cheer her up.

As Rebecca stood to go, she silently gestured for Dr. Swanson and Francis to follow her out into the hallway. "Dr. Swanson, how bad is Richie? Is he going to live?"

Dr. Swanson explained he didn't really know at this point since Richie was very weak, and his immune system was almost nonexistent. He reviewed the several things going on at once in Richie's body and explained that his body was providing no defenses.

"Becky, I'm using powerful antibiotics. They're helping a little, but the prognosis is not good."

Dr. Swanson's face reflected pain, sadness, and professional stoicism all at once. To Francis, the look in the doctor's eyes said he knew he was giving understanding and pain, yet he regretted the need for them. He was clearly struggling to remain professional and was hurting terribly.

"Simply put, he's in critical but stable condition. Richie was right. Go and get something to eat and some sleep. I'll stay with him until you get back and will call you if there's any change."

Rebecca reached up and put her arms around the doctor's neck and clung to him. "Thanks for all you're doing. I'll eat but I'm staying here."

"Shall we go together to the cafeteria then?" Francis said, nodding at the doctor in silent gratitude and understanding.

+ + +

Eventually, hours later, Rebecca finally realized she needed to get some rest or risk collapsing. Richie was stable for the present, and Rebecca kept falling asleep in her chair, so Francis gathered her luggage from the front desk, and they took a taxi to the apartment.

Once she had settled in and come out to the kitchen, Francis opened a bottle of Chardonnay and prepared a simple salad for their repast. She sat on one of the stools at the kitchen island staring distractedly into space. He knew she was drained from her arduous flight and the stress of the situation, but he wanted to engage her, if he could.

He said quietly, "Richie mentioned you live in Aspen. I've heard it's beautiful there." After launching his question, Francis realized it was rather lame. Foolish or not though, the silence between them was not a comfortable silence.

"Yes, it is rather pretty, but I guess I've gotten used to it. I haven't really looked at the view for as long as I can remember." She looked over then and looked him in the eye. "You're very kind to have helped Richie the way you did."

"Well, as it happens, Richie helped me a great deal as well. When I met Richie on the flight from Frankfurt, I had no plans and no place to stay," confessed Francis.

"You don't seem like the spontaneous type. Why are you here?" asked Rebecca, her curiosity piqued.

"Well, that's a long story, but suffice it to say I'm trying to escape an awkward situation."

"Oh, that must mean a woman," replied Rebecca, warming to the topic.

"No, there's no woman," replied Francis with a chuckle.

"If there's no woman, then you must be an international jewel thief or a spy, running from Interpol or the Mossad," teased Rebecca, enjoying that Francis was squirming under her good-natured assault.

"No, I'm not a thief or a spy. I'm a disgraced priest being punished by the Roman Catholic Church," explained Francis, his own candor surprising him. *What was he thinking, blurting out his story?*

"Oh, I see. That's why there's no woman involved. Why were you thrown out? It sounds exciting."

"Well, I did nothing I'm ashamed of, if that's what you're asking. I wrote a book about the universal Church, which my superiors found annoying. My research apparently threatens them, and they reacted to protect their authority," explained Francis tentatively.

"Yes, I suppose I can see why they would. I was tossed out of my church too," Rebecca admitted as if she were speaking to a close friend who understood such things.

Francis' heart melted at her innocence and openness. She was so uncomfortably beautiful, and her childlikeness enhanced both her beauty and Francis' discomfort. He remembered how Chloe and her beauty had discomfited him when they were young. While he had been a full-fledged priest, he had not had an issue with beauty, so he thought this must be some kind of deeply buried weakness, or perhaps his new freedom was releasing his heart to feel.

Rebecca explained her experiences with the two churches she had attended, and she elaborated enough about what she had been taught for Francis to understand her dilemma with Richie and the treatment she had received when she had left her husband.

"I was taught," Rebecca explained sorrowfully, "that it was my responsibility to be acceptable to God. I could never quite figure what the standard was. The preachers all said God would judge my acceptability, but inevitably, they described the elements of acceptability as being based on how well I followed the rules and regulations they set out."

She paused to accept the wine Francis silently offered her. She took a sip and gestured at Francis with the glass as she continued. "I remember one sermon in which the preacher illustrated his point by likening Christian life to a hurdles race. The participants had to make it over the hurdles *and* keep up the pace. If I tripped or fell, I should feel ashamed, and if I succeeded, the hurdles would become higher to match my maturity. He summed up by saying he was close to the finish line, but when he looked around, there weren't many people around him. I felt shame all the time and always felt unworthy. That little voice whispered in my head and told me I was worthless and useless—damaged goods—particularly after my divorce. How could I be worthy if I had been rejected by a Christian spouse and the Christian Church?"

When Rebecca finished telling her story, Francis realized he had been standing the whole time in rapt attention, an opened bottle of wine in his hand. Once again, he felt like a foolish teenager. Yet he had had more emotional discipline when he was a teenager because he knew he had been on the road to becoming a priest. What was he on the road to becoming now?

+ + +

Drago was bored. He was accustomed to boredom, but this was the least exciting assignment he had ever had. Following this priest was too easy, too predictable. There was no danger. It was like hunting an animal that couldn't fight back.

He looked into the ICU from an adjacent corridor as the gay boy lay dying. He watched the priest as he spoke to the boy, seemingly trying to ease his passing. Drago continued to watch as the priest comforted the young woman, who, from the look of her, was related to the boy. Unbidden, his mind returned to his own experiences with death and grief, and a grudging admiration for the priest surfaced as he watched the ease and professionalism he showed when dealing with the hospital staff, the dying one, and the girl. Even though this priest was obviously a pussy and deserved his scorn, there was still something admirable about him. *Perhaps it was something like admiration for a job well done*, Drago thought as he watched the priest and the girl finally leave and he followed them out.

CHAPTER 9

Endings and Beginnings

The next morning dawned cloudy and drizzling. As Francis got ready for the day, he heard Rebecca urgently talking to Dr. Swanson on the telephone, her voice muffled by the distance from his room to the living room but still distinct enough for him to understand her side of the conversation.

"That's disappointing …" he heard her say. "I'll get ready and come right over. Thanks for spending the night with him. I'll see you in thirty minutes." After she hung up, he heard gentle sobs drifting from the other room, which broke his heart. The depth and power of the emotions he was feeling was new to him. In his previous pastoral duties, he had often intervened in tragic circumstances to bring comfort and solace, but this was different. He was feeling the emotions himself, and he had no filter in place to lessen the blow. He was mourning. He was grieving. When a pastor, there had always been a professional distance between him and those he comforted. The bottom line, emotionally, was that their problems were their problems. He had been taught never to take someone else's problems into his inner world, and though he was compassionate, he never allowed the pain of others to be his pain.

As he pondered this, he recalled the accounts of Jesus in his ministry. One account of Jesus weeping over the city of Jerusalem had always struck him as odd in light of his own training about not becoming emotionally involved. Even the biblical accounts had always been taught to him in a clinical fashion, without reference to the emotional elements of the stories. One story had particularly stood out for Francis, of a woman caught in adultery. It had been presented as a study in the theology of sin, grace, and sanctification rather than as the story of a real woman in a real-life conundrum, feeling real fear, anxiety, and humiliation.

As he stood before the mirror, Francis tried to imagine what that woman must have felt as the priests caught her having sex with a man not her husband. The embarrassment she must have felt when they dragged her out of her house and into the street in front of her neighbors, and the soul-sucking horror she must have experienced when they threw her like a piece of rotten meat in front of Jesus, as bait. She had been valuable to the priests only for her sin. She must have been terrified she would be stoned as an example. Her story was one of life in the raw, and Francis was now gnawing on raw life now. This was life outside the shelter of the corporate Church, life without his shield of professionalism to protect his untested sensibilities. He felt frayed and tattered, but fully feeling was exhilarating. He finally felt fully human. *Yet*, he thought, *that exhilaration came with a price.*

+ + +

Rebecca heard his footsteps as he trod on the hardwood floor down the hallway. She turned to greet him as he approached, not bothering to hide her tears

"How is he this morning?" he ventured.

"Dr. Swanson says he's worse. I'm going to the hospital as soon as I'm ready. Will you come with me?"

"I'm ready," replied Francis.

Rebecca pulled herself together in minutes, and Francis hailed a cab outside the building. They reached the hospital in less than twenty minutes. As they came within sight of the ICU, it was obvious something was going on. Nurses were scurrying in every direction, and a group that included Dr. Swanson rushed into Richie's room from the direction of the nurse's station pushing a cartload of equipment. By the time they reached the glass door into Richie's room, the team was preparing to administer the paddles to Richie's pale, sunken chest.

Rebecca stood in horror with her hand over her gaping mouth, staring as if unbelieving at the scene unfolding before her. Her brother was dying. Everything that could be done was being done, but a feeling of outrageous helplessness overtook her. She began pacing like a caged animal, emitting a desperately whispered wail. Francis drew near to her and tried to put his arm around her, but she pushed him away almost viciously and continued her desperate pacing.

Just then, the doctor yelled, "Clear!" and Richie's torso arched in response to the electric current coursing through his body. Everyone in the room stared expectantly at the screen with the green line above Richie's bed, willing it to bounce. The line across the monitor remained flat, the tone steady. The doctor once more slapped the paddles on Richie's chest and sent another tremendous shock into him. Breath exploded from Richie's mouth as his body convulsed upward, involuntarily. Again, each face turned to the monitor, and they were rewarded by a *bleep, bleep, beep*, the green line rhythmically climbing its little hills and valleys on the screen. There was an audible sigh of relief from the gathering in

Richie's room. Dr. Swanson immediately slipped out the door and approached.

"That was close ..." he breathed.

"What just happened?" blurted Rebecca.

"Richie's heart stopped," Dr. Swanson explained. "There's a buildup of fluid around his heart from the pneumonia that put pressure on the heart muscle. We got his heart going again, but I'm afraid we're fighting a losing battle."

Rebecca's lips pursed in concentration, and then her shoulders sagged with resignation. Richie was going to die, and there was no avoiding that.

"Can we see him?"

"Yes, of course. He's awake but not very comfortable. He's having great difficulty breathing."

Rebecca and Francis scrubbed and gowned together in silence. When they pushed the glass door open, Richie turned his head and smiled weakly.

"It's good to see you two. Were you here for all the excitement? I guess I had everyone on the floor in my room, by the sounds of it. I don't remember a thing, but the nurses filled me in," Richie said, wheezing, attempting to be lighthearted. He was rewarded with a smile bursting across Rebecca's face behind her mask, her eyes reflecting her smile.

"You always enjoyed being the center of attention," she teased quietly.

Once again, Rebecca sat and lay her head close to Richie's and they talked. What they said to each other was less important than the love flowing freely from heart to heart. Both knew this may be their last moments together, and they were not going to waste a second of it. After several minutes, Richie became obviously weary and nodded off. Rebecca stood and went to Francis' side, putting her arms around him and seeking the solace he desperately wanted to give her.

"Have courage," he said, thinking as the words came out of his mouth how stupid they sounded. But Rebecca's expression showed her appreciation of his support and encouragement. As they stood together, Richie awoke once more, a look of peace on his face.

"It's good to see you're getting to know each other," he said. Speaking directly to Francis, he went on. "Francis, please promise me you'll look after Becky when this is over. I don't want her to be alone. She'll have no one, and there's no one I would rather she be with than you."

"Yes, I will," answered Francis, not trying to avoid the inevitable by lamely trying to tell Richie he would be all right and he would be back on his feet in no time.

"I'm so cold. But I feel peaceful. I happy you both are here. I spoke to God last night, and I feel certain now he loves me and will welcome me when I meet him. I'm not afraid."

Tears streamed down both faces as Francis and Rebecca went to stand on either side of the bed, each holding one of Richie's hands. Richie's face took on a decidedly blue tinge, and his eyes stared, not really seeing. His breath came in shallow gasps as he tried to fill his congested lungs to no avail. The next thing they heard was a shallow gurgle in Richie's throat, and then he was still. The heart monitor sang out its monotonous song until a nurse came in and turned it off. Richie's life on this earth was over. Francis moved to Rebecca's side, and she held onto him as if she never wanted to let go. Tears dripped from her eyes, but when Francis looked, a small smile lingered at the corner of her mouth. It was a peaceful smile, a smile of love, and a smile of bittersweet joy in the midst of terrible sorrow. It was a smile that was the essence of a paradoxical relationship with God where opposites exist together without contradiction.

+ + +

The pontiff was lighthearted and whimsical after the pomp and ceremony of the Easter weekend. He could not help himself. He had to smile. A thrill coursed through him like a bolt of electricity, and he was tempted to pump his fist as he had seen athletes do when they scored a goal or won a game, but he restrained himself just in time as one of his aides entered his chambers. Easter was the highlight of his year and the pinnacle of the religious calendar. He felt tremendous satisfaction leading the faithful in the age-old traditions of the Roman Catholic Church as his predecessors had done for millennia. The papacy was much more than a job or a position. To be the pope was more than an honor. It was a mixture of the spiritual and secular, the profane and the divine, humility and pride. He had always felt his responsibility and knew it was greater than he was, though he knew he was only human, even if those around him and the faithful attributed to him infallibility and superhuman powers.

When playing his role, he presented himself, as pontiff, as the direct descendant of the Apostle Peter, as the Rock, as the defender of the faith, but in the privacy of his inner self, he knew the truth. He was not divine. He did not possess superhuman or supernatural power, and he really did not fully understand his own faith let alone the faith people had in him.

His reverie was interrupted by a gentle knock at his bedroom door. "Your Holiness," his aide said quietly, almost in a whisper. "Cardinal Carducci asks for a word."

"All right. I'll be right out."

Meeting with Carducci required the pontiff to be fully engaged. Carducci was a cunning politician and a useful fellow for cleaning up messes and handling difficult situations. He wore an air of gentleness, but the pontiff knew he was cold as steel on the inside, an unrelenting foe if he ever became a foe. Carducci must never become an enemy, so he must be commanded with strength to funnel his energy away from his ambition. The pontiff was aware of Carducci's incursions in papal authority but tolerated it as long as Carducci knew his limits.

"Your Holiness," began the cardinal, "you wished a report on the Father Bauer situation?"

The pontiff quietly waited for the report without further acknowledgment. Silence, he knew, was such an excellent way to communicate authority.

Chafing under the naked power play, Carducci reported, "I still have a man monitoring Father Bauer's movements and activities. He is ready to intervene as we direct."

"What has your man reported?"

"Father Bauer is in New York. He has been living with a young gay man."

The pontiff's eyebrows rose at this revelation. "Is this something we can use to discredit him?"

"Perhaps. My man reports they became acquaintances on the flight from Frankfurt to New York, and Bauer was invited to stay in the young man's apartment. As far as my man knows though, there was nothing *unusual* about their relationship. The young man had AIDS and has just passed away. Bauer had been active in making arrangements."

"Has Father Bauer made contact with anyone of concern in New York?"

"No. My man is confident he has had him under surveillance at all pertinent times, and he has spoken to no one we should be concerned about."

"Good. Keep your man on Bauer and report to me if anything changes. We are not out of the woods yet. Bauer has not been missed, but he will be soon, and we must be prepared to protect papal authority. I will not have Bauer undermine me. Understood?"

Carducci nodded his head slightly, acknowledging the pontiff's wishes. Carducci's mind was not on papal authority as an abstract concept or even in terms of the authority of this man. No, his loyalty to this man had limits. He must be seen by his fellow cardinals to be tirelessly serving this man, but his loyalty rested comfortably in the pocket of his own ambition. His own concern with Bauer was his threat to the authority of the papal office that he hoped someday to wield himself. The authority of the papal office was in danger, and that was personal indeed.

+ + +

Francis and Rebecca slowly made their way back to the Manhattan apartment. They decided to walk to take advantage of the brilliant New York spring day. The sun was shining, and while the warmth enveloped them, their hearts were cold. The darkness of mourning was upon them as they walked along, hardly acknowledging each other's presence.

Francis' thoughts were on Richie and how Francis had become so attached to him over such a short period. It was ironic that they would create such a close relationship to have it last no time at all. The concept of God having a plan for individual lives was mysterious to Francis. In his own life, he had often felt it was his own initiative and energy that moved things along, but then, every once in a while, a coincidence would occur that would make him wonder. Francis looked up at the dozens of faces passing by on the sidewalk, knowing he would never know any of these people, yet his and Richie's paths had crossed and joined. Was there a plan or was it just coincidence he and Richie had met and become like brothers? Was there a master planner that directed the lives of men and women to come together and to draw apart? It seemed at times there had to be a plan, yet at other times, Francis was convinced his life was a random series of unrelated events orchestrated by chance alone. His life was a mystery to him, and mystery was upon him as he walked along.

+ + +

Rebecca's heart hurt. She had watched the life pass from her twin, her best friend. She was tortured by the guilt of discarding that friendship in favor of a boyfriend, then a husband, and then a religion. That Richie had so easily forgiven her and accepted her back into his life as if nothing had happened humbled her and made her realize what humility and forgiveness were really all about. We do not try to forgive. We forgive or we don't. There was nothing she could do to change things, but she was determined to follow Richie's lead and cultivate and grow the virtue he had defined for her.

As she made this commitment to herself, she sensed the presence of this other person that had dropped into her life. She had sensed in him the same virtues Richie had demonstrated in the last hours and moments of his life. She wondered whether this man had influenced Richie in some way, and her curiosity to know him better overcame her mournful mood.

"Are you all right?" she asked him.

"Yes, I think I am. I was just thinking about how much Richie had influenced me and how much he meant to me. He had a tremendous zeal for life, and he drew me out of myself. I realize now I have comfortably existed in an artificial bubble that protected me from real life. It put my soul to sleep. I'm awake now and don't know what to do with myself. I feel guilty for the freedom I feel. I feel exposed and afraid and vulnerable. I feel like a child who wakes up to a bright sunny morning and cannot wait to get outdoors and play. And I'm also so very sad. Does that make any sense?" responded Francis.

"I can relate. I've been depressed so long about my marriage, my divorce, the loss of Richie's closeness, the death my parents, and everything else negative in my life that I feel like I have finally come out of a black tunnel and into the light. I think I'm ready to live again, just like you, but I feel so guilty at the same time. I should be mourning my brother and parents, not thinking about enjoying life."

"Perhaps we can do both at once," Francis said in a whisper. "When we experience trauma, tragedy, and pain, we often wonder whether God has left us. In truth, if God had abandoned you and me, we would be the only two human beings in the history of human beings, except Jesus, to have experienced such abandonment. I don't think we're that special."

He paused to look at everyone around him again, bathed as they were in sunlight, and then back at Rebecca. "We human beings often misinterpret God. We think of him wrongly. The truth is, God is not opposed to trauma, tragedy, and pain. The Bible is full of stories of people experiencing these things, but modern believers think they ought to be immune. Think about the life and death of Jesus. Much has been taught about his story. Most teachers say Jesus experienced these things so we would be spared. It just is not true. Traveling the world as a priest, I saw much evidence to the contrary. While local churches and television personalities in rich countries teach that God will make all believers healthy, wealthy, and wise, believers in the Third World experience tragic lives where death, famine, excruciating pain, and loss are common. Believers that suffer such things are not diminished in value in the sight of God. Believers in Rwanda who experienced the trauma and pain of genocide are not worthless."

"Wow," Rebecca exclaimed. "I've never heard anyone say that before. It makes sense, but in some ways, I would have preferred to hear that God will make everything better and easier."

"I know, Rebecca. We all crave simplicity and a life without pain and suffering, but that's not what we've been promised. We have been promised that, notwithstanding the trials of life, God will not leave us or toss us aside. In my experience, God keeps that promise."

Rebecca took that nugget and silently stewed over it as they walked. The newly grieving friends strolled the rest of the way to the apartment, lost in their own thoughts.

+ + +

Chloe Romano had grown up all her life in Zurich, where she had experienced the rigidity of Swiss life combined with the oppressive control that permeated her neighborhood thanks to the Catholic Church. Her parents went to Mass each and every day without fail. Their life was indelibly intertwined with the local church and the clergy who acted as directive leaders, religious counselors, and judge and jury in the event of perceived sin.

Chloe had always felt there was a different life out there somewhere and that she would be smothered by her life at home until she broke free.

That freedom had come as a result of Chloe's extraordinary beauty and grace. The symmetry of her face and form came from genetics, the grace from years of gymnastics classes. Her promising gymnastics career had ended at age fourteen when she had experienced a growth spurt that had not ended until she reached almost six feet tall. She had become too tall for the sport of tiny girls. Her disappointed coach of almost a decade suggested basketball instead. The loss of gymnastics had sent Chloe into a depression that had lasted for more than a year. She had moped her way through her days feeling ungainly, ugly, and useless.

But then at nineteen, she had been *discovered* in a sidewalk café near her home by a modeling agency on the lookout for new and unique looks. Chloe's was not a classic beauty, which to the icons of fashion was boring. Instead, she was tall, lithe, and sinuous. Her face had both the high cheekbones of her Italian Swiss heritage and the pure-white, flawless skin that can only come from alpine living. The combination created the exotic but still European look the agency had been looking for. The offer the agency had made was an offer that could not be refused.

Initially skeptical, Chloe's parents had eventually succumbed to the flattery of the agency's pitch woman. After all, this "divine beauty," this "genetic wonder," had come from their union. Chloe's mother, in particular, had been overwhelmed by the comparison of her Chloe to the rich and famous models regularly seen on Europe's runways. So, Chloe's parents had allowed the agency to whisk the innocent and naïve teen off to her first training assignment in Paris without restriction or parental oversight.

Her career had started immediately, and most of her life after that had come under the control of others. Diet and exercise programs had been put in place. Her schedule had been filled until she had had no time for anything or anyone. Her friendships at home had withered, and her parents had worried. Chloe went a whole year without going home, relying on the phone to keep in touch, but it had not been the same as being there in person. She had felt so alone and lonely. In many ways, she had still been just a child, but a child committed to her career by an ironclad contract. Her life had not been her own, and she had felt that fact deeply.

CHAPTER 10

Aspen

It took a month to complete the arduous task of dealing with Richie's estate. When the process was proceeding on its own, without the need for Rebecca's presence, she made the decision to leave New York, intuitively rather than cognitively. Rebecca just began to pack.

While she was stuffing her suitcase, she turned and said to Francis, "This city feels too crowded. We have to get away."

There was no question of Francis staying in New York. He was moving on, and he didn't question that. He and Rebecca were together now, but were they a team or a couple? Those distinctions had never occurred to him before. Since he had been a youngster, he had avoided girls as they conflicted with his inevitable life as a priest. His friendship with his childhood best friend, Chloe, had been willingly sacrificed on the altar of the priesthood, and he felt she likely had never forgiven him for that unilateral sacrifice. He wondered where Chloe was at this moment and what she was doing. The acrimonious end to the friendship of their youth had hurt Francis, but he knew it had hurt Chloe more.

Had something changed in him? Had his commitment to the priesthood weakened? He didn't know, but something grated on his conscience. Until this very moment in his life, his relationship with Rebecca would have seemed wrong, yet it did not seem very wrong now. He, a man, and Rebecca, a woman, were friends.

As she packed, Rebecca mumbled something about Aspen. She was still emotional and somewhat reclusive at times, yet being together was comfortable for them both. Francis had no idea where Aspen was but understood it was Rebecca's home, and he was coming along. No discussion was had.

The morning of their leaving, they packed their belongings into Richie's fire-engine red BMW roadster. There wasn't much room in the trunk, but they were traveling light. Francis had only a few things to his name, and Rebecca had come in a hurry and had not brought much. Rebecca got behind the wheel out of habit, and in a distracted daze, began to drive, paying little attention to Francis as she followed the highway out of the city.

+ + +

As she drove, Rebecca's mind traveled back through her life. The monotony of driving triggered reverie. She mused on the golden years of her childhood, when everything had been safe and happy. Her home had been full of fun and lighthearted optimism. Her parents had provided for her without question of want. She had been innocently secure in the knowledge that everything would always be good. She'd had no idea whether her family was wealthy or poor. It had never crossed her mind.

Her teen years had been only slightly more turbulent. She had wanted desperately to rebel but had had no real excuse. Her mom and dad had been supportive and level-headed. They had been neither soft nor hard, neither strict nor easy, and she had known beyond any doubt they loved her. She had loved and admired them too, so her rebellion had found no roots, though adolescence had tortured her inner self. Overall, she had lived a lovely, rich, sheltered life.

Rebecca's soft smile became a grimace of pain as her mind snapped back to the present. "What's happened to my ... to my life ..." she choked. "It's all gone. Everyone I have ever loved has left me. There's no one left."

+ + +

From the corner of his eye, Francis caught a glimpse of her pain when her smile disappeared. And then he heard Rebecca's lament. What could he say? Anything he did say would be in poor taste. He had heard his colleagues at times like this quote the Bible, often using the story of God caring about the bloody fallen sparrow. He had heard them spout ridiculous platitudes about hope and perseverance citing Job as an example. In fact, he himself had done the same thing. Everyone seemed to forget that the story of Job is incomprehensible to justice and incompatible with a constantly loving God. It was all a load of crap dumped on suffering people by insensitive, self-righteous, religious, emotionless Neanderthals as he saw it now.

Nothing would comfort Rebecca except quiet companionship. It was irrelevant to her that God cared for her. How was that relevant when her world had been destroyed? How caring did He seem to her, or even to him for that matter? *My world is gone too,* he thought, *trampled under the jackboots of evil men claiming to be God's representatives. What did God do to help me?* If God cared so much, why the pain, why the intolerance, why the corruption, why the unbridled arrogance and deceit? Blaming it all on mankind just didn't satisfy. God was to blame too. If God, too, was to blame ... what did that mean? If God was responsible for loss in our lives, then how was that compatible with love? Both he and Rebecca had experienced loss, yet Francis had no answers for either of them.

+ + +

Francis had never driven so far so fast. The miles literally disappeared under the wheels of the car. The first night, they stopped in St. Louis and awkwardly decided on two rooms in an interstate motel. Everything was a first for Francis while in America, and even staying in a nondescript motel eating in a nearby diner was interesting. He avidly people watched. The people from Missouri were so different from New Yorkers. They actually spoke to him and Rebecca and seemed glad they were visiting their state. Francis also immediately noticed the prevalence of African American and Hispanic people and noted the apparent economic discrepancy between the races.

Beyond that, his prevailing impression of America was sameness. Every gas station looked the same, every highway restaurant looked the same, and every mile they traveled initially looked the same. After passing through the hills that Eastern Americans called mountains, the land seemed to have been crushed by a massive press. So flat was the landscape at times that one could see a limitless horizon, mile, after mile, after mile. And where were the trees? He was in awe. The enormous sky made him feel uncomfortably like an insignificant microbe.

And then there was Aspen. What a magnificent change from dreary flatness. The Rocky Mountains suddenly erupted out of the prairie in magnificent fashion. The climb from Denver was dramatic and a little scary. At times, it seemed they were driving straight up the mountains. The town reminded him of the Monaco version of a quaint Swiss village. Aspen attempted to be European but just could not shake being very American instead.

The mountains could be the Alps, although higher, but the town itself was only a façade.

Once through the center of town, Rebecca, still quiet and introverted, pushed the car into a dizzying climb. Francis turned in his seat and could see for miles toward the rising sun. She soon turned into the drive of a magnificent structure of peeled honey-colored logs. The paved driveway was lined with immaculately landscaped beds of Colorado blue spruce and junipers. The house itself was dominated by an enormous, covered log portico that could accommodate several vehicles.

"Home sweet home," said Rebecca quietly. "Welcome to Aspen."

"What a lovely place. I have never seen a structure made from trees before," replied Francis.

"It's my father's design. It was his dream to have a log house in the mountains. It was a lot of work but … well, let's go in and get settled. I'm exhausted from the drive."

Stepping through the front doors was like stepping into a bright, golden world. The sunshine burst through the southwest-facing windows that drew the eye to the unobstructed mountain views. The golden hues reflecting off the log walls created a surreal atmosphere both soothing and exciting. Francis could only stand and stare.

+ + +

Drago watched the couple enter the large, elegant home. He was sure they had no idea they were being followed. He had taken precautions, and they were inexperienced lambs. Just as he was pulling past the driveway, his cellphone vibrated.

"Ja."

"Report," the cardinal demanded curtly in Italian.

"I am with them in Aspen, Colorado. Everything is under control. What are your orders?"

"Keep them under surveillance and keep me informed. You are to take no unauthorized action, but be ready to act on short notice," instructed Carducci in his classic condescending manner, always ensuring Drago knew he was the servant and Carducci the master.

"I am ready and will wait for your instructions before the lamb is processed."

+ + +

Carducci was nervous about acting alone in this plot. His Holiness knew of Carducci's predilections regarding the priest, and Carducci was no wallflower when deciding what had to be done to protect the Church, but nonetheless, if he acted precipitously, it could come back to bite him. The Church could not afford another scandal after the endless sex scandals coming out of America and the financial scandals closer to home.

"What to do with this runaway priest?" he thought. His inclination was to bring the matter to a close if it could be done with no recourse to him. Drago was trustworthy enough to do the dirty work, but could he be trusted to keep his mouth shut? Carducci needed a backup plan, and he gleefully knew exactly how it should unfold.

+ + +

As Francis sat in an overstuffed chair in the enormous living room looking over the mountain panorama, his thoughts returned to how his life was unfolding and where it might go.

It's a good thing we live mostly in our own heads, our thoughts safe in the privacy of our own consciousness, he thought. For healthy people, thoughts are a safe place, a place to test out theories and try things on for size in a way that is inoffensive to those around us. People cannot be offended if they have no idea what we're thinking. Conventional wisdom would suggest, however, that our thoughts are not hidden from God. That is a real problem when it is God we are considering.

Francis was thinking of how God must interact with human beings. He had heard many people say God had spoken to them. In charismatic circles, even in the Catholic Church, God speaking to you was practically a mandatory element of salvation. If God didn't speak to you, or you were too honest to lie about it, in those circles, you were seen as somehow spiritually challenged.

God doesn't speak to me. Over the years, I have yearned to hear the voice of God, yet it has never happened. Why not me? Why not send an angel to me to bolster my faith? If one saw an angel shining like the sun, it would ease nagging doubts, wouldn't it? But God doesn't treat me like that.

To say either that He does or does not talk to you results in hubris. On the one hand, you are either so unimportant to God or so stable that he does not need to speak to you directly. On the other hand, if he does talk to you, then you must be much more important to God than those not hearing his voice. In either event, just thinking about it is depressing, and as with many things in Christianity, there seems to be an annoying balancing act required to stay sane. Opposites do balance, but that is unhelpful to the person in the middle. *Therefore,* thought Francis, *we must live our own lives in accordance with our own experience and not think much about the experiences professed by others.*

Returning to an assessment of his situation, he thought, *I have been discarded by my peers, and I am cut off from any meaningful interaction with the wisdom and guidance, if any, of my superiors. The* latter circumstance, though, may be a godsend given Cardinal Massey's suspicions of physical danger from those very superiors. *How can that be? How can they want to hurt me? It should be impossible to believe in the twenty-first century, yet it's not.* He sighed and leaned forward in his chair, resting his elbows on his knees. *I've seen careers end in spectacular fashion without just cause, and I've seen incredible injustice inflicted on others with seeming impunity and without consequence. If there was no accountability for the wrongs committed by leaders, would they be emboldened to remove someone they considered a threat?*

He shuddered and pushed the thought from his mind. The next thought that pressed into his consciousness was of Rebecca. It was less than a thought really. It was more a subtle, undefined, unformed impression. Somehow, he was attached to her in a way he had never allowed himself before. He was devoted to her and would give his life to protect her. He felt powerful in his need to protect her and powerless to resist her as though he was Superman and a young boy all wrapped into one. Was this love? He had always thought he was forbidden to love a woman. Yet he saw nothing wrong with it now. He determined he was smitten.

That's a good word for it, he thought. *Smitten.*

+ + +

Drago, typically, was not a deep thinker. Thinking too deeply only caused him pain, so like Pavlov's dogs, he naturally avoided the pain and chose pleasure instead. If he mused, inevitably his thoughts returned to his failures and losses.

This assignment should not be causing him to overthink. As a soldier, he was supposed to follow orders—just follow orders. The problem this time was his prey were innocents—civilians without a clue—who could never hurt him or anyone else for that matter. At first, he had just thought if the priest had stepped in it, then it was no concern of his. It was a payday. Now he was mulling over what was happening, and he had far more questions than answers.

The priest must be a real danger to his employers, or they would not have sent him after Father Francis. The lamb was lousy at hiding, so Drago's task was ridiculously easy. And that was what was bothering him. The priest wasn't running, wasn't even hiding effectively. He was unaware of his danger. Maybe he was just a moron, but Drago was unsure. He would watch and wait.

But what if the cardinal asked him more of him?

CHAPTER 11

Easy Living

The days and weeks passed with unusual rapidity for Francis. He had never lived like this before. Life in Aspen was easy. He and Rebecca did whatever they wanted each day. Sometimes they would stay at home. Sometimes they went for walks or hikes in the mountains. The one constant was that they did everything together. Rebecca no longer had friends in Aspen, so there were no mandatory gatherings or appointments. They were alone with each other, but neither felt lonely nor confined.

After several weeks though, Francis noticed a vague stirring in his mind and body. For decades, his life had been filled to overflowing with people and responsibilities. The vague stirring matured into powerful guilt. He knew the Catholic Church was famous for producing inordinate guilt in its adherents, and he had tried throughout his life to avoid falling prey to false guilt. He had also spent considerable time alleviating it in others. After all, human beings have enough to feeling guilty about without being overly creative about it.

Upon reflection, he discovered he felt guilty about the inactivity and leisure that filled his days and nights and his pleasure in spending time with a beautiful young woman. Had he turned to sloth? Each time this thought surfaced, the corresponding realization came hard on its heels that he had been chased out of the mainstream by circumstances and powers beyond his control. Keeping this in mind, he would relax once more. This cycle of guilt, self-analysis, and reaching the same inevitable conclusion swirled around in his head for several days, but eventually, he had to just give up.

Rebecca noticed he was particularly pensive and asked him if anything was wrong. When he did his best to explain his dilemma, she responded with her characteristic charm. "Don't worry about it. You deserve a rest, and anyways, I need you."

Rebecca's last statement brought to Francis' mind another dilemma that was his to analyze. What was he doing here, living with this beautiful young woman, unsupervised, at this vulnerable time in his life? His priestly training warned him his salvation was in imminent danger, but frankly, he didn't care. His feelings for Rebecca were ... complicated, but brotherly, he told himself. Being there for a sister could not be wrong, but when his internal "lie-o-meter" went off, everything remained "complicated." Right now, he decided, he could live with complicated.

Being a man and a priest was complicated. There was nothing one could do about being a man. Notwithstanding that religious teachers suggest otherwise, there is no magic inoculation for the "Y" chromosome. Given most religious teachers are men, they are being disingenuous when they glibly suggest that every ill of being male can be avoided with prayer and self-control. Self-control would suggest maleness was not real. It was all in one's mind. The prayer element of the equation would suggest God would help one not be male. How had that worked for the clergy in North America? Every denomination was plagued by men acting inappropriately. It seemed to Francis this endless stream of misconduct negated the theory of purity through self-control and prayer alone. Ignoring his current predicament, he thought, men had to want to act properly and be equipped to act properly or nothing would help.

The problem was not the mind. The problem was having a hard-wired body with hormonal responses that bypass the brain. Certain stimuli cause certain responses, no matter how much self-control and prayer are brought to bear. That is not to say all men are slaves to their natural responses, but the responses happen notwithstanding belief systems or good intentions or religious conditioning. The fact that God wants men to be men is a conundrum for most religious folks. Men should want to be men too, but decent, wholesome, well-adjusted men.

Francis, throughout most of his life, had been insulated from women. That was the primary religious defense mechanism employed by the Catholic Church. If women trigger unhelpful responses in clergy, keep the clergy away from women. Now that he was spending large blocks of time in the presence of a woman, the hormonal responses were no longer hypothetical incidents that could be explained away or justified in the confessional.

Rebecca is awesome, he thought. *She is incredibly awesome, in fact.*

At just this moment, Rebecca walked out onto the deck wearing a bikini top and very short shorts. Francis had seen her in the same state of undress before, but his musings about hormonal responses and maleness had warmed him up for the view this time. The splendors of the natural beauty around him disappeared in favor of the splendors of real physical beauty that sat down next to him and handed him a glass of wine.

"So, Francis, I've been meaning to ask you about something," Rebecca began as if reading his mind. "What's it like to be a priest? It seems to me it would be an unnatural lifestyle, to be forced to abstain from sex and live separate from half the human population. Have you ever fallen in love? Have you ever considered having sex? Do priests think like other men, or are you all different, like gay men?"

Francis was shocked by Rebecca's questions and shifted uncomfortably in his chair. He wasn't so shocked by the questions themselves but by her obvious confusion about the priesthood. All the theology that had been pounded into him about the priesthood came flooding back to him, and all his conditioning and preconditioned taglines were instantly on the tip of his tongue, but he could not say them. None of the theology and preconditioned responses fit this situation. Rebecca was obviously confused about his behavior and his profession. He was behaving as both a man and a priest with her. Nothing physical had happened in his relationship with Rebecca, but though he was a virgin, he knew passion and was experiencing passion now.

Considering his internal conflict, he just could not answer Rebecca's honest queries with platitudes. Platitudes inevitably resulted in a breach of trust. Relationships demanded honesty and transparency. Without honesty and transparency, no healthy relationship could exist. Francis' desire for a deep relationship with this woman was overwhelming and demanded he be transparent or lose something important to him. His standard platitudes, he knew, would relegate him to an acquaintance at best.

"I am not gay. I am a man like any other," began Francis, carefully. "Until recently, being a priest was all I had ever known since I was a young boy. Even as a young lad I knew I'd been dedicated to the Church, and I started my training at a young age with a plan that unfolded over many years. I am still a priest now, just one the leadership of my Church doesn't appreciate. That doesn't change my commitments, though. I made commitments to God."

"But you're not answering my question. What's it like to be a priest, to be celibate? Is it even possible to be celibate? Do you even *believe* in being celibate? The whole concept seems crazy.

Pastors in my church married and supposedly remained pure," continued Rebecca, leaning closer to him.

Francis was quiet for several minutes as he considered his response. "A priest is taught celibacy is a state of spirit, mind, and will. The Church believes it's part of one's commitment to God. Women who dedicate themselves to the Catholic Church are also expected to remain celibate."

"Yes, I know that, but what about you? What do you believe? I don't care about all the other priests. I want to know what you believe," Rebecca repeated, looking directly into his eyes earnestly.

"From my study, I have concluded celibacy should not be a requirement to be a priest. Celibacy was a concept imposed on men and women as a spiritual discipline like fasting. The problem is the hunger for food and the hunger for sex are different. I don't believe in celibacy, but I do believe sex should only occur within a committed relationship; otherwise, it's just a shallow physical act akin to animals breeding. Even within a committed relationship, the Catholic Church has, in the past, taught that sex should be restricted to procreation; otherwise, it becomes a pursuit of pleasure, of sensuality.

"So that's what you believe. Sex is for making babies and shouldn't be pleasurable? And what does the commitment you're talking about look like?" asked Rebecca, shifting sideways and looking out at the mountain panorama.

Francis leaned forward and rested his elbows on his knees. "I'm not an expert on sex, Rebecca. And your question about commitment is a good one. The Church teaches that a committed relationship is a marriage between a man and a woman, performed in a church by a priest, that only ends at death. The Protestant Church, I believe, teach something similar. Frankly Rebecca, I don't know what commitment looks like. I've always chosen to believe in the teachings of my Church, but my belief system has taken a beating lately. My thoughts are changing at an alarming rate on an equally alarming number of subjects. Why should the Church make a sacrament of marriage, which is, most essentially, a civil contract for legal purposes? I'm beginning to think the Church ought to get out of the marriage business and perform blessings on relationships instead. Requiring marriage to be performed by clergy in a church smacks of control. Marriage could be less sacrament and more relational and spiritual. That would reflect the actual situation better. However, I realize I'm not answering your question. The real answer is I am just not sure anymore."

Following that in-depth, honest statement, Rebecca leaned over and kissed Francis, her lips barely touching his in a tentative exploration. Francis' initial reaction was to pull away, but his strong emotional attachment and a deep loneliness bred from a lifetime of separation from people led him instead to cling to Rebecca and return her kiss, as gentle as a whisper. His first kiss gave Francis a heady feeling. He felt heavy from head to toe, the blood rushed from his head, his vision became reduced to a tunnel, and he saw stars.

Rebecca ended the kiss and eased back, noticing the blood had left his face and he was blinking and struggling to stay upright by grabbing at the arms of his chair. She instantly found the whole thing comical and giggled. "Well, I've never seen a grown man faint from a kiss before," she chortled.

Francis' immediate embarrassment became mirth as he thought of how his face must have looked going white and then crimson, all in a few seconds. They shared the humor, but something profound had changed. Francis felt the change in him as he was liberated from his priestly conditioning and artificial self-definition. *Good thing my vows didn't specifically mention a kiss*, he thought.

+ + +

Drago was so bored. His target was doing nothing and going nowhere. He wished his boss had given him more latitude to act against the priest. If asked, his professional opinion would be to put pressure on the man with an appropriate end result in mind. Just watching was accomplishing nothing. He thought of contacting the cardinal to make a case but immediately thought better of the idea. This was not his op. He was just the soldier. Soldiers only acted at the direction of politicians.

+ + +

Chloe's first few assignments as a runway model had gone well. She had loved all the attention she received, having her hair done, letting makeup artists work on her face and body, and wearing the elegant and stylish clothes—sometimes being the first human being ever to wear new designs. And the money ... she got paid and paid and paid. The money had seemed to flow like water. She had never experienced having more money than she could possibly spend. The only constraint was time. With no time to shop, the money built up in her bank account to her delight and awe. She had been primped and pampered, and she thought she had gone to heaven.

The attention from the men in the fashion industry had also initially been welcomed. She had been treated as a royal, offered more engagements than she could attend. Her agency had run her ragged trying to show her off and advance her as an asset. Initially, the more exposure the better, they had told her over and over. The pace would slacken as time went on and then she could have a life—but not yet. Her life had been theirs to command and Chloe obeyed to succeed.

Through the amalgamation of two agencies, Chloe's agent had become Sylvia Benson, who, originally a Brit, now enjoyed life among the jet set. She had homes in Los Angeles, London,

Paris, Madrid, and Rome, each big enough to house her stable of working models and blossoming prospects. Chloe had been herded from place to place, assignment to assignment, party to party. Time had become meaningless in the rush and tumble of the glamour world.

One beautiful spring day in Madrid after she had been in the business a while, she and her cadre of colleagues had been relaxing on the terrace of Sylvia's flat in the bright morning sun when Sylvia had approached Chloe and asked her for a private conversation. Sylvia was a combination of mother, employer, and guardian to half a dozen young women, so one-on-ones were not uncommon. Chloe had followed Sylvia to her elegant office decorated in an ornate Spanish style with expensive furniture.

As they had sat, facing each other across the solid oak desk, Sylvia had said, "Chloe, I have a special request to make of you. Mr. Thompson, an important American fashion buyer, has asked to meet you personally. He's a pleasant gentleman. He noticed you during our last show. It would be good for your career to be his friend and spend some time with him."

Chloe had initially accepted the advice from Sylvia but was afraid of what might be expected of her. She had fretted more and more about it as their meeting time grew closer. Was this where her future was headed?

CHAPTER 12

Dangerous Outing

Life with Rebecca went smoothly. There was no conflict or discord. The fact that they were each unsure of what their relationship was or where it was headed prolonged a period of peace. They did not behave superficially exactly, but they weren't investing heavily in a future together either.

"Let's go downtown this afternoon. We need some groceries, and there's a conference I'd like to check out."

"As you wish, my dear," answered Francis. As if he could say no to anything Rebecca suggested. "What's the conference about?"

"It's a Christian conference about why the universal Church is experiencing dwindling attendance in North America and Europe," explained Rebecca.

At this, his heart went cold. Cardinal Massey had told him categorically to stay away from churches of any stripe and gatherings associated with Church. He had to maintain his anonymity. But what harm could this do, so far from anyone he knew or anyone who knew him?

Francis' anxiety increased during the drive into Aspen. Until today, Aspen had seemed a safe haven, so far from anywhere that he felt secure. Ignoring Cardinal Massey's warning frightened him even if this conference was a Protestant conference unlikely to attract Catholics.

The conference turned out to be a three-day event. The first day was dedicated to exploring the problem: declining institutional churches. The second day focused on the extent of the damage: how far the decline had extended and what the future looked like. The third day was dedicated to potential solutions: what a recovery looked like. Despite his misgivings, Francis had to admit he was fascinated with the summary of the event. This was obviously not a Catholic event. The Roman Catholic Church conducted these kinds of analyses in private. Asking these questions in public would be seen as exceedingly dangerous and unpredictable. The Roman Catholic Church shied away from unpredictability. He was living proof.

Because Rebecca had expressed such a strong interest in hearing the panels, Francis reluctantly agreed to attend. Rebecca's experiences with the Protestant Church matched in most ways what Francis was experiencing. Both had been rejected by their Christian tribes, and both had felt they had to flee from their respective organizations for their own good. During her ordeal, Rebecca had felt strongly there was something seriously wrong with her to have attracted violence from her husband and then ridicule and shunning from her Church. Francis, for all his temerity, had similarly attracted ridicule and rejection along with vague threats of harm. Rebecca had eventually concluded the fault was not hers and wondered whether her experiences reflected fault instead with the Church. Francis was not in a position, yet, to consider, let alone judge, his contribution to his circumstances and the contribution of others. His experience was still unfolding.

Both found the conference topics of interest because they were both truth seekers, and though they were both currently alienated from their respective Christian traditions, they were both still unambiguously hopeful of a change that would appeal to those believers that, like themselves, had found their Church experience painful or damaging.

Today was Day One. Rebecca and Francis found chairs in a corner in the back of the auditorium. The question posed to the gathering was, "Is the institutional Church in decline?" The panel members represented a diverse group: a polling company that researched cultural trends in the United States, Canada, and Europe; the Southern Baptist Convention; the Presbyterian Church of America; the Church of England representing itself and the Episcopalian Church of America; and the U.S. Assemblies of God. Francis was familiar with all these organizations and knew the basic theological tenants of their particular brands of Christianity. Rebecca was only familiar with South Baptist Convention since that had been her only experience.

The panel session was launched by a presentation from the pollster, who reported dramatic drops in various indicators of Church involvement in North America and Europe. She reported that European and North American societies were revealing a steep trend away from active involvement in institutional churches and Christian organizations. Many people still identified with Christian traditions and saw themselves as Episcopalian, Catholic, or Baptist, but there was a dramatic falloff in regular church attendance. Further, polling revealed a growing biblical illiteracy even among people that attended church regularly. The report also included a section regarding leadership failures within the universal Church summarizing thousands of examples of physical, emotional, and sexual abuse of Church members by clergy and other forms of misconduct including financial misconduct, spiritual manipulation and in particular the horrific abuse of aboriginal children in Canadian church-run residential schools. The report was obviously depressing to hear, and the crowd was somber and contemplative at its conclusion.

Francis was astonished at the openness of the presentation in outlining obvious failures within present-day Christianity. He had heard and read these statistics and was very much aware of the serious issues facing the Catholic Church after the multitude of cases of misconduct by priests and leaders had come to light around the world, particularly here in the United States. The presentation did not directly connect decline in Church involvement with clergy misbehavior, but the connection of the misconduct as a symptom, if not a cause of the problem, was not a stretch.

The panel discussion commenced at the conclusion of the presentation. Each member was given time for a short opening statement and then discussion would follow. The opening statements were eerily similar. Each denominational leader described the good works their organizations were doing and how they were impacting their constituencies for God. They gave statistics about how many churches operated in their organizations and how they were all healthy and growing. They were upbeat and optimistic. None interacted with the pollster's presentation or the facts it revealed.

Francis thought, *This was more like it.* This was the Roman Catholic approach: no bad news, ever. The panel discussion too followed this general trend: ignore the issues and speak positively and passionately about whatever good things they wanted to showcase notwithstanding the elephant in the room.

Rebecca and Francis remained with the crowd after the first session. From the discussions they overheard in the small groups gathered in the foyer of the auditorium, the convention crowd was not impressed with the first session.

One man said he was a Baptist without revealing what branch. He said he was shocked none of the leaders on the panel had anything to say about the depressing polling data. "They're living in a dream world," he said. "How can they not see there's a serious problem, and that churches everywhere are dying? How many old churches in your town are now restaurants or bars? How many of you go to a growing church?" he asked those in the group. The group fell silent. Nobody wanted to comment, and eventually people drifted away.

"Well," said Rebecca to Francis on the drive home. "That was depressing. Why won't people see what's clearly written on the wall? Are these Christian organizations so sick they can't even recognize their own illness?"

Francis replied, "Those folks are afraid. It's better for them to pretend everything is fine than admit there's a problem. They're hoping for the best, and some are betting on a revival or even the return of Christ."

"What good does hoping and pretending do, compared with realistic analysis and problem-solving?" Rebecca exclaimed, waving her arm in her frustration, narrowing missing Francis' cheek. "Sorry for making you duck," she added with a giggle.

Francis smiled at Rebecca's antics but added seriously, "In Church circles, hoping and pretending is called faith. Christian organizations have been doing the same things over and over and over for several thousand years. That kind of entrenched paradigm is difficult to adjust. Those leaders have no idea how to change or even what to change. The rut is so deep they can't see the top. And I feel sorry for them and for the leaders of my Church. They're afraid their institution is dying on their watch but don't know what to do. That's partly why I did my research and wrote my book. I was hoping to stimulate creative discussion. Instead, I stimulated defensiveness and hostility. I suspect all Church leaders are afraid anything other than a good news story will also stimulate defensiveness and hostility against them personally. Most have invested their lives in their institutions. They end up worshiping their organizations, which becomes indelibly linked to their faith in God. In return, the institutions sustain them in their lifestyles and give them support systems. The nurturing and eminence they receive traps them in their chosen profession. They become unsuited to any other way of making a living, let alone thinking."

"I noticed that about the pastors I knew," said Rebecca. "Their job was their life, and they had no useful skills that could be adapted to anything else. The job of pastor insulated them from the world outside the Church and only provided opportunity to develop Church-related skills. They might be able to do menial jobs, but they wouldn't be suited to business or professional roles." After a moment of awkward silence Rebecca asked, "Is there hope?"

"Oh yes, there's always hope with God. But part of the problem with what we call Church in the twenty-first century is that it focuses on the wrong thing. In God's economy, the currency has a single denomination: one. One human being, one individual."

"What do you mean by that?" asked Rebecca, glancing over at Francis as she drove.

Turning to watch the landscape flash by out the window, Francis replied, "Well, if we look at my Church, it sees the 1.3 billion people noted in their records as Roman Catholic. The Roman Catholic Church has a theology that recognizes masses of humanity. It doesn't recognize non-Catholics and doesn't see their own followers as individuals. If it does have to recognize a person for some reason, then it then fits them into one of two genders, into an age group, and into a hundred other categories. Their success is determined by the total number. What they fail to realize is that God only sees 1.3 billion *individuals*, all infinitely valuable to Him."

"Interesting. Well, tomorrow, a panel is supposed to examine how far the Church has declined. Won't these leaders have to be more transparent about what is really going on?" asked Rebecca.

"We shall see," responded Francis. "But I'm dubious."

+ + +

Day Two started with a plenary session that introduced a much different panel. In fact, the senior leaders of the denominations were gone. The Day-Two panel was composed of the pollster from Day One, Church historians, Christian commentators, and Christian journalists.

The same format was followed, with each panel member giving a brief introductory statement outlining their qualifications to comment on the topic, which was the extent of the damage, how far the decline had extended, and what the future holds.

The first panelist to speak was the young woman from the polling organization that polled on subjects of interest to Christians and Church organizations.

"My name is Jessica Talbot, and I represent The Church Door," she said, leaning into the microphone. "We are a Christian, non-aligned, not-for-profit think tank located in Colorado Springs. We poll internationally on a wide variety of topics of interest to the Christian community. We ensure that we touch a variety of demographics. Much of our extensive polling is directly related to the question asked of this panel," she began, leaning back and away from the microphone almost passive aggressively, her voice growing progressively louder in her assertion. "As such, my opening statement is brief. My answer to the question is, apart from rare exceptions, the worldwide Church is absolutely in decline, notwithstanding the reports we heard from the first panel."

Then she grew quiet and moved back to the microphone. "The worldwide Church is not maintaining a steady membership, and is in fact, losing its membership at a material rate. Except for a few places in Africa and South America, the worldwide Church is not replacing members who pass away or leave their organizations. The decline is across the board but is more prevalent in the liberal traditions such as Presbyterian, Anglican/Episcopalian, Lutheran, and Methodist. Even the largest denomination in the Unites

States, the Southern Baptist, is shrinking," she said, again leaning in for emphasis, her amplified voice echoing in the large room.

"Further, when examined from a historical perspective, the worldwide Church is shrinking, even if one ignores the growing human population. So, not only is the Church not growing, but it is dramatically losing ground against world population growth with the attendant reduction of overall influence over humanity. The data is clear."

A buzz of conversation grew in the gathering after Ms. Talbot's opening statement before easing into silence while the crowd waited for the next panel member to start.

"My name is Bruce Robinson. I am a long-time member of an Assemblies of God Church in Denver. I am also the editor and publisher of the Christian Chronicle, a magazine whose chief goal is to bring transparency to all things Christian. My opening statement will also be brief."

Sitting up straighter in his chair as if he was gathering courage, he said, "I cannot comment on the worldwide Church as Ms. Talbot has done, but I consider myself an expert respecting Christianity in America and Canada. Our magazine has done considerable research into cultural trends in North America, and, how those trends are influencing and affecting the Christian communities of those two countries. Is the North American Church in decline?" he asked, turning his head right to left, acknowledging each segment of crowd.

"As Ms. Talbot most ably pointed out, the numbers don't lie. Christianity is declining in North America. I won't repeat the statistics we've already heard but will instead comment on why the decline is occurring from a cultural point of view. Simply put, the expression of Christianity we're experiencing in the twenty-first century is institutional in structure and nature. Christianity has adopted a corporate organizational model. This corporate model is the only model employed by Christianity in North America.

Large denominations represent giant corporations with corporate subsidiaries in sometimes thousands of locations. They have corporate leadership, they have corporate jargon, they have corporate goals, and they have corporate methods. These corporate expressions of Christianity have lost touch with humanity, and humanity is increasingly not buying their products. Local churches, like local shopping malls, are losing business for the same reasons."

A mixture of confidence and resignation shone in his eyes, and he fidgeted in his seat as if he was beginning to feel claustrophobic. Taking a deep breath as if afraid, he continued, "The products are outdated, and the methods used to sell and deliver the products are not convenient. Local churches, selling Sunday performances that involve theater seating, artificial power furniture, and other gimmicks to increase the power differential between speaker and listener aren't cutting it in our rapidly changing postmodern culture. The structure, leadership, and methods of local churches are driving folks out the door. Just like shoppers initially gravitated from small shops to megamalls, churchgoers moved to megachurches, but that trend is reversing, just as it's reversing for retailers. Brick-and-mortar locations will be a thing of the past in short order for twenty-first-century Christianity as it is for twenty-first century retail."

Rebecca and Francis looked at each other and grimaced. The fantasy world of Day One was clearly not going to survive Day Two.

The third panel member turned on his microphone and introduced himself as Jeff Simpson. He was a thirty-something with a beard, hipster haircut, tight pants, plaid shirt, and bow tie. He introduced himself by saying he had earned a PhD in software engineering from Stanford and he was working in the tech industry in Seattle, Washington. More importantly, he said, he was a member of a postmodern emerging network of Christian believers. He clarified that he used the term "postmodern" to describe the culture of our current era rather than expressing any alignment with postmodernity itself, which, he said, he opposed for its Marxist roots. "I'd like, first of all, to welcome all of you in the audience and thank you for coming to this conference," he began, nodding warmly to each side of the room.

He waited for the associated applause to subside before continuing. "None of you would be here if you didn't love the people of God and humanity as a whole. All believers should feel familial bonds with each other regardless of what tribe we may currently associate with. I'm excited to be here. So, to answer the question of this session—Is the Church in decline? I say yes because the statistics say it is, and notwithstanding the statistics, we all feel it in our bones. Is there hope for the Church? I'm not sure how to answer this question because I make a strong distinction between the people of God who make up God's Church and 'the expression of Christianity we see in the twenty-first century,' as Bruce Robinson put it in his opening remarks. There is definitely hope for the people of God. However, I am much less certain about the institutional things we call churches. My guess is that most of the local churches in North America will run out of money over the next couple decades and disappear. We're seeing that happen already. The future is bright for the people of God, though."

He cleared his throat and sipped from the glass of water beside him before continuing. "I had a conversation with a friend of mine, just the other day, about churches. He's not familiar with churches and told me he sees churches everywhere in every town he visits, and he always wonders, 'What do people do in there?' I asked him why he didn't go in one and check it out. He said it was like the time his wife had asked him to pick something up she had put aside at a Victoria Secret store in the mall. He had told his wife that that would be too weird, and he just couldn't do it. He had the same feeling of dread about going into a church: 'too weird man, can't do it.' My friend represents one segment of the American population that is the responsibility of the people of God to know personally and disciple. How do we do that?"

He paused for effect, looked a few audience members in the eye, and moved on. "I have another friend who has attended various local churches for more than forty years. He's fulfilled most roles except senior pastor and eventually ran out of faith in the institution. Now, he may have run out of faith in the institution, but he has a vibrant faith in God. He has not regularly attended Sunday services for almost a decade and feels the need for fellowship beyond his immediate family and friends, but not fellowship in a local church where he feels only discomfort. My friend and his family represent a growing segment of the people of God that is the responsibility of the rest of the people of God. They live in the space between God and the institutional Church. How can we help?"

Still mulling over the potential answer to that question, the panel session broke then for coffee. Francis and Rebecca stood off by themselves. Francis was not willing to mingle, much to Rebecca's chagrin. He was abiding by Cardinal Massey's warning to avoid Church people if he could. Then the unexpected happened. Jeff Simpson approached and without hesitation said, "You're Father Francis Bauer. I've read your book."

Francis shuddered, but recovering, immediately extended his hand to shake Jeff's firmly and resolutely. "Yes, I am."

"Could we meet after the session today?" asked Jeff.

With trepidation Francis responded, "Certainly."

+ + +

After the session, Francis and Rebecca sat waiting patiently at a small table in the foyer for Jeff to run the gauntlet of well-wishers and questioners. He finally emerged from the auditorium and made directly for them.

"Father Bauer, it is so good to meet you in person," Jeff said as he reached the table.

Francis stood and shook Jeff's hand again and said, "Please, call me Francis."

"I'm a great fan of yours. I read your book a bunch of times and worked through all the references. Your scholarship is remarkable, and your conclusions are revolutionary for all of Christianity. Thank you for having the courage to put it out there. I read somewhere the book didn't make you very popular with the Catholic tribe."

"No, it did not make me popular," Francis responded with a cautious smile.

"What brings you to Colorado?" Jeff said, waving his arm to indicate the mountain panorama revealed by the floor-to-ceiling windows. Oh, I'm sorry," he said, catching himself and turning to Rebecca, "I've ignored you. Please, forgive me. I'm Jeff. I got caught up in meeting Father Bauer. I recognized him from the picture on the jacket of his book."

"I'm Rebecca Mossman," said Rebecca, "I'm quite impressed with him myself."

"So, what are you doing here?" asked Jeff. "I'm very glad you are, but it seems strange that such an eminent Christian scholar would end up in Aspen and at this conference."

"I'm staying with Rebecca, on sabbatical from my work, and she was interested in the conference, so we decided to attend the first day to gauge the agenda and atmosphere," Francis said vaguely. "Please have seat."

Jeff was first to speak after sitting. Words avalanched out of his mouth in a flurry. "The conclusions you reach in your book, if adopted broadly, would seem to make the long-term viability of Christian institutions a bit tenuous. There might have to be another Reformation of sorts. It would a complicated one this time given the complexity of modern Christianity. Do you have a sense of what the result would look like if the principles in your book resulted in real change?"

Francis responded with, "I really don't. I didn't write the book to trigger another Reformation. I'm no Martin Luther. My purpose was academic. I wanted to publish my findings and that is all. I had no other objective."

"The same general principles of change might apply, though …" Jeff mused, thinking out loud, referring to a great revolution that could sweep the globe. "But surely you anticipated the strong reaction your scholarship has triggered?" Jeff said earnestly.

"Actually, I didn't. When a scholar writes a scholarly book that's pretty dense, he wonders whether anyone at all will read it. The fact that the book is widely read is a surprise to me. Having said that, I did expect some negative reviews from people with a vested interest in the status quo. My point that the Bible had not anticipated giant institutions with powerful, controlling leadership structures didn't make the powerful, controlling leadership structures happy."

Jeff responded with directness that surprised both Francis and Rebecca, "Hence the sabbatical?"

Rebecca responded to this to relieve Francis' growing distress. "Francis is touring the United States to take a rest and is making friends in the process. I'm glad he has some time to spend with me." She tried to finesse the fact that she and Francis were not lifelong friends.

Jeff smiled knowingly but did not challenge Rebecca's account.

Francis nodded at Rebecca and thought, *I guess my presence in America is no longer a secret.* Fear rose within him.

Jeff was sensitive enough to feel the fear and said, "Well, you probably want some privacy while you're here, so I'll keep it to myself. Could we keep in touch though? I would love to follow up with you on some of my thoughts."

Visibly relieved, Francis thanked him for his discretion and assured him they could stay in touch. Francis had no plans to visit Seattle, but one never knew. Francis' belief that there would be little likelihood of anyone recognizing him in America had been false security as it turned out. He hoped it would not result in a security breach contrary to Cardinal Massey's explicit instructions. He would pray no harm was done, and they would give Day Three a miss.

During the drive home, Rebecca sensed Francis' discomfort at having been recognized. "I guess you're more famous than you thought."

"I'm fearful," replied Francis. "Under other circumstances, I'd be flattered that someone who isn't clergy and or an academic actually read my book. But now I'm not flattered, just worried. I was supposed to remain hidden here in America."

"What should we do?" asked Rebecca.

"Perhaps we should consider going somewhere else for a while. After being recognized and talking to Jeff, I realize I've been anxious for some time. I have a strange feeling we're being watched, but perhaps I'm just being paranoid." Francis unconsciously looked behind them.

"Let's take a trip. I have a friend in LA—Los Angeles—the City of Angels. She's always offered me a place to stay if I ever visited. She's a successful modeling agent and has a big beach house. We can stay with her. I'll email as soon as we get back. Are you famous among models?"

"I hope not," Francis said with a laugh. "I am just a humble priest."

+ + +

Drago dutifully watched his target from his rental sedan through the large windows of the log cabin's foyer. All was well with his assignment. Little effort was required, and he was easily in almost constant visual contact while the priest and his girlfriend were in town and not at the large house on the mountain. He had heard nothing from the cardinal, so his instructions were static for now. Just as he finished that thought, his cell rang.

Without preamble Cardinal Carducci barked, "I want more from you. Search the place where the priest is staying and see what you can find. Look for anything that might discredit him." The line went dead before Drago could respond.

Drago immediately formulated a search plan.

+ + +

Jeff was not a gregarious person, often preferring his own thoughts and his own company. At the same time, he was invigorated by conversations involving complex subjects and philosophical conundrums. He was widely read and particularly interested in Christianity and how it had and could influence humanity.

Having become a Christian in his early twenties through a series of events and relationships, he had spent much of his life inhabiting Christian institutions. Unfortunately, his curiosity and natural tendency to think through challenging questions had not endeared himself to clergy and others in charge of the institutions.

Initially, leadership and clergy had been flattered to have Jeff around. He was unusual: a highly educated and intelligent young man evidencing a relationship with Jesus Christ not stemming from a generational Christian heritage. Jeff found churches thrived on the longevity of Christian families adhering to the heritage of Christianity without much thought or inquiry of their own. He quickly discovered there were unwritten, and sometimes written, rules governing the questions one ought to ask and ought not to ask. In fact, when he had asked what he considered obvious questions about what was being taught and thought about in his churches, he was reminded that faith was not enhanced by questioning. Occasionally, he was even told his questioning put his faith and standing with God in doubt.

Jeff had not agreed and kept up with his study of a wide range of material that spoke to and commented on Christian thought and philosophy. He discovered, the more he read, that many Christians who had thought deeply throughout history had significant struggles with theology and the then current school of Christian thought. He found himself to be in good company with Saint Augustine, Martin Luther, Thomas Aquinas, and others. He did not consider himself to be in their league but felt a kinship with them as fellow seekers of truth and fact. He was not interested in fantasy and magic.

What great fortune to have met Father Francis Bauer, Jeff thought as he mused over his dinner? *I hope I get to spend more time with him sometime.*

CHAPTER 13

The City of Angels

Two days later, Rebecca and Francis were back in the roadster, once again heading west. The twelve-hour drive from Aspen to LA was too arduous to manage in a single day, so Rebecca suggested a stop in Las Vegas, which was a bit more than halfway.

"So, we haven't talked about our 'moment' the other day," Rebecca said suddenly.

"I assume you mean the moment when you made me faint?" Francis replied as he fidgeted nervously before catching himself.

"Yep, that's the one."

Looking down at his now-clasped hands, he explained, "Well, as you can tell, I'm not very experienced with that sort of thing. My dedication as a young boy to the Church limited my exposure to girls and women, and once I became a priest, anything near to intimacy was out of the question."

"Surely, women paid attention to you. You're very good looking, you know."

"No. Not really. If they did, I failed to notice. I must have had a professional force field around me that said, 'I'm not available, so keep your distance.' I don't think women are interested in priests,

But when I was in my teens, my best friend was a girl. She wanted a romantic relationship, but I was focused on becoming a priest, so I didn't understand her motivation."

Rebecca chanced a quick glance at Francis. "I don't know about other women, but I don't see you as a priest, only a gentle, charming, lovely man."

"I don't have my uniform on, and I'm afraid I've let my guard down with you. I should not have. But I have begun to hate maintaining my guard. I really appreciate you, and I appreciate you being close to me while everyone else seems far away. I cannot tell you how valuable that is to me," he said with real feeling. "You are a unique friend, a woman for whom I have no solid barriers. You are helping me explore areas of myself I never knew existed. During our short time together, I've grown to love you."

"Wow, buster. Don't use the 'L' word on me," Rebecca said with a chortle. "Although I know what you mean. My feelings for you are complicated, but I love you too, in a way I didn't know existed. It's like we've always known each other. We've been through some things together already in our short relationship."

"Sorry, I didn't mean … what I meant was that I have … oh, I don't know what I mean. But is there such thing as love without too much complexity? That's what I'm talking about."

After a brief silence, Rebecca said, "I miss Richie," with a strangled sob.

After his initial alarm at the abrupt change of subject, Francis put his hand gently on her arm, thinking, *Comfort for the grieving doesn't need many words.*

Francis wondered if perhaps it had been sharing Richie's death that had brought them so close so quickly.

After a long silence, Francis spoke his thoughts. "My best friend growing up lived next door." Once the words were out, he felt guilty about changing the subject from Rebecca's loss but continued to avoid another awkward apology. "We did everything together. We went to the same school and spent all our spare time together until I moved to Rome. I remember she was achingly beautiful, and she triggered emotions and physical responses in me as a youth that frightened me. I didn't think I could be a priest and respond to those emotions and urges. I couldn't give her the relationship she wanted, and she was angry with me. I think she thought I was rejecting her rather than pursuing a calling that couldn't involve romance. But it was just that I accepted celibacy as part of the uniform of being a priest. I haven't seen her since. I love her and miss her, even now."

"That's a sad story," said Rebecca, tears still on her cheeks.

"It is sad. It's sadder still because I didn't really decide to be a priest. It was just the way it was ever since I was small, and I perhaps lacked the fortitude to question that. I accepted it and was, for the most part, excited about it. Until recently, I was satisfied with my life and my accomplishments. I loved being a priest and loved the Church. Now, I feel a bit empty and lost."

After the exchange, Francis felt he had inadvertently equated the loss of a childhood friendship with the death of a twin brother. *What a fool I am,* he thought, but then the moment passed, and he could not rectify the situation.

As if she had read his mind, just as Francis had comforted her with a gesture, Rebecca reached over and took his hand. They held hands for a long time, until they had to stop for fuel, each in their own thoughts of loss and pain.

+ + +

Drago was panicked. He had taken up his station near the Aspen house as usual one morning, this time about to execute a break and enter, when he had noticed a change. The lights in the house were not on, and there was no sign of movement. He realized, to his horror, that they were gone. His mind raced. Where would they go? Back to New York? Somewhere else? He cursed himself, *I was lax. I wasn't paying attention. This was too easy, and I lost them. Damn it!*

He had to take a chance: east, west, north, or south. He flipped a couple coins in his head and chose west since that was the direction they had always headed since they had gotten together in New York. He raced onto Interstate 70 in his rental and drove at breakneck speed. He knew they drove a BMW roadster and watched for it as he raced west. He sped past Glenwood Springs, Castle, Rifle, De Beque, and Palisade and was driving past the first truck stop in Grand Junction when he saw the BMW at a gas station. Relief flooded through him, and he took the exit. He needed fuel anyway and pulled into the gas bar three stalls away. He was comfortable they would not notice him in the crowd of vehicles, and he sure wasn't going to lose them again. He had left all his kit in Aspen, but he had not left anything irreplaceable. This shit-show would certainly not appear in his next report to Carducci.

+ + +

"Did you notice the white car in line for the pumps on the opposite side of the gas bar from us?" asked Rebecca.

"No, why?"

"I think I've seen it around Aspen, and the driver ... I think I recognize him from New York too. I must be wrong. After you said you felt like someone was watching you, maybe I'm just being paranoid too."

Francis felt dread infuse him. *Was there really someone following them?* Cardinal Massey's words came back to him, *"You're not safe here."* Francis no longer felt safe in America either.

+ + +

Francis' first thought upon arriving in Las Vegas was that it must be the strangest city he had ever visited. He remembered it was called, "Sin City," and he recognized immediately how appropriate the name was. They sold the things traditionally labeled "sin." Gambling, prostitution, excesses of all kinds. It felt weird and distasteful as if the air was too dirty to breathe and left a residue on one's skin. The dirty, distasteful feeling was pervasive.

He and Rebecca walked through casinos and high-end stores, and he was astonished at the superficial extravagance. Even some of the casinos were replicas of several wonders of the world in miniature. Very strange. But once one left the main road, everything changed. Then it became an ordinary desert town. Whatever Las Vegas was selling obviously sold well.

He could not help comparing some of the pomp and circumstance with that of the Church, such as official events orchestrated by the pope with their ancient costumes, extravagant pageantry, and glorious displays of wealth and power. Pomp and circumstance sold in many different environments. Human beings loved the celebration of something bigger than themselves.

"We don't have a place to stay yet, so let's splurge," said Rebecca abruptly. "We've been living like hermits for weeks. I have an idea that will give us a little holiday from that."

"I'm not familiar with the word 'splurge,'" responded Francis, not really knowing what else to say.

"Splurge means to spend a ridiculous amount of money on something extravagant and completely unnecessary," explained Rebecca.

They returned to the parking lot where they had left the BMW, and Rebecca drove down the strip until she saw what she was looking for: the Wynn Hotel. She pulled up to the front entrance. The first impression of the building was of an oddly shaped, giant ship. The bow shape and distinctive rose-brown color created the impression of movement, not jerky movement but rather the gentle rocking of ocean swells. The effect was both stimulating and disconcerting and created the impression of instability. As they approached, uniformed attendants surrounded the vehicle with a flurry of car door opening, luggage retrieving, and welcoming.

They were ushered into the lobby where Rebecca conspiratorially whispered to Francis, "I've always wanted to stay here but have never had the opportunity before. It's outrageously expensive but should be an experience we won't soon forget." The lobby itself ascribed to the theory that if something was worth doing, it was worth overdoing. The large room was a riot of luxurious interior design details that overwhelmed the senses of ordinary people, which was the point.

At reception, Rebecca took charge. "We want two of your Fairway Villas on the same floor, close to each other."

The guest services specialist responded, "Two separate villas, madame? We have two-bedroom villas."

Rebecca responded, "Yes, two separate villas."

The persistent specialist replied, "The two-bedroom villa is a favorite of our more affluent guests. They're very private and very romantic."

Rebecca smiled pleasantly and insisted. "Thank you, but we require two villas." She made this statement without consulting Francis, assuming he would wish it.

"As you wish, madame," the young woman responded, trying hard to hide her knowing smile. Unmarried folks in want of privacy often booked separate rooms for appearances' sake.

"With our discount, the total will be $2,500 per night per villa. Is that acceptable, madame?"

Hearing the cost of the two rooms, Francis felt his throat constrict, and he found it strangely harder to breath. He had never considered "splurging" as Rebecca described it. He had never had enough money. Almost $5,000 for one night's accommodation? What was she thinking?

"Yes, it is, thank you," confirmed Rebecca, ignoring the small smirk on the clerk's face.

"Your luggage will arrive in your rooms in about ten minutes if you would like to have a complimentary refreshment at the lobby bar. I will have a bellman find you when everything is ready."

"Thank you," Rebecca and Francis said in unison.

As an afterthought, Rebecca turned back to the clerk and asked, "Oh, and could you please arrange for tickets to the Celine show this evening?"

"Of course, madame, I will arrange for you and … Mr. Smith to see the show from one of our VIP booths, which offer privacy."

"This is all very extravagant, Rebecca. Spending so much money. I wish to pay for this adventure. I have sufficient funds to splurge this once," said Francis trying to speak confidently without being completely sure.

Rebecca smiled gleefully. "This is a once-in-a-lifetime splurge, so thanks for your willingness to pay. But how about you just pay part, but not all, of the cost? I'm so excited to see Celine. Are you familiar with Celine Dion? She's a Canadian singer."

Francis nodded at her suggestion before answering her question. "Yes, I've heard of Celine Dion. She has quite a voice. A large range, perfect pitch, and brilliant clarity."

"That's her," confirmed Rebecca. "Going to the Celine show is part of the splurge. I pay for food and accommodation; you pay for entertainment. Deal?"

"Agreed. We have a bargain," responded an amused Francis. Rebecca could be so charming. Once again, he felt that strong emotional pull in her direction. *I thought I had vanquished that*, he thought sadly. *After all my years as a priest and my efforts at developing self-control, you'd think I could do better.*

The bellman arrived in the lobby to show them to their rooms so quickly they'd had only a few minutes to relax with a soft drink.

"This way, please," he said as he led them toward the elevator bank.

The bellman opened the first door with a flourish. "Madame, this is your villa. The gentleman's villa is next door." He followed them into the villa and showed each of them the features of the accommodation.

Francis must have been standing agape at the luxury of the rooms because the bellman said imperiously, "Only the best for our VIP guests, Mr. Smith." Rebecca's villa reminded Francis of the Vatican. The Vatican was itself a piece of art, ostensibly dedicated to God, but those that resided there were privileged to live within the walls of that piece of art. It was magnificent and opulent in every way.

Rebecca's villa was a twenty-first century attempt at emulating the opulence of a similar royal residence. The colors were designed to mute what would otherwise be overstimulation. Every surface was beautiful golden-brown marble and every appointment matched and enhanced the rest. Francis was cynical enough to assume the rooms were designed specifically to create the exact reaction he was experiencing. He felt like a king in a palace. Unbidden, he felt on a visceral level that the cost was worth the experience. Again, he realized he had been masterfully manipulated.

"This way, sir. I'll show you to your villa. It is the mirror image of this one," the bellman informed him.

"I'll freshen up and knock on your door," said Rebecca as the bellman led Francis out the door.

"I'll be waiting," responded Francis.

As the bellman had promised, Francis' villa was the mirror image of Rebecca's. After having fallen prey to the well-designed first impression, Francis felt a little foolish. He realized now how easily he could be influenced. This realization firmed his resolve to be more self-aware and cautious in this place.

He gave the bellman a tip and bade him farewell at the door. He only had to wait a few minutes before he heard a soft knock.

"Well, what do you think of the accommodation?" asked Rebecca as she strode through the door. "It's crazy opulent, isn't it? I find this much opulence a bit amusing and a little repulsive all mixed together."

"It is impressively elegant, but I admit I have the same mixed impression as you," Francis said sardonically. "What's your plan?"

"The plan is dinner in my villa, which is all arranged, and then Celine at 8:00 p.m. Does that meet with your expectations, sir?" asked a smiling Rebecca.

"It does, madame," replied Francis officiously as they both laughed at the parody of the hotel staff.

Dinner arrived in Rebecca's villa exactly on time—delivered by her personal butler. He set a beautiful table on the balcony so they could enjoy a bright city view as they dined. That night, Las Vegas delivered the perfect weather and the perfect atmosphere for a perfect meal.

Rebecca had ordered rack of lamb for two. As the butler served each plate, Francis caught a whiff of the gravy, which formed a deep-brown, lustrous sheen on the lamb. It reminded him of the fragrance of a similar dish he had once enjoyed in a mountain-top chalet in Switzerland. The delight of this recognition made him nostalgic and homesick. The side of sauteed green beans and broccoli, steamed, made his mouth water in anticipation. The butler went about his business professionally and unobtrusively, rarely speaking but always attentive to every detail. He poured a Tuscany red, which was rich and flavorful, perfectly accentuating the subtle taste of lamb.

At the conclusion of the service and enjoying a glass or port, Rebecca and Francis were completely satisfied and comfortable. The view of the extraordinary lights from the surrounding hotels created an air of expectation in them for the rest of their evening.

"That had to be in the top ten meals I have ever had. It couldn't have been better," said Rebecca.

"I agree. The whole affair was lovely and the company second to none. Thank you so much for planning this experience. It is something I will never forget. I'm afraid I'll be spoiled forevermore," replied Francis with a relaxed sigh.

"Don't get comfortable, my dear. We still have Celine to enjoy. And we should get going," prompted Rebecca.

On the short walk to Caesar's Palace, where Celine Dion was performing, Rebecca and Francis enjoyed the closeness of the occasion. They held hands and enjoyed each other's company, oblivious to everything going on around them.

After the show, which both thrilled and enchanted them, the pair walked slowly back to the Wynn. The desert night was pleasantly warm, feeling like a cocoon especially built for human beings. Their pleasant physical closeness and emotional connection soothed and comforted. At this moment, life was good, the concerns and anxieties of the previous weeks and months forgotten. They didn't have a care in the world.

They rode the elevator to their floor at the Wynn. As they approached the door to their respective rooms, their pace slowed. Neither want this feeling to end. As they unlocked their respective doors, they looked at each other longingly, both thinking what might make this evening even more perfect and how much that perfection would fulfill and soothe. They each stood still for a long moment, looking intently into each other's eyes for signs of encouragement. They simultaneously made the same decision, and in unison, said good night and entered their respective villas.

Each had, during that long pause, weighed the options and the strength of their commitments. Their commitments to God and each other had held. Francis had renewed his vows, and though Rebecca had felt the longing for intimacy and comfort, she knew her commitment to her faith and to her God superseded her immediate desires. She had renewed her surrender to her Lord and Savior in that moment. Both commitments, though tenuous for a moment, had held, and they were both satisfied. The transient comfort they may have experienced was fulfilled instead with eternal comfort.

+ + +

To Drago, they looked like lovers. Walking and standing close together, holding hands, talking in whispers as they walked with their heads nearly touching. He wondered if all priests were so blatant about their affairs. He felt the burning disgust of this hypocrisy rise like acid in his throat. How he hated this priest. "At least I know what I am and don't pretend," he thought savagely.

I want to hurt them both, he thought. *But perhaps I could just hurt the priest.*

+ + +

The next morning, they drove to Los Angeles. The drive was interesting since Francis had never seen a real desert before. One cannot help but feel a bit helpless and vulnerable in a place where human beings so obviously could not survive for long. His thoughts turned to the story of Jesus in the desert during a time of contemplation and temptation. Las Vegas and the surrounding desert provided exactly the mixture of discomfort and danger Jesus had faced. Francis would be glad to get to Los Angeles alive and undamaged.

Rebecca broke the prolonged silence, turning to Francis as she drove. "How have you been processing what we heard at the conference?"

Francis replied instantly, revealing he, in fact, had been processing what he'd learned. "I think most people familiar with Christianity realize its current institutional expression is losing its appeal in the world; therefore, the number of people involved in Church is dwindling. The polling data we heard certainly would verify that trend. And Jeff's distinction is integral to analyzing the situation. God's people are the big "C" Church. Even though institutions downplay this distinction by emphasizing *their* Church is *the* Church, people intuitively know that is not true," Francis said with a wave of his hand. "Christian people, those that think deeply, evaluate their experience in the institution, compare it with sensible interpretations of the Bible, and find there are significant gaps between what the Bible says about the Church and their experience week to week," he added, his voice becoming quieter, his face creased with concentration.

After a brief pause and another vigorous wave of his hand, he added, "For example, the Bible says the Church is the bride of Christ 'without spot or wrinkle,' which would imply a level of personal holiness under God's grace. What, in fact, we human beings have created are institutions. We have created institutions unable to assist individual believers in becoming the bride of Christ. The institutions are self-serving and more interested in their own longevity than in the human beings inhabiting them. In many countries around the world, religious institutions have proven corrupt and even abusive," he said, the intensity showing in his face. "Leaders have often proved untrustworthy with the lives of those supposedly under their care, and women and children have been victims of this corruption. The shepherds have abused the sheep, and abuse is not restricted to any denomination or tradition. It's widespread and has become notorious within those institutions, but the institutions corruptly choose to protect themselves instead of the innocents. And this type of corruption is only one example," he exclaimed breathlessly.

"Wow, you really have given this some thought," Rebecca remarked turning her head slowly to look into his eyes before turning back to the road before her.

After a deep breath, he continued, "The type of corruption you experienced, spiritual abuse, is just as disheartening and damaging as sexual abuse. Leaders that believe men can abuse women physically because men are superior and dominant, in biblical terms, are not fit to be shepherds. And leaders who advocate or condone bigotry against certain groups of human beings corrupt the message of Christ. A leader who preaches that homosexuals will burn in hell and we should hate them is wrong. Nowhere in the Bible does Jesus advocate such things. The man who spoke from a pulpit to that effect in your presence led you to believe you should shun your own brother," said Francis, sorrow evident in his expression. "That was a corruption of biblical teaching. Our families and friends are our primary ministry responsibilities as Christian people, and shunning is not loving. Shunning splits families apart and leaves individuals without support and encouragement just as it left Richie discouraged and alone."

Sadly, Rebecca made an observation. "I guess Christian people have a right to be wary of Church."

Again, Francis paused to consider, then decided to speak his thoughts plainly as he turned in his seat. "And nonbelievers are wary of Christian institutions not only because of the exceedingly bad press surrounding abuse, but also because they don't see the relevance of religion in their lives. That would indicate that whatever is being said and done in Church isn't impacting the people in their communities. The Christian message, the Gospel, is not a religion and is supposed to be the Good News, yet the way it is being presented is not good news in the ears and hearts of many human beings."

Francis stopped abruptly, realizing he had given Rebecca a lecture. "I'm sorry, a simple 'it was thought-provoking' would have sufficed."

"No, that wouldn't have been enough. I want to hear from you. So, how should we change things?"

"We? I'm a disgraced priest of the Roman Catholic Church, and you're a Jewish Protestant. Does that sound like a team that can change the world?"

"It does to me," replied Rebecca. "About as likely as a poor Jewish carpenter changing the world."

"Touché," replied Francis with a laugh. "I have been giving the subject a lot of thought over the past several decades. Change does not come easily to institutions that have operated under the same basic paradigm for two thousand plus years. However, during periods of crisis, meaningful change can occur, and paradigms can be adjusted. A crisis of sufficient magnitude has not occurred yet. I have a feeling it's on its way, but it's not here yet. A disruption of the status quo of sufficient proportions could create the crisis."

"What does a disruption look like?"

"I would suspect circumstances striking at one of the roots of the paradigm, like the inability to meet in buildings with large groups or government disfavor resulting in the institutions' financial support eroding would do it. Something that makes local churches disappear in large numbers and the large organizations governing the local institutions become irrelevant. Like what's happening in the retail industry, the brick-and mortar locations of religious organizations may become obsolete. If that happens, everything changes."

"Well, what do we do when the crisis hits?" Rebecca asked, raising an eyebrow and revealing earnest interest and concern.

Francis took a moment to reply. "I'm not exactly sure, but lots of things have to change. The corporate organizations that house the people of God are strong, defining, and controlling organizations that have to give way to more organic structures that do not try to maintain order and discipline to define adherents but disciple and maintain freedom."

"And …?" Rebecca prodded when Francis fell silent.

"Well, our faith must be in God. Today, most believers have more faith in the Church than in God. Part of the institutions' strategy is to ensure that alignment with them and attendance at their locations becomes a sacrament. Attending a Sunday service or Mass in the Catholic tradition is not a sacrament. Baptism is a sacrament; church attendance is not. Baptism is relational, church attendance is not. It makes sense to teach that attendance is a sacrament if you want to ensure the long-term continuation of an institution, but it does not align with the Bible. It is institutional conditioning. Believers should gather, but they don't need an institution for that. And if we feel obliged to attend a particular gathering, our faith is in the wrong place. The biblical accounts of believers gathering immediately after Pentecost were gatherings of family and friends. That is the biblical principle we should aim for. Meeting like we do today is mostly a spectator sport. We often don't know the people sitting in the seats around us, and we don't participate meaningfully. Most gatherings are little different from sporting or entertainment events, and our relationships are equivalent to regular attendees of sporting events. They're not familial relationships as are contemplated in the New Testament. People in the pews must be figuratively, and perhaps literally, turned to face one another."

"I can relate to what you're saying," said Rebecca. "For most of my Christian life, I thought faith was about going to church and doing what I was told. I did that until what I was told became too bizarre."

"Agreed," said Francis vehemently as he looked out at the view and ran a hand through his hair. "Those who speak for Christianity must stop being silly. Fighting against what humanity knows through science, for example, is silly. I had a professor in seminary who insisted the world was only about six thousand years old, having counted up the generations listed in the Old Testament and then adding in the New Testament time period. His argument was tortured, at best, and he maintained it because he was afraid the biblical accounts must each be verified, or the veracity of the Bible would become fluid. From science, we know, without much doubt, that the world is very old, and that should not frighten us as long as we don't have to interpret biblical stories literally. I have often seen statements from Christian leaders attesting to the inerrancy of the Bible and a tenant of their faith. What they really mean is the inerrancy of their interpretation of the Bible."

Shifting sideways to again face Rebecca, Francis continued, "We must accept that some biblical accounts of things are metaphorical stories through which principles for life are communicated, but the stories themselves are not intended to be literal words of God beyond God communicating through story. The story of creation, for example, is not required to be a literal account to have great meaning. Each human being makes decisions regarding learnings from the Bible, and theology in general, even if they're not aware of the process. Theology is very personal, and everyone's personal theology is different because of our individual emotional and psychological makeup, our backgrounds, our cultural experience, and our education. What we all share is the ability to decide to believe in something positive rather than something negative. The Bible contains a positive message. Yet most of what we believe, we cannot prove. We cannot prove the existence of God. Nor can we disprove the existence of God. Faith, then, is the decision to believe in the existence of a loving God—which we cannot prove."

Francis' face, when she glanced over, had such an earnest expression that Rebecca hung on every word, finding Francis' thought process fascinating and enlightening.

"Because every human being decides what they wish to believe, our message to the world, as believers, must be culturally sensitive, and the Bible must be interpreted acknowledging that some writers were reflecting cultural biases of their times that aren't applicable today. For example, the Old Testament seems to condone or advocate slavery and even genocide. The average highly educated and literate modern Christian person reading the Bible today intuitively discounts these things as anachronistic and misguided."

The sudden realization that this was true shocked Rebecca into considering her own Christian education and resulting personal belief system.

Francis continued in a rush, "An example of this is the Pauline epistles. Paul clearly reflects cultural biases about the roles of men and women, marriage, and sexuality that aren't helpful in our society. If one applies what Paul said literally in every instance, the message is highly misogynistic, divisive, and repellant to most modern human beings. Christianity ought to be able to look beyond the ancient culture of the first few years after Pentecost and reflect the positive principles Paul often presented of inclusion, love, and respect for human beings of every stripe."

Not being able to sit still, Francis crossed and uncrossed his arms, crossed and uncrossed his legs. "Many scholars contend that discounting inconvenient parts of scripture is dangerous, and control of the outcomes would be lost by departing from a literal interpretation. I say nonsense to that. Belief systems accepted by modern believers are already not identical or even consistent. Each person's belief system is unique in many respects. If we, as Christians, do not have a relevant message, then we are not who we say we are. If we focus on the principles of the messages related by Jesus, without cultural add-ons and layers of institutional conditioning, the message will be as relevant to all human beings today as his message was when he lived."

"Wow," said Rebecca. "That was a lengthy answer to a very simple question."

"I'm sorry for the complex answer," said Francis sheepishly.

"No, don't apologize," said Rebecca.

After a quick glance at Francis, she explained, "I've been feeling so unsettled in my faith for long time, and what you just said makes me feel much better about myself. I've felt so lonely in my church, and I condemned myself for being unfit to have good relationships. When church members met me on the street, they would often either pretend not to have seen me or look impatient to get on with their lives rather than spend a few minutes with me. And I've done the same thing. Even when I worked in the church, I was just another volunteer doing low-level, inconsequential work, keeping the machine running. I was ashamed I wasn't good or valuable enough to be part of ministry to people. Leadership and 'real' ministry were restricted to professional clergy deemed qualified. Plus, I was always uncomfortable with the concept of church members being holy and non-adherents being unclean unbelievers, as if we had built a fortress to live in, keeping all the riff-raff out."

"Sorry, I'm not familiar with the term 'riffraff,'" said Francis.

Rebecca explained, "'Riffraff' are the lowly, unworthy, unsophisticated people we should not associate with because of our superior station."

"Ah, I'll remember 'riffraff,'" said Francis, nodding with a grin. "But yes, from what I've seen of local churches and church organizations everywhere I've been, the concept of being 'special' is alive and well. Those on the inside are special, and those on the outside are not. Those on the inside are loved by God as his children and too bad about those on the outside. And to qualify as a child, one must pass the entrance examination designed by those on the inside. Plus, you could lose that standing anytime according to the rules created by the insiders. It's just so unfortunate because it divides humanity into 'haves' and 'have nots.' God, on the other hand, does not distinguish between human beings. He only sees the ones, not the many. One characteristic that makes God, God, is that each human being is equally precious to Him, and there is nothing one can do to enhance their standing and nothing they can do to detract from that standing. That's just God's grace, which doesn't create special people."

"But surely some people are more important to God than others," protested Rebecca, looking directly at Francis as she drove. "What about a pope for example? Your Church says he's infallible. I've heard that in some places, it's even taught that priests were infallible. Doesn't that make them more valuable? Southern Baptists seem to believe their clergy are special. Aren't pastors more valuable than I am? I've always been taught that, and I thought so myself."

"No, they are not more valuable than you. Clergy have occupations in the institutional Church but are not more valuable to God. A more pressing question is how valuable to God is the institutional expression of Christianity that is the modern Church? The institutional Church is not *the* Church, notwithstanding its claims to the contrary. The institutional Church is also not the Kingdom of God, notwithstanding its claims to the contrary. *The* Church is human beings, and the Kingdom of God is in the hearts of those human beings. *The* Church includes every human being who has acknowledged God, which primarily happens through acceptance of Jesus' life and message. It may also include those that have yet to do so."

Rebecca harrumphed her agreement and understanding, her gaze darting between Francis and the road.

Francis continued at that. "Institutions are only vehicles, and they should be discarded or changed if they are not driving well or driving in the wrong direction. It is only the people that are important. Each one individually, no groups other than families and familial groups, which is the New Testament model. Dynastic institutional religion is an Old Testament model reflected by Israel, and the success of that model wasn't great. We have recreated a failed model. If one studies the kings of Israel, it's easy to see they were corrupted by the power of their positions. Even King David, who is portrayed as a great king of Israel, was guilty of sexual misconduct and murder. And now we emulate the kingdoms of Israel with our dynastic institutions. The Catholics have a kingly pope and cardinals and priests, and Protestants have their kingly leaders, some with their own impressive dynasties. Why would we do such a thing? The simple answer is because human beings create paradigms and hold onto them without regularly thinking things through carefully. Human beings hold on to paradigms. Reverence for kingly leaders is a paradigm, and, in essence, is the worship of authority not the worship of God."

"So, to repeat myself. What do we do?" asked Rebecca.

"The first, and main thing, is for us, individually, to decide to change and perhaps to abandon the status quo if the status quo is no longer relevant and working. If asked, I would say as long as a local church is working well for the people that congregate there, and everyone is happy and fulfilled, stick with it, but if that is not the case, then make a decision to change. Each person must mature and take responsibility for themselves and their family and friends. That means taking personal responsibility for one's own faith, one's own spiritual development, and one's own spiritual responsibilities while not forgetting those closest to us. Not deciding opens us up to confinement and abuse."

Rebecca was silent for a long time, thinking. "But what happens to all the churches if people decide?"

"I don't think that's a relevant question," responded Francis without realizing how harsh that sounded.

Rebecca looked a little hurt but also determined. "It is a relevant question. What about the money that's been donated and the programs?"

"I'll answer your question with several questions to you. In the unlikely event that all the local churches disappeared, what would God think? Would He think, 'What a disaster! What will I do without all that money?' Or would He think, 'What will I do without all those volunteers?' Instead, might he think, 'Finally, my people are awake and free'?"

My goodness, he his Martin Luther, concluded Rebecca silently.

+ + +

Chloe was in a serious funk. *How could I have gotten myself into such a mess?* she thought. *I'm bound to an ironclad contract that keeps me a slave, I earn more money than I can ever spend, but I work all the time, and I'm forced to do what I'm told, including "favors" for big clients. They're not terrible favors but degrading things I hate. I have to let people touch me, grope me, and fondle me. My body isn't my own. I can't stand it anymore. I have to find a way out.*

"Chloe, I need you to focus. You're just going through the motions out there. Engage! Bring some emotion. If you're not engaged, you're not selling product. Your job is to sell the client's products. What is wrong with you?" an exasperated Sylvia Benson barked.

"I'm sorry, okay? I feel weak and tired. Maybe I'm coming down with something."

"No. I don't accept that. You are a highly paid professional. Be professional," responded Sylvia insistently.

"All right. I've got this." Chloe took a deep breath and refocused on giving the photographer the emotion he required for the shots on his list. She was a professional and could conjure believable emotion.

After the shoot, Chloe sat alone at a small table near the front door of the studio. She knew she wasn't performing but had no energy for what she was doing. In her mind, she inventoried her life and career. She thought back to her childhood when she had no serious cares or needs. *I had been a mostly happy, fulfilled child,* she remembered. *What had happened to that child?*

Her best friend, Francis, came to mind. Part of what had happened to that kid was Francis. He had become a priest, a priest, instead of staying her best friend and boyfriend. This was a news reel she had played in her head many times before. When she thought this way, betrayal and shame always surfaced. Why hadn't she been good enough for the best person she had ever known? He had rejected her and left her, going off to live his dream. It still made her feel worthless after all these years. His goodness, kindness, and gentleness had slapped her in the face, yet she regretted rejecting him back when he had tried to stay in touch.

+ + +

This assignment was bordering on embarrassing. Drago was back in sight of his quarry, but he kicked himself for almost losing them. Good thing there was no scrutiny from his employer. These little pigeons might even have noticed him if they were not constantly engaged with each other rather than being aware of the world around them. He could have driven next to them waving a red flag and would not have been noticed.

+ + +

While Drago groused, Cardinal Carducci was scheming.

Cardinal Carducci's staff continually monitored Bauer's book. They reported growing sales and exponentially increasing social media attention. It appeared the dangerous ideas of the problematic priest may go viral. What to do?

I haven't heard from the bloodhound since I told him to search the priest's rooms, he thought. What was that fool doing? It had been meant to be a small escalation to better understand what the problematic priest was planning or to use to discredit him if necessary. The priest's book was still a bestseller and still raising all kinds of questions that he, in his role of guardian of orthodoxy, was responsible for answering.

He thought back to his own thorough study of Church history. The closest comparison to what he was facing had happened in the sixteenth century when the Roman Catholic Church had faced the troublesome Martin Luther. *Luther had been a priest and professor at an insignificant German university,* he recalled. Luther had taken issue with an age-old method of raising money employed by bishops, archbishops, and cardinals.

As it does today, the priesthood had stood between God and the common folk, as it should in Carducci's mind. The priesthood granted, on behalf of God, forgiveness for sins. The archbishop Luther had clashed with had put a price on sin and had extracted that price. In Carducci's view, this was a crass practice, but he understood the need for money.

In 1517, as in the twenty-first century, the Church had needed money. Luther, it had turned out, was a fire starter. He had started the fire of so-called reform, which had created a new Christian sect named after him: the Lutherans. Luther had taught that grace and forgiveness were free and were the privilege of the faithful. Carducci scoffed at this notion. *He* was the judge, for his generation, of what was true and what was not.

History had given Carducci many examples of how the Church dealt with heretics. The most common practice was public burnings. Carducci understood the motivation for such executions. If Christian faith dealt with life and death eternally, then protecting the orthodoxy of the faith was of prime importance. Threats to orthodoxy must be dealt with savagely. Coercive force was justified to keep the faith pure. He chafed under weak and spineless leadership.

When it came to his troublesome priest, he may not have burning in his arsenal, but he could still make a powerful statement to all that would teach dangerous nonsense.

+ + +

The rest of the drive to LA was dominated by silence. Rebecca spent the time thinking through Francis' answers to the questions she had posed. She had never met someone who had thought so deeply about God, the people of God, and the Church. His answers were satisfying on one level and extremely disconcerting on another. If Francis was right, another Reformation was required to get Christianity out of the rut it was in. From what she remembered about history; Martin Luther's Reformation had been a turbulent affair.

+ + +

When they finally arrived in Los Angeles, Francis was dumbstruck by the city. It seemed to be a city designed for automobiles with its spiderweb of huge highways, like autobahns in Germany. Unlike the autobahns, the design had not kept up with demand because the highways were crammed with vehicles often stopped or crawling along. Thanks to the bumper-to-bumper traffic like he had never seen before, it took hours after they had reached the city limits to arrive at Rebecca's friend's home.

+ + +

"Sylvia Benson is one of my oldest and dearest friends," Rebecca explained to Francis. "Richie and I got to know her in London while Richie was dancing. That was before I met my ex and got married. I didn't see Sylvia or Richie much after I married, although they continued their relationship. I touched base with Sylvia after the divorce, and she has been a real support to me since then. I still don't see her much though because she's always on one of her photo shoots in some exotic place. I don't envy her lifestyle. She's never in one place very long. She actually isn't in LA either right now, so we'll have her house to ourselves for a couple days. She'll arrive with her cohort on Friday."

Francis was relieved to hear there wouldn't be a welcoming committee. He had been feeling a bit embarrassed to be traveling with Rebecca and having to explain himself to a complete stranger once again. Misunderstandings about his and Rebecca's relationship, what they were doing together, and why they were together at all were all complex concepts difficult to accurately explain without obvious misinterpretations. Did the perception of others really matter though? His and Rebecca's relationship was platonic and loving, but such an explanation was probably incomprehensible to most people.

+ + +

"Drago, Carducci. Where is the priest?"

"He's with his girlfriend in Los Angeles. I'm unsure where they're headed, but I'm surveilling them."

"What did your search reveal?"

"I was unable to search because they left immediately after our conversation," responded Drago. A lie works best when it's near the truth.

"No matter. Stay close and report to me every two days. I will give you further instructions shortly. That search may still be necessary."

Carducci hung up and leaned back in his red leather desk chair contemplatively. How to take momentum away from the priest? Discredit him: probably not effective. Ignore him: would not stop the damage. Frighten him into recanting: might work.

Carducci abruptly stood up and headed for his office door. "Call His Holiness," he barked to his assistant. "Tell him I'm on my way."

CHAPTER 14

Discomfort and Fear

Arriving at Sylvia's Malibu beach home reminded Francis of arriving at Rebecca's Aspen home. *This is how the other half lives,* he thought yet again.

As a priest, Francis had never owned property and had never had much money. He had more money at this very moment, thanks to Cardinal Massey, than he had ever had in his life. His book had generated royalties, but he had donated those funds to Church development projects in Africa. His needs had always been provided for by the Church but in spartan fashion. The rooms in which he had lived since he was young had a bed and desk, each many years old, but that was the extent of the luxury. Austere utility was the principle, not comfort. The higher one rose in Church hierarchy, though, the less austere utility and the more luxury. Francis had seen that the Holy Father and his cardinals lived in extraordinary luxury surrounded by priceless furnishings, artifacts, and art, but that did not extend far down the food chain. There was an inverse relationship between the breadth of one's position in terms of numbers in your cohort and the level of luxury. Francis had always been in a large cohort of priests.

There were more than four hundred thousand priests worldwide. But Francis had been happy with his contribution to the Church and had never been concerned with missing out on the pomp and circumstance.

Sylvia's beach house was a large two story, with a walkout at ground level that emptied right onto the beach. The couple maintaining the house, the housekeeper, and the chef, met them and made them immediately welcome, having been teed up by Sylvia. The warm, welcoming couple had been told to expect them at 4:00 p.m., and it was 4:15 p.m. now. The two were admirably organized and efficient and had made the place look as though Rebecca and Francis had always lived there. The home had nine bedrooms, so when they were shown to a large bedroom with a bath and asked instead for separate bedrooms, the housekeeper, Brenda, an older woman with silver hair and laugh lines, was able to accommodate them right away.

"I was unsure if you were a couple or not. I'm sorry I assumed more than I should have. Sylvia just said her friend, Rebecca, would be staying for a while with a guest."

Rebecca replied, "Don't worry about that in the slightest. We're just happy to be here. I can't wait to see Sylvia. Does she have an ETA?"

"She does," said Brenda. "She'll be here later tomorrow evening with her girls. She asked Stefan and I to prepare dinner for you and make you comfortable."

"Thank you very much for your kind welcome and for looking after our needs," replied Francis. "I must say, I feel a bit out of place in such a lovely setting."

"Your accent," said Brenda. "Is it Swiss? Is sounds a bit British but also a bit German or French."

"Yes, I was born in Switzerland and went to school in Italy before moving around Europe."

Brenda looked curious. "So, what do you do that involves so much moving?"

"I'm an academic," replied Francis, turning to Rebecca and asking, "Would you like to freshen up or take a walk on the beach? I am at your disposal."

"I vote for a walk on the beach," said Rebecca enthusiastically.

"Perfect," said Brenda. "Dinner is in ninety minutes."

The beach looked endless in both directions, but they chose north as it looked less crowded. As they walked, Rebecca described her relationship and history with Sylvia.

"Sylvia is a high energy, driven businesswoman," said Rebecca. "I'm pretty sure she wants to join the billionaire's club. She has properties all over the place and travels from place to place as her business demands. Her modeling agency is one of the biggest and busiest in world. And she's the consummate traveler. I love her dearly, but we don't see each other much. She wasn't impressed with my choice of husband and was even less impressed with the reason Richie and I had fallen out. She blamed me and couldn't understand my 'Bible-thumping ways' as she called them. Her opinion mattered to me and made me think many times that perhaps I had been naïve and might have trusted the wrong people."

Francis gently placed his hand on Rebecca's shoulder saying, "I'm very sorry you were led down a path that separated you from your brother. Christianity should never separate a family. If we see anything clearly about the life and the philosophy of life communicated by Jesus, it's inclusion and joining, not separating. Local churches acting as spiritual castles, with moats and drawbridges to keep dangerous people out, are so sad and misguided. Once that process begins, it only ends in exclusion and avoidance of anything unfamiliar."

Dropping his hand and gazing out at the long stretch of beach before them, Francis continued, "I once heard of a local church that, through various circumstances, developed a strong ministry to drug addicts in rehabilitation programs because all the residential treatment centers near the church liked bringing their clients to the church for spiritual training and inspiration. Exposure to the church services had proven beneficial to recovery. Hundreds of addicts attended. Initially it worked well. Then discontent rose among the regular church attendees and leadership. They became afraid of such people coming into their assembly. The addicts, when they felt comfortable and welcome in the church, were themselves. And when they were being themselves, they were unpredictable, which required considerable patience from other church members. Eventually, the church invoked a rule that no one could smoke on or around the premises, and the ashtrays at the front door were removed. Most of the drug addicts smoked, so the vibrant and effective ministry ended by exclusion. The recovery centers appealed to the leadership of the church, but the leaders were unrelenting, stating they could not build a church with 'those people.'"

Francis paused and turned to Rebecca once again. "Banishing the unclean is the opposite of how Jesus lived. Jesus did not distance himself from those around him, particularly those viewed as unsavory by the Jewish institutions of his day. He didn't have much admiration for the Pharisees who advocated that distance. Pharisees are alive and well in the twenty-first century."

Francis shook his head, sighed, and continued. "I'm an example of how that works. Since I was disciplined and relieved of my duties, I have been completely shunned by everyone I once knew in the Church. In our institution, even those on the inside can become unclean. Those I thought were close friends, not just colleagues, distanced themselves. My former colleagues treat me like the proverbial leper. Out of hundreds, I have only one real friend left. He's the one who counseled a quick excursion to America. He loves and cares for me, but he's the only one that doesn't hope I'm quickly forgotten. I no longer exist to the rest." With a small, sad smile, Francis finished with, "This all sounds like self-pity, I know. I'm sorry, Rebecca."

"Well, while it is self-pity," said Rebecca with a grin, "It's justifiable self-pity, and your situation is a sad illustration of what's wrong with Christianity right now. It makes me sad to think how far we are from Jesus' words and deeds."

Francis stopped once again and earnestly said, "Thank you from the bottom of my heart for understanding me. I have not had the benefit of a friend like you in a very long time. As a priest, those around me always expected something from me—understanding, forgiveness, wisdom—but we were taught only God could provide the same to us as priests. That always seemed to be a hollow principle. I'm sure the same principle exists for Southern Baptist ministers as well. It doesn't work well, though, because everyone needs others around them that don't treat them as a priest or pastor but as a friend or family member with problems, cares, and needs too. We're no different from anyone else, which is obvious given the trouble priests and pastors get themselves into. Thank you for being such a fine friend to me."

Rebecca reached out and took his hand, and they walked on in silence for a few minutes, taking solace in the sound of the waves lapping the shore.

"Exclusion is only one example of the relational desert Christianity has become in many churches. Jesus related intimately with those around him, but he could only manage such relations with a group of twelve individuals or so without creating some emotional distance. Given that we're not Him, we can't aspire to that level of intimacy because of the drain on ourselves and others, but we should be able to manage familial relationships in our closest circles. One's closest circle might be his or her family, but it could also include non-family members. How many people could be in that circle? Judging by Jesus' example, not many. The trouble with churches is that the paradigm doesn't promote familial relationships that last a lifetime. At best, they encourage working relationships between clergy and volunteers and volunteers and each other. Lack of true lifelong relationships is one of the tragedies of Christianity in the twenty-first century despite having unprecedented prosperity that ought to make relationships easier."

Rebecca interjected, "I heard a story from a pastor once. I met him when he visited my church. The story he told was terrible, and I remember it as if it was yesterday. Apparently one day, a man came to the church where this pastor worked and asked to see a pastor. The one I heard the story from was the only one around, so the receptionist delivered the man to his office. The man, a large, burly gentleman in his early fifties, gruffly said, 'My wife is dying.' The pastor didn't recognize the man but felt tremendous compassion, so he said, 'I'm so sorry to hear that,' and waited for the man to continue."

It was Rebecca's turn to stop walking and gaze out at the water as she continued with her story. "I guess this wasn't an ordinary interaction from what the pastor said. Anyway, the man said, 'I'm Stan. My family and I have attended this church for nineteen years. My wife, Mary, and our two children, that is. We don't know anybody, and you're the first pastor I've ever met personally. I need to make arrangements.'

'Arrangements?' the pastor asked.

'Funeral arrangements,' he said, looking down into his lap. 'I don't know how anything works around here, and … and I need to know for when—' It was at that point Stan burst into tears and sobbed uncontrollably for several minutes.

After Stan's sobs had abated the pastor asked, 'How can I help you?'

'I don't know what to do … and, and I can't make sense of it. We were saved in this church almost twenty years ago and attended every Sunday. We gave money. Doesn't that count for anything?'

The pastor said he thought being faithful to the church should count for something, but it doesn't make us immune from pain or tragedy. It doesn't enhance our salvation. Despairing, he told Stan, 'But it counts a lot to us.'

Stan retorted, 'Who is 'us?' I keep hearing you and the other pastors say 'we' and 'us,' but who is 'we' and 'us?' It doesn't include me because none of you have ever met me and my family.'

The pastor told me he felt terrible but only gave this lame response: 'It's a big church …'

'Sure, it's a big church, but what good has it been to me?' Stan asked. 'What good is it now when we're in trouble?'

The pastor telling the story told me he had no answer for that question other than platitudes. He said he and Stan went on to make advance arrangements for a funeral. He said the whole incident made him unbearably sad.

At the time, I felt the story was an unusual admission for a pastor to make. Most sermons I had heard weren't personal. Preachers seemed to love illustrations in their sermons, but I never heard many personal examples like this one, particularly when the result was unflattering. I'm still not sure how I feel about his admission, but it did make me think, especially now that you brought it up."

Francis too looked out over the water, perhaps processing the story Rebecca had shared. After long moments, he sighed and turned to Rebecca. "It is a sad state of affairs, isn't it?"

+ + +

Returning to the beach house, Rebecca and Francis noticed a commotion in the driveway. A passenger van and two cars were in the driveway along with enough people to fully fill all those vehicles.

"That would be Sylvia and her retinue," said Rebecca. "She's a day early. The house will be full tonight."

She and Francis hurried to get to the house so Rebecca could greet her friend. As they approached, Rebecca saw Sylvia waving from the balcony and waved back excitedly. Francis was a bit nervous to be thrust into a crowd but followed along dutifully.

As they approached the beach level of the house, the door flew open, and a woman emerged at a run. Rebecca ran forward, and they met in a flurry of arms wrapping each other up.

"Becky, I am so glad you're here," Sylvia said with tears running down her face. "Please forgive me for missing Richie's funeral. I miss him so much, and I've missed you. And who is this?"

Rebecca turned to Francis and introduced him to Sylvia. "This is Francis Bauer. He was a friend to Richie at the end and has become a dear friend of mine. Francis, this is Sylvia Benson. She is the older sister I never had."

"I am very pleased to meet you, Sylvia. Rebecca has told me much about you."

"You're from Italy, Germany?" asked Sylvia. "I can't quite place your accent, and you don't speak English like a native."

"Switzerland," answered Francis.

"Ah, yes, but with lots of Italian I'm thinking."

Francis did not reply to that comment, feeling it would expose him to further questioning and not wanting someone else to recognize him. They proceeded into the house and climbed the stairs to the main floor foyer where eight young women had gathered.

"Girls, this is Rebecca, my best friend, and Francis, my new friend."

Rebecca noticed a most beautiful young woman in the midst of the beautiful young girls push to the front. She called out in a small, strangled voice, "Francis?" And then in a louder, excited voice, she shouted, "Francis!" She ran to him and threw herself into his arms, almost knocking him over.

Rebecca and everyone present was startled into speechlessness.

Francis was far more than shocked as he stood holding the woman, dumbfounded. "Chloe?"

+ + +

Drago watched the target walking on the beach and then returning to the house. His view from a turnout on the highway was exceptional, and he recorded the priest's movements in his notebook, which would form part of his report to Carducci. Just as he was composing his report in his head, his phone rang, and he saw Carducci's name appear.

"Drago, Carducci."

"Yes, sir," responded Drago.

"You have contact?"

"Yes, sir."

"Frighten him. Make sure he knows he must recant his book. Do what you need to do but without crossing the line. If this does not provoke the proper response, we will escalate. Understood?"

"Understood."

The call ended as abruptly as it had begun.

Frighten the little priest, thought Drago. *I can do that.* Finally, something concrete to do.

+ + +

"What's going on, Francis? How are you here? I can't believe you're here. What has happened? Are you well? What are you doing? I haven't seen you forever. Who is this woman you're with? *Why* are you with a woman?" The questions, in German, poured out staccato fashion from Chloe.

Francis took Chloe's arm and directed her away from the others.

"I'll explain everything in a minute, but right now, I just want to look at you and enjoy the moment. It is glorious to see you," said Francis with real emotion. "It has been so long."

At Chloe's nod, he pulled her close once more in a long, meaningful embrace. He truly had missed his best friend.

Releasing her once more, he took her hand and guided her back to the group where he said, "Chloe, Rebecca, could we speak in private, please?" He was still unsure how to proceed. The mixture of shock and delight had robbed him of rational thought. He did, however, have enough presence of mind to introduce the two women closest to him. "Rebecca, this is Chloe, my best friend from childhood I told you about."

Rebecca smiled and nodded at Chloe but said nothing.

"I'm coming as well," said Sylvia. "I must hear this."

Francis nodded to the rest of the young women and outstretched his hand in the direction of the house. On the short walk inside, Francis' mind raced to come up with a plan. He could not think straight though, and on impulse, decided his only approach was the unvarnished truth. He would not lie to protect himself, not with Chloe of all people. Once the four were seated, Francis turned to the three women and said, "I have a story to tell you, and it will take some time, though you know everything, Rebecca, so I understand if you want to go freshen up."

"Oh no, you can't shake me that easily. I'm here to stay." Rebecca gave him an encouraging smile.

"And I love a good story," said Sylvia. "We have an hour until dinner."

Francis nodded and began. "Sylvia, I'm Father Francis Bauer."

Francis noted that Sylvia did not, thankfully, recognize his name but was very, very curious about his identity. Over the next hour, he explained the situation. He explained how he had met Richie and then how he had met Rebecca. He explained his research and the writing of his book. He described how, outside

Church leadership, the reaction to his book had been positive and how, within the Roman Catholic Church hierarchy, he had been vilified, censured, and stripped of his positions. He then went on to tell of how his mentor had planned and facilitated his leaving for America to avoid potential danger.

Both Chloe and Sylvia raptly listened to the story without question or comment. When he finally paused, indicating he had concluded his tale, no one spoke for a long time.

"I don't care, Francis," Chloe finally blurted out. "I only care that you have come back to me after so long. I missed you so much, and I need you so much now."

Sylvia and Rebecca were alarmed for different reasons by Chloe's almost frantic declaration. Chloe was Sylvia's biggest money-maker, and the younger girl had but a few good years left in her. Sylvia was also alarmed because she had, before this moment, felt all was well with her protégé.

Rebecca was alarmed by Chloe's outburst because of the strong feelings of jealousy that had erupted out of nowhere. Even though Chloe undoubtedly had beauty worthy of a supermodel, how could Rebecca be jealous of her? It was ridiculous, wasn't it? She and Francis weren't involved. He was a priest. She inwardly tried to shake off the disturbing thought.

+ + +

Francis noted the reactions of the two women to Chloe's fervent cry but was unsure what they meant.

Suddenly seeing Chloe again after so many years was enough to lay waste to his equanimity. She still smelled like baking cookies, and her close proximity upset his emotional balance just like it had when they were young.

Since leaving Rome, Francis' emotions seemed to constantly be in tatters with the fear instilled by Cardinal Massey, his short but intense friendship with Richie, Richie's death, mourning Richie's death, meeting Rebecca, the strong affection they had developed, and now Chloe's return. Seeing pain and desperation in her face tore the last tethers of his heart. His priestly reserve had dissolved into excruciating vulnerability. He was out of control and ill equipped to handle this. He knew his cloistered priestly life would not serve him well now. Everything crashed in on him now, and he had no choice but to just gave up. *Lord, I'm a mess. Help me*, he breathed silently.

He thought how little all his training and experience as a priest had equipped him for real life in the real world. It left him unarmed and unprepared. The principle of cloistering had derived from a philosophy of separation from the world to remain pure, which meant following a carefully scripted lifestyle because the world was dirty, and the cloister was clean. The world was unholy, the monastery or convent was holy. The people outside were impure and the people inside holy. *What rubbish*, Francis thought. Location and walls made no difference to a person's spiritual standing. Attempting to achieve purity begged the question, what is purity, and how much does it matter if it cannot be effectively evaluated? On a scale from one to ten, what is pure or holy? Self-evaluation is just self-delusion. In his experience, some of the most distasteful people he had ever met sincerely believed they were righteous and pure.

Meditation, contemplation, and spiritual formation were all excellent pursuits, but they did not require separation from the world. In fact, meditation for its own sake was worthless. Contemplation without interaction with other human beings was a waste of time, and spiritual formation requires life experience, the more the better.

A knock at the door of the study brought the four back to reality. "Dinner is served, Madame."

"Thank you, Brenda. We're coming now." Silvia turned to the others. "Shall we continue this conversation after dinner?"

+ + +

At dinner, Francis sat between Chloe and Rebecca. Throughout the meal, Rebecca kept glancing his way questioningly, and Chloe spent most of the time contemplating the contents of her plate. As was he, they were still digesting the reunion, and they each remained thoughtful. Sylvia reintroduced Francis as a friend of both Rebecca and Chloe and asked that each of the women make him feel at home. He smiled calmly but felt nothing of the sort. He must have had a pained expression because each of the girls looked at him with a mixture of pity and interest. They were probably thinking he had been caught in a love triangle. If only they knew the truth. The truth was much harder to believe.

When Francis was finally able to compose himself, he looked cautiously around the table. He marveled at the striking femininity represented. In fact, he felt awash in femininity. It became obvious he was not in the presence of typical human beings. These women were different and unusual. Other than Rebecca, they presumably were all supermodels schooled in their craft. It occurred to him there was more to their profession than just being attractive. Their natural beauty was obvious, but that could not be enough to trigger emulation in women and fascination in men. He was unsure what they were selling, but the whole subject was uncomfortable for him as a man and terrifying as a priest. As a priest, he had not been exposed to a group of women cultured to be irresistible. *What pressures accompanied irresistibility?* he wondered.

His reverie was broken by Rebecca's hand on his arm. "After dinner, can we talk?"

"Certainly," he replied.

+ + +

After dinner, Rebecca and Francis met on the balcony overlooking the beach. The temperature was neither hot nor cold, perfect for just sitting quietly.

"What was your impression of the group?"

"I have no context to understand this crowd, I'm afraid. They make me feel like a thirteen-year-old boy again with my mouth agape. I've lost my priestly demeanor. Plus, I'm concerned for Chloe."

"Why?" asked Rebecca with renewed jealousy.

"We haven't seen each other since I moved to Rome. We were both in our teens then, but even though I know she should have changed, she seems so unhappy. She hides it well, but we were very close when we were young, and I sense significant suffering."

Just then, Chloe came looking for him. He stood and strode toward her carefully. He was not sure what she thought of him being a runaway priest in the company of a woman.

"Francis, could we walk together?"

"Of course," Francis replied, looking back at Rebecca, pleading for understanding.

Rebecca, having been ignored and interrupted, was not happy. She just turned and retreated into the house.

Once on the beach, Chloe immediately asked, "What really happened to you? I can't believe you failed as a priest. When we were young, you failed at nothing. You were born to be a priest, or so you said. You were never in trouble, even though I tried very hard to take you off the straight-and-narrow path you'd chosen. Are you still a priest, or are you free?"

"I am a priest. I was not stripped of that, at least. I have been banished from most of the Church institutions but continue to be ordained."

"I wish you were free. I never stopped loving you, even though you left me. I was devastated when you left and felt so abandoned and worthless. My only true soulmate left me for the Church and never looked back." She paused thoughtfully for a second before adding, "I think I've been waiting for you all these years. I haven't had much romance."

"I am so very sorry I hurt you. I thought I was doing God's will by becoming a priest, so I could not let anything stand in the way of that goal. Not even you. It took all my resolve not to stay with you, even though we were still children. I am still a priest, though, and have made vows and commitments to God and am determined to maintain those commitments."

"But you never came and found me. Just one letter, and then you never wrote to me again or even cared enough to find out how I was doing. I thought the Church had turned you into some kind of monster. Holy on the outside but dark on the inside." Chloe clutched her hands together tightly as confessed her darkest feelings.

"Chloe, please forgive me for being insensitive and unkind to you. I missed you terribly but could not reveal anything contradictory to my education and training. Even as a young boy, I was encouraged by my mother not to have close relationships that could cause me to fall."

"Have you fallen now? You're living with Rebecca."

"I have not. Appearances deceive. We aren't intimate."

"From what I can see, Rebecca wishes otherwise."

"Perhaps so. I cannot judge that. I may well be set free from my calling against my will, in which case, I will need to re-evaluate everything, but as of today, my vows remain intact, and I will keep them."

"What good have your vows been to you? They kept you a slave." Then her intensity abruptly dissipated as she took a deep breath. "Tell me everything about your life since we were last together. I want to hear it all."

Francis did his best to fill in the details of the previous decades of his life, including summarizing the story he had told before dinner. His life had revolved around his training and career in the Church. He described his education, his doctoral studies, his postdoctoral research, his pastoral assignments, and finally his downward spiral from respectability.

By the time he was finished, he was exhausted, and so was Chloe. In fact, he realized they were lying on a dune quite a distance from the house and Chloe was asleep, her head comfortably in the crook of his arm. He did not recall how they had gotten into this position, but he felt calm and peaceful, and at that moment, the world was in harmony. He was together again with Chloe, and everything felt so right. He realized he was happy and content for the first time in so very long.

Just then, the world tilted. Francis was bodily jerked from his position and thrown with force several meters away. When he regained his equilibrium, he saw a huge figure in the darkness holding Chloe from behind with what looked like a military knife at her throat. An enormous hand over her mouth choked off any sound but for helpless squeaks.

Francis launched himself to his feet and toward the figure, but the stranger just put up his knife hand in a command to stop. Francis slid to a stop.

"Stay where you are," a deep rumbling voice said in Italian with a heavy Eastern European accent. "Do not move and she will not be harmed. This is a warning, priest. You must not continue spreading your lies. You must tell the world you were wrong. You have one week. Do you understand? You will get no further warning."

Francis nodded mutely, not knowing what else to do or say. The hulking man suddenly propelled Chloe into Francis. When Chloe and Francis had untangled themselves, the apparition was gone.

Francis noticed a tiny trickle of blood running down Chloe's neck from a small puncture under her chin. He reached for his handkerchief but realized he did not have one and just sagged to the ground, shaking from the aftereffects of adrenaline. Chloe followed suit.

"Are you hurt?" he asked Chloe shakily.

"No," she replied weakly.

They were both badly shaken, and it took some time before they moved to stand.

"What are we going to do?" Chloe asked.

"I don't know. I am so sorry I put you in danger."

"I don't think I was really in danger. He wasn't holding me like he was serious about doing me harm. I've been grabbed before with malicious intent, so I'd know. But what was that all about? He spoke to you as if he knew you."

"It was a warning, like he said. My mentor, a cardinal, told me some individuals bore me ill will, but he thought me coming here to America would be enough to keep me safe. Obviously, that didn't work. Again, please forgive me for putting you in harm's way."

"Don't apologize, Francis. That wasn't your fault. You did nothing wrong. But those Church men must really not like you. Should we call the police?"

"I don't know what the police could do. Perhaps this will be enough for those that are so offended. Let's get back to the house."

"But he said you must tell the world you were wrong. Are you going to do that?" asked Chloe.

"I will not," replied Francis with resolve.

When they arrived back at the beach house, Rebecca was waiting for them. One look was enough for her to know something was not right.

"What happened? You two look like you've seen a ghost."

Francis replied, "We received a visit from a ghost with a warning directed at me. Apparently, I am not incognito after all."

"Tell me," said Rebecca.

Francis explained they had been talking on the beach, and a huge man had grabbed Chloe and threatened her while delivering the warning. He had then shoved Chloe away and disappeared.

"Did he hurt you?" Rebecca asked Chloe, holding her at arm's length and looking her over.

"No, he gave me scratch under my jaw but that was all. He wasn't overly serious. I was just a prop in the drama," she said with a shaky laugh. She chose not to mention the knife at her throat.

"What are we going to do?" Rebecca asked Francis pointedly. "We can't stay here if they know you're here and if you're in danger."

"I'm more worried about everyone else here being in danger. But yes, we should leave. The problem is, where do we go and how do we shake him?"

"Let's sleep on it and decide on a strategy in the morning. I'm just glad neither of you were hurt," she said, hugging Chloe as she spoke, looking pointedly at Francis over Chloe's shoulder. Tears of worry and relief leaked down her cheeks as she spoke.

Francis, in the moment, thought, *What a mess I've created for myself and everyone around me. Is it all worth it? Perhaps I should write a retraction and be done with it. But how can things change if everyone is intimidated by power? What of speaking truth to power? I believe my book is truthful, so I cannot just capitulate. I'll have to find another solution.*

His moment of reflection over, Francis said, "I agree. We could all use some sleep. I'm sure a solution will present itself in the morning."

Chloe pulled out of Rebecca's embrace and nodded, wiping a lone tear from her cheek. Rebecca took her hand as they all made their way upstairs.

They retired to their bedrooms after bidding each other goodnight, each falling into fitful sleep.

+ + +

In the morning, the three met early to discuss next steps. They had decided not to include Sylvia in the caucus because the fewer in danger the better. Sylvia was unaware of the incident the night before, and the three thought it best to leave it that way.

While they were talking, Rebecca's phone pinged. She looked and saw a new email from Jeff Simpson. As she read the email, the shards of a plan started to come together in her mind. "Jeff Simpson has been trying to contact you, Francis, but he only had my contact information. He's asking us to come visit him in Seattle."

"Who is Jeff Simpson?" asked Chloe.

Francis answered, "He's a fellow we met at a conference in Aspen. He recognized me from the picture on the cover of my book. He read my book and was interested in my research."

"If you go to Seattle, I'm coming with you," said Chloe. "I'm not letting you out of my sight, Francis. You left me before. You're not leaving me now."

Rebecca looked at them both with significantly mixed feelings but responded that three heads were better than two. *Human relationships are unpredictable,* she thought. Like a priest with no experience, Francis was, she observed, blissfully ignorant about what was going on around him. If she had to share Francis, though, she would share with Chloe. Chloe already felt like a long-lost sister, but she knew Chloe's feelings for Francis, like hers, were not sisterly. Even the jealousy was not sisterly, Rebecca was sure. Francis was a perplexing man at the best of times, and his being a priest just made everything even more complicated. And he had no clue.

"How do we leave without our 'friend' following?" asked Francis. "He must have followed me since Rome."

"Remember the man in the white car I told you about on the drive from Aspen? He was a large man. Maybe that was him. Maybe he *has* been watching all along. But Francis, unless we can throw this man off our trail, we'll be putting Jeff in danger, won't we? I wish I'd thought of that before I said anything."

"I hadn't considered that either, Rebecca. We must throw him off. But how?"

"We need a different car," mused Rebecca. "Mine only has two seats anyways. We can leave mine here and ask Sylvia for one of hers. Maybe then we can leave without being seen."

They all agreed it was a good plan, so they went to discuss the planned trip to Seattle with Sylvia. They neglected to mention the reason for the trip and the incident the night before saying only that Rebecca's car wouldn't fit three of them. Sylvia was not happy to hear Chloe was taking unscheduled leave, but after her outburst the previous day, Sylvia knew something was off, so she relented. She hoped spending time with Rebecca and Francis would sort out Chloe's personal issues and get her back to work in top form. In the end, Sylvia told Rebecca she had a vehicle she kept in downtown LA they could use.

"How long do you plan to be in Seattle?" asked Sylvia.

"We're not sure, a few weeks, a month perhaps. We'll stay in touch. Thanks for letting Chloe come with us. It means a lot," Rebecca replied for all of them.

"Choe, I had scheduled a shoot in Milan starting next week, but when your vacation is over, you can catch up with us in Rome."

"Thank you so much, Sylvia. I just need some time."

"I know. I hope it helps and you come back to me refreshed and ready to give all you've got," Sylvia replied, pulling Chloe into a farewell embrace.

She let Chloe go and turned to Rebecca. "Goodbye, my dear," said Sylvia with feeling. "I appreciate you so much, and I'm so sad about losing Richie."

"Thanks, Sylvia. I appreciate you too. I'll see you again soon."

+ + +

"So, how do we get to Sylvia's car without being noticed?"

Chloe offered a solution. "We take an Uber and tell him not to let anyone follow us. It works when we're trying to avoid persistent admirers and paparazzi jerks. Then, we jump out in the middle of traffic and get in a cab going in the opposite direction. I mean, all we have to do is get to Sylvia's vehicle without being followed, and we're golden. We'll take some hats and sunglasses, maybe some coats, to change our appearance at key times."

"You sound like an evasion expert," said Rebecca. "That's a skill that may come in handy from now on."

+ + +

Drago was satisfied with his altercation with the priest and his woman. For a priest, he sure had relations with lots of beautiful women. Not for the first time, he thought the little priest was a prime example of hypocrisy. Celibacy was a thing for priests yet look at this priest. The media was right. Priests don't walk the talk.

Drago reported to Carducci that he had effectively scared the priest, and Carducci was satisfied for the moment. If nothing of substance came from the priest, there would be more asked of Drago, he was sure. He would watch very carefully now that he had made first contact. He certainly expected the priest to run.

+ + +

The sunrise was stunning the next morning. The golden hues spread magnificently over the sand, and in the shallows, the early-morning light turned the water's surface into an effervescent pond with gradations of shining green flowing into dark blue. The effect stimulated the brain and invigorated the soul.

The three travelers were up early getting ready to make a break for anonymity. Cheerfulness replaced the foreboding of yesterday.

Retrieving Sylvia's spare vehicle was uneventful and went strictly according to plan. The three travelers were confident of their execution and sure they could not have been followed. Unfortunately for them, they were amateurs in a world of professionals. Drago was amused by their attempts at evasion and concealment and was waiting for them when they emerged from the parking garage in their new set of wheels: a white Cadillac SUV. He loved that. He could pick out the SUV from a mile away. It was a shining beacon. He had changed vehicles as well and drove a nondescript, dirt-green Toyota Camry. No one gives a Camry a second look. It was the ultimate granny car.

In a further effort at evasion, the trio decided to take Highway 101 and the Pacific Coast Highway running along the coast of California, Oregon, and Washington to Seattle. It would be a slow journey, but they all agreed it would be the road less traveled—or so they thought. They gave themselves a week to travel to Seattle and had communicated that schedule to Jeff and warned him they were fleeing peril.

Given their confidence in their dubious evasion skills, the trio took no further action to misdirect. Drago was unsure of their intended destination but following them was child's play. He relaxed and enjoyed the scenery. In fact, the seascapes were so spectacular he felt a semblance of peace. Feeling peaceful on assignment was evidence of weakness and it annoyed him. But on a different level, he felt, well, peaceful.

CHAPTER 15

Seattle

The drive from LA to Seattle was congested and slow. Long sections of the Pacific Coast Highway were just two narrow, multiuse lanes. Dodging cyclists and pedestrians became a nail-biting drama. The travelers stopped at many of the sights and reveled in the display of creation's glory. If there were more physically beautiful landscapes on earth, none of them knew where. They made touristy stops at quaint towns like Morro Bay, with its population of sea otters, then drove through San Francisco to the Monterey Peninsula and on to Bannon, Oregon.

The Oregon coast amazed with its coastal rock formations, sand dunes, and seemingly endless perfect beaches. The majestic redwoods towered so high and were so old it made them feel young, feeble, and small. They thought Oregon beaches had to be the best in the world, though the climate was a bit chilly to enjoy them fully.

It took the whole week plus a day to get to Seattle. Only Chloe and Rebecca drove because Francis was not an experienced driver. Francis had to put up with good-natured teasing about not being able to drive. Most men, they both claimed, wouldn't surrender the keys to a woman, ever.

Upon arrival, Rebecca texted Jeff for directions to his loft residence. It was located near the center of the city. Remarkably, they wove through city traffic effortlessly, without a single incident or wrong turn. The women congratulated themselves. After Rebecca had made arrangements with Jeff to proceed to the loft, she had also made arrangements to head out for dinner. That was something they were all looking forward to, that and no more driving for a while.

+ + +

Jeff sat on his comfy sofa in his loft musing about his Christian life as he waited for his guests. While attending different churches, Jeff had observed the discomfort many Christians had with their Christian experience but had also observed an even more profound discomfort with change. From his study, he knew Christian institutions, including local churches, had essentially the same design and governance as business corporations. Corporations resisted change because they carefully designed a set of principles and assumptions, thought to be recipes for success, and then they stuck to those principles. Those principles and assumptions were paradigms, and he knew human beings stick to their paradigms.

The best example of a corporate paradigm Jeff had discovered in his reading was the Disney Corporation. Disney has a simple slogan and strategy that governs how they structure and implement their businesses. Walt Disney, the founder, had decided to "make people happy." He had determined that would be an attractive and valuable undertaking. Using the idea of making people happy as a guideline, Disney created a corporate structure and a suite of products and services designed to do just that. Nothing more and nothing less. Anyone who has visited a Disney theme park would likely say Disney is achieving its goal. In fact, Disney does make people happy and charges large sums of money for the pleasure. As a result, Disney is one of the most successful businesses in history.

Jeff had noticed local churches engaged in a similar process. Leadership would develop mission and vision statements intended to convince those inhabiting the church of the value of their underlying principles and the veracity of a strategy projecting into the future. The result was a corporate paradigm. The corporation—the local church—would then relentlessly convince its members, and then, if they were unusually energetic, would aggressively implement its chosen paradigm. Most Church paradigms, once boiled down, were just as simple as Disney's. Most decided to design and produce Sunday morning gatherings for the members of the corporation that would generate enough resources to sustain the corporation into the future. The Sunday morning productions concentrated effort and marshaled resources.

Jeff knew from the history of the Church since Pentecost that little had changed in the breadth, scope, and effectiveness of the paradigms employed between the first century and the present. Almost immediately after Pentecost, early Church paradigms developed. Some of those principles were revealed in letters written by Apostle Paul and others, now codified as parts of the New Testament. The Church, throughout history, had interpreted and reinterpreted biblical text in an effort to organize the perfect institution to house Christian people. Twenty-first century churches still did the same thing. And though the basic Church paradigm developed in the first century had survived, conversations about trying new things had dwindled over time. As a result, acceptable and available changes to the paradigm were insignificant. Jeff had discovered human beings stick to their paradigms and change them only when the paradigm is destroyed or rendered impossible by circumstances.

Jeff had studied the Roman Catholic Church as the oldest surviving Christian institution. He found it to be organized very much like it was hundreds, if not thousands, of years ago. It was the quintessential corporation. Arguably, with over a billion members, it was the largest corporation in the world.

The problem with corporations, particularly religious ones, thought Jeff, was that they bound and gagged the people that inhabited them. He too had, until he had chosen otherwise, been bound to a strict paradigm and gagged by those fearing dissension in the ranks.

Jeff suddenly awoke from his reverie and realized his guests were about to arrive. He was interested in meeting Chloe, of whom he knew nothing, and was looking forward to lengthy conversations with Rebecca and Francis. He had questions he felt Francis may be willing to discuss.

+ + +

Carducci sat at his desk, agitated, thinking about his wayward priest. Nothing he had done had changed the situation. Increasingly, he was coming under fire from the Holy Father for having no effect on the impact of the Bauer book.

"Is this book heresy?" the Holy Father had asked him just that morning. "If it is, something must be done. Shall we publish a condemnation of the book? What *do* you intend to do? This is within your authority, is it not?"

All the questions without suggestions or desired outcomes had only made the matter worse for Carducci. His job clearly included guarding the Roman Catholic Church against theological error. His problem was that the inquisition had not found heresy. He must make the priest recant and formally repent without the threat of the age-old tool of excommunication. How to do that?

Then Carducci felt an idea taking shape for the next phase of pressuring the priest. Drago was the only tool he had, so he would use the mercenary.

+ + +

"The priest must feel his betrayal and disobedience in his body as in the Bible," Carducci ordered Drago.

"Understood," said Drago, ending the call. *A step beyond threats then,* he thought. He felt nothing. It was just a job after all. A plan started to come together as he followed the Cadillac through the streets of Seattle.

+ + +

Francis, Rebecca, and Chloe arrived at Jeff's home in midafternoon and buzzed the front door of his loft building. It looked remarkably like an old fish cannery or factory, and it sat on the water in a distinctly industrial area of Seattle.

"Hello?" asked the voice in the speaker.

Rebecca answered, "It's us, Jeff."

"Okay, great. I'll come down and show you where to park."

Before they could comment on their new surroundings, Jeff opened the front door and warmly greeted Rebecca and then Francis. Then, looking past his two friends, he stared agape at the woman that must be Chloe. He had known she was a model but clearly, he had not known what to expect.

"Oh, ah, you must be … be Chloe. I'm, I'm … ah … ah, pleased, happy … I mean, good to meet you."

At Jeff's stumbling greeting, Rebecca and Francis couldn't help but chortle. During their travels with Chloe, it was obvious her effect on people and Jeff's reaction was typical. Chloe was used to the phenomenon and warmly hugged Jeff as if he was an old friend.

"I've heard so much about you I feel like I've known you forever," she said.

Jeff just stood frozen, his jaw still slack. Once he realized his arms were hanging loosely by his sides, he quickly recovered and gave Chloe a perfunctory embrace including a quick, brotherly pat on the back.

Still staring unabashedly at her, he gave himself a quick shake as if waking from a pleasant dream and said absently, "Sorry, sorry, sorry. Come with me and we can park your car in the garage and unpack your luggage."

Rebecca slid back into the driver's seat while Jeff opened the large garage door a few steps from the front entrance with a code. Rebecca drove into the parking garage, following Jeff down the ramp to a visitor space marked for 201, Jeff's spot.

"Here's a card for the door, Rebecca. You can come and go as you please."

"Thanks, Jeff. We're so very grateful for your hospitality."

Jeff acknowledged Rebecca's thanks with a small shrug of his shoulders.

The loft was huge. It turned out to be one full floor of an old fish-packing plant that had been converted to lofts designed for millennials wishing to live near downtown. It had a giant great room comfortably furnished with leather and solid-wood furniture and floor-to-ceiling windows overlooking Elliot Bay. It was an interesting, if busy, maritime scene. Elliot Bay was full of all sorts of watercraft seemingly going in every direction at once.

Jeff showed them around and let them choose bedrooms for their stay. Francis chose the bedroom next to Jeff's, and the two women shared a room next to his but further down the hall. All the bedrooms had a commanding second-floor view of the harbor.

And to top it off, each room had its own full bathroom. Each traveler thought it could not be a more comfortable arrangement.

"Change of plans, folks. Instead of going out—thanks for that though, Rebecca—I've arranged for dinner to be delivered at 6:00 p.m., so you still have time to freshen up," Jeff said. "We can meet for wine around 5:30 p.m. in the great room if that works."

"Absolutely!" Chloe replied for them all as they disappeared into their respective rooms.

Jeff proceeded to his office, letting out a sigh while sitting down heavily at his desk. *Whoa,* he thought, *definitely made a fool of myself that time.*

+ + +

Drago watched attentively as the priest and his women rang the buzzer at an industrial sort of building on the Seattle waterfront. A young man of about thirty greeted the group at the door and ushered them into an underground garage. Drago evaluated the neighborhood once they had disappeared. It was imperative he find a way to access the residence and the surrounding buildings if required, plus a suitable place to carry out his encounter with the priest.

He would have to catch the priest alone and out of sight of his entourage. He felt sure an opportunity would present itself. If not, the encounter would have to be here in this building. Drago himself would stay in a shabby, nondescript hotel nearby. He would watch this building closely to ensure he found just the right time for his engagement. There wouldn't be time to plan much, but he wasn't concerned. After all, strategic violence was one of his specialties. Drago had no problem using violence as a tool to achieve his employer's goals. Lately, he had cooled to the use of ultimate violence, but ordinary violence was well within his boundaries. He had taken many lives in war, but taking lives in peacetime was, to Drago, distasteful. He wasn't sure exactly why, though while he did not spend a lot of time thinking through the philosophical underpinnings of his profession, he did at least have standards.

+ + +

Jeff called out to the others to let them know he was serving the wine. They had all had a chance to rest and clean up and were in an effusive mood.

Rebecca started the conversation. "This place is so interesting and comfortable. How did you come to live here?"

Jeff said he had gotten a large bonus from his employer once because of the success of a new software, and he had bought the loft with it so he could be close to his work and downtown. "Most of my friends live down here. Many don't drive, so they have to live close enough to their jobs to walk or bike. Not driving is pretty common among people my age."

"How old are you then, if you don't mind my asking?" asked Francis

"I'm thirty."

"Practically a baby," said Chloe, making Jeff blush.

Jeff asked, "So let me throw the question back at you then. How old are you, Father Francis?"

"I'm forty-four, three years older than Chloe, who was by far my best and most disappointed friend when we were growing up. I was committed to becoming a priest at an early age and regretfully abused Chloe's friendship by leaving her and going off to Rome." His abandonment of Chloe was bothering Francis immensely, and even though he and Jeff were not close friends, he shared his regret without thinking.

Chloe replied, "For a long time, I couldn't accept the Church stealing you from me, but I did eventually accept God had called you and you had answered. I was mad at God for taking you, but I'm over that after all these years. I'm so just glad to have you in my life again. Maybe I can have that little piece of you the Church doesn't want."

"Well," said Francis, laughing. "We shall see who is entitled to what as the future unfolds."

"I want a piece too," piped up Rebecca, a little petulantly.

"That makes three of us," said Jeff and they all laughed.

Francis blushed and tried to hide his discomfort at being the center of attention by taking a sip of his wine. "I'm flattered, but really, I am pretty ordinary," confessed Francis.

"But I have a bunch of questions," blurted Jeff.

"And I'll do my best to answer them, but I'm not a counselor, and I'm not really known for being a great pastor."

"Don't worry about that. My questions are philosophical and theological. I want to know more about what you discovered in your research that caused such a stir."

"All right, what would you like to know?"

Jeff didn't know where to start, so he stood and paced. His own Christian experience had started in a Pentecostal Church, and he had eventually found the institution to be oppressive, and in some ways, tyrannical. He felt the institution had insisted he conform to an artificial standard. It had been run like a business with a board of directors and salaried clergy and staff and looked very much like his employer, the software developer, only the software developer didn't relentlessly try to convince him of things he questioned. The leadership, a group of men with a vested interest, wanted his obedience, his money, and his time but had nothing much of value to give in return. The whole experience over many years had been vaguely offensive and had not accorded with his personal beliefs, so he had left that local church and immediately lost all the friends he had made. He had been left with less than nothing to show for the experience.

Compared to others he knew, he had a deep faith, and he thought deeply about issues and contradictions apparent to him. He asked deep questions and had been told that focusing on mysteries was unproductive. Supporting the ministry of the local church leadership was the most important objective of all believers.

After leaving his Church, Jeff had discovered a network of believers in Seattle that had no formal structure. They met regularly and discussed any topic anyone brought up. There was no preaching, no pressure, and no asking for money. The network cost nothing to belong to, and the groups met in coffee shops, pubs, and restaurants, depending on what time of day the group decided to meet. The only formal organization was deciding on a time and place to meet. Someone with Alcoholics Anonymous experience had thought similar groups would benefit non-alcoholics too. So, these groups concentrated on learning, prayer, and long-term relationships. There were so many groups, he couldn't hope to visit them all.

"Okay, what about leadership?" asked Jeff. "Do believers need the clergy and boards of elders? The elders of my church were just the richest men in the congregation who liked to be in charge."

Rebecca seconded Jeff's question. "Yeah, after my experience with bad leadership in my church, I've wondered about the same thing."

+ + +

The obvious passion behind the questions confused Chloe. She hadn't known what to expect from this conversation. Though she was Roman Catholic by birth like so many of her generation, she wasn't a practicing Catholic. She had never understood Francis' dedication to the Church, so she sat forward in her chair, interested to hear Francis' answer.

Francis frowned in concentration, wanting to do the question justice but knowing how daunting it was to answer such a complex question simply.

"My research showed me that what presents as Christianity in the twenty-first century is really a human creation, not a God creation. Well-meaning people since Pentecost have assumed they had God's blessing in building what we see today. The simplest answer to your question is that the Bible doesn't support monolithic structures that define and control those that inhabit them. The builders built these structures like the Tower of Babel in the Old Testament: the structure is supposed to bring us closer to God. God didn't intervene to tear down the Tower of Babel but instead changed the people. Was his lack of direct intervention a tacit blessing to the undertaking? I would argue it was not tacitly blessed, and our giant structures must be examined from the point of view of their value to the individual believer. The question that must be asked is what value are our structures to the ones God recognizes as the capital 'C' Church rather than the small 'c' institutional churches of our design? Clearly our organizations are not the Church, and they are not the Kingdom of God since both of those concepts are human-centric. The Church is human beings who acknowledge God as Father and Jesus as Savior, and that is the essence of the kingdom."

Once again Jeff paced and interjected, "I understand and agree with you that the Church is only people. That's clear, but what about what we see? My church ran like a business, and the clergy in my Church treated their positions as a career and wanted to move up the corporate ladder and get paid more, just like the staff of a business. Is that a justifiable model?"

Francis responded carefully, not wanting to diminish faith with excessive analysis. "From my understanding of scripture and Church history, I understand why this situation has developed, but no, it is not a justifiable model. Immediately after Pentecost, biblical accounts suggest there was no strong core leadership in gatherings of believers. The Gospel was moving so fast among Jewish communities that bureaucracies could not really develop. In fact, in the Book of Acts, Chapter 6, there is an account of the apostles delegating part of their role to others for convenience. To settle a dispute over who was getting what services, the apostles decided on delegation, so they would not need to be bothered with mundane day-to-day matters in the group. Whether this was a good decision or a bad decision is hard to say, but unfortunately, we have used this small example, and others, as a foundation for a model to build bureaucracies. As time went on, the bureaucracies became larger and larger and more dominant, and now, they really have become present-day Christianity for all intent and purposes. They make up a religious industry separate from human beings."

Jeff sat down and leaned in, "I get that, but what can be done? You represent the biggest Church of all. What is best for us believers?"

Francis sat pensively for some time. The others waited patiently, not daring to break his train of thought. He did not have a ready answer for Jeff's question, so he asked prayerfully for help from above and then launched into his answer, hoping. "Things have to change. Our structures are increasingly unsuccessful in our Western culture. They have become cumbersome and domineering. The average person living in the Western world is highly educated and highly intelligent. We are not more intelligent than our forefathers, but we are far more aware of our world and our universe. No longer will it be acceptable to give trite answers to life's most difficult questions. Peers must be able to discuss life with peers."

Francis paused here to think through the rest of his answer, crossing his arms as he did so. "Preaching from a power position is not effective or acceptable. No thinking human being is prepared to accept, without question, a priest's or pastor's word. They want to think on their own and find the solutions they feel are culturally and personally acceptable and are inclusive rather than exclusive. Leadership failures have only enhanced this attitude. I shudder to say this, but I think we need a Reformation. Ultimately, every believer must find or invent circumstances in which his or her relationship with Christ can grow and flourish. The biblical model is family, not business. Can we all seek healthy familial relationships in a group of manageable size, keeping in mind that Jesus had a core group of twelve, not twelve hundred?"

"Actually, that's exactly what I've found," said Jeff, leaning back and crossing his own arms. He rubbed his chin before continuing. "Although I've often felt bad that none of my friendships from my local church days survived."

"There's a reason those relationships may not have survived," replied Francis. "Part of the reason behind building our large structures was to convince people that part of their salvation involved coming to the local church. Inside the building was holy and outside the building was not. Therefore, if you chose 'outside' instead of 'inside,' there was no acceptable category for you, and you were shunned, even though your relationship with God had not changed. I'm sorry that happened to you. Rebecca experienced the same thing."

Rebecca nodded at Francis in silent response as Jeff glanced at his phone and said dinner was on the way. But he had one more question before dinner. "What about all the sexual, spiritual, and physical abuse by clergy?"

"You leave the most difficult question for just before dinner?" Francis joked. "Yes, we have to acknowledge that something is amiss in Church organizations. My theory on this is two-fold. First, there has been a lack of candor and transparency in our organizations that allowed people to hide their failures. In turn, failures continued and multiplied unabated. Secondly, there's something about ministry by clergy that's been unhealthy for everyone involved. Historically, there's been a power differential between clergy and their followers. Perhaps that power differential is at the root of the abuse. If we were to focus on familial relationships instead, the trappings of power would evaporate. Family relationships can be really messy too, but at least they seem to last, and to varying extents, support family members."

"Thanks for your input, Father Francis. I've been dying to ask these questions for so long. I have plenty more, but dinner has arrived," said Jeff jumping up at the buzzer.

Chloe met Rebecca's gaze before she got up to fill her glass. Her thoughts were spinning wildly in her head as she processed the conversation.

+ + +

Drago situated himself across the street from the young man's home and put the final touches on his plan. He needed what the military called, "shock and awe," to execute his plan. He would wait for the chance to catch the priest off guard when it was either dark or he was alone in a confined space with some privacy. A few bruises, maybe a broken rib or two, even a mild concussion might stun the priest and reinforce Cardinal Carducci's message. At the very least, the priest would know the stakes were being raised and his superiors were serious.

+ + +

Dinner was a lighthearted affair full of reminiscing, teasing, and laughter. After the table was cleared and the kitchen cleaned, the host and guests once more launched into dialogue.

Jeff started once again. "During services in churches I attended, I often listened to someone standing in front of a congregation saying something like, 'We are very glad you came out this morning,' and I would immediately think, 'Who is included in this 'we'? I was pretty sure I wasn't included. Father Francis, who do you think 'we' is?"

Rebecca chimed in. "Now that you mention it, Jeff, I've heard that very thing, although it never occurred to me to ask the question you're asking. The one that sticks in my mind now, is 'We thank you for your giving,'" she intoned in a replica church voice. "I often thought, who is thanking whom and why?"

Francis thought about an answer for several minutes. The others waited patiently again. It was a good question he had not really thought about before. "Now that you've asked, Jeff, I'm not sure who the 'we' is. I've heard popes and cardinals say that, in fact I've said it, but it never occurred to me that the turn of phrase was odd, but it is."

He pondered moments more, resting his chin in his hand as he thought until an answer came to him. "I would presume the 'we' is the institution speaking with a human voice. Thanking a group of believers for their attendance or their tithes and offerings is the institution communicating. The institution is really saying, 'You're a guest here in my building, and I'm in charge.' It also implies that I, the institution, ought to be important, and you, its guests, perhaps are less important."

"I agree with your assessment," answered Jeff. "But that doesn't paint a pretty picture. If we've submitted ourselves to dominant institutions all this time, what does that mean for our faith? How does that define us as believers?"

Again, Francis thought through the ramifications before responding. Jeff was certainly keeping him on his toes. He was impressed with the depth of Jeff's analysis. "One of the conclusions I came to in my book, though not as starkly as I'm about to say now, is that the institution demands faith from us to encourage us to support it with our time, money, and effort."

All present were stunned by this revelation. The three went to respond simultaneously, but Rebecca was fastest, leaving the other two open-mouthed as she blurted out, "But we can't have faith in an institution. It's not God."

"So true. Where does that leave us then?" Francis replied, one corner of his mouth quirking upwards as he enjoyed the exchange. "One thing I know is that how we view ourselves, our self-definition, is our greatest limiter. In the case of a churchgoer, if they define themselves using the paradigm of a Christian institution, it results in a reduction of freedom of thought and deed. One of the powers of an institution is the power to persuade. So, to achieve long-term life, an institution must convince people of several things. In the case of a religious institution, it must convince people it is holy and worthy of their admiration. As a counterpoint to strengthen that argument, it must convince them that outside the walls of its building is profane. Further, it must convince them that what happens within its walls is God's will. It has to convince them that the leaders of the institution are special, unusually spiritual, and authoritative."

Here Francis paused to sip his drink. Answering all these questions was making his mouth dry. After using the time to find the right words once again, he placed the glass down on the table but continued to hang on to it as he spoke once more. "Finally, it must convince them to give money to the institution to further its particular goals. The institution then employs relentless convincing to create a form of unanimity, which has the effect of adjusting each person's self-definition to support the institution's goals and objectives. This convincing has been going on for generations in local churches, so we now have generational church-member families and generational church-leadership families, elites that form the core of the institution's strength. Once this convincing has molded a person's self-definition, freedom of thought and action are dampened. It's much more comfortable to go with the flow than swim against the current. Seeking comfort rather than challenge and chaos is human nature. I think you found that out, Jeff."

The weight of the discussion had exhausted everyone, so as Chloe looked at the group, she suggested, "Perhaps we should break for the night and resume the discussion in the morning? I, for one, have a lot to think about."

Each nodded at that, though each mind was busy weighing the consequences of faith in an institution and thinking of elements of their own self-definition that perhaps were not really their own.

As she followed Chloe to their shared room, Rebecca asked her, "Can't we just have faith in God, without all the rest? What freedom that would bring. So simple and so powerful. I feel so much better now that I understand the discomfort I had with my Church experience. It's sad that I spent so much of my Christian life having faith in something that wasn't God. I invested a lot of time and energy there."

Reaching into her luggage for her night things, Chloe said, "Well, I guess we better get some sleep if we're going to be prepared for tomorrow's conversation. It certainly won't be light with those two!" she laughed.

Rebecca chuckled in reply.

+ + +

Francis decided a short walk was in order. He had spent so much time in vehicles and comfortable chairs that his body was rebelling. Jeff gave him the codes to both the front door of the building and the loft and let him out the front door.

As Francis absentmindedly began walking down the street, not paying much attention, he thought about the revelation he had had because of Jeff's question. The answer he had given was novel to him in its simplicity and consequence. Francis had spent his entire adult life in pursuit of his vocation as a priest. The foundation of his goals had initially been at his mother's persistent insistence before it had become his own ambition. His faith in the institution of the Roman Catholic Church had cracked because of his comprehensive research into ecclesiology but had not broken until just a few minutes ago. What did that mean for him? What did it mean for him as a priest? What did it mean for his relationship with God?

These deep thoughts were interrupted when he instinctively felt a presence darting at him from his left. The shadow threw a punch to his left kidney that landed heavily before Francis even knew what was happening. Because of his training, the blow met only a solid core. The acute danger released an adrenaline surge in his body, heightening his senses and lessening the pain, and the hours Francis had spent in the gym dampened the disorientation that imminent danger would normally instill. Instinctive muscle memory took over.

Although Francis had never had to defend himself in this manner, he felt the events take on a surreal slow motion. He saw his attacker with uncharacteristic clarity. The darkness was strangely not so dark, and the streetlight lit the large man's outline so Francis could see with brilliant clarity his assailant's posture. After throwing his punch, the assailant had rotated beyond center mass and was now out of position for a follow-up blow. Francis had no context to analyze the situation with, but his training helped him respond without thought.

+ + +

Drago was alarmed. He had stalked his prey perfectly and thrown his best body blow. It should have leveled the priest, but his fist had struck iron. The priest had moved laterally from the punch but had remained standing. Drago sensed rather than saw the torsion in the priest's body and in that moment thought, *What is going on* here? *This is impossible. This man had responded like a warrior, not a priest. The priest should have fallen and been stricken with fear, but he hadn't and wasn't.*

Drago had been startled into inaction before, but not like this. This was a priest. How could he move so quickly and absorb the blow Drago had administered without going down? He thought all this as he watched the priest shift laterally and then twist on his axis to deliver a counterblow. *A counterblow? What it this?* The blow was heading toward Drago's throat. And in that moment, with regret, Drago thought he might die. The blow came like lightning, and it was a killing blow. He blocked the blow instinctively by lashing upward with his right forearm, which connected with the priest's fist and instantly became numb, rendering his whole arm useless.

The appropriate counterblow to a straight punch to the throat was a left hook to the side of the priest's temple, which would render him unconscious. Drago started to execute the punch with his left fist and was again shocked as the priest expertly countered the blow with his own forearm and went on the offensive again with another blow emanating straight from his shoulder.

Drago's eyes closed involuntarily while his brain cataloged and processed the data it was receiving. In the microsecond he knew it would take for the priest's fist to reach Drago's larynx, his brain rebelled, and a fight, flight, or freeze reflex made him freeze in surprise. Such a blow, he knew, would crush his larynx, and blood would immediately flood his lungs. He would be dead within a minute. He knew this.

Killed by a priest. Unbelievable. Life had always been strange to Drago. He felt foolish and ashamed now. The events of his life flew across his mind's eye, and he felt in that instant the pain and anguish of losing his family. He felt the shame of who he had become and what he had done. For the first time in his adult life, he felt remorse, he felt the fear of death, and he realized he wanted to live.

The blow never landed. Drago's eyes blinked open, and he felt the priest's second knuckle gently resting against his larynx, the other fist held at the ready.

"Don't move," the priest said in an angry whisper in Italian. "You are the man that has been following me?"

Drago wordlessly nodded.

"You were the man that put a knife to my friend's throat on the beach?" Francis' voice rose in a crescendo of rage.

Again, Drago nodded.

"I guess they didn't mention I studied martial arts. It wasn't priestly, so I kept it quiet. But I've been expecting you. What is your name?" Francis said, his voice firm and insistent.

Drago hesitated and then realized he had no choice. Any move would result in him being disabled at best, killed at worst. He could run but even then he wasn't confident of a positive result. He chose to answer instead. "Drago."

"Drago who?"

"Drago Milanovic."

"I guess you know my name."

Drago nodded dumbly.

+ + +

Francis was unsure how to proceed but was filled with a perhaps unjustifiable confidence that he should at least try to engage with this man. It was the last thing he wanted to do, but he could not shake the feeling. *How should he fix this mess?* He looked the man over and Francis saw his response to the attack had unnerved Drago and left him in disarray. Francis certainly could not trust him, but perhaps they could talk. His own words came back to him: "God sees every human being as a valuable individual worthy of salvation and love." *Oh no,* Francis thought. *Not this man. He wants to hurt me, badly, or worse. He's a hired thug. No, I will not just talk with him.* He wrestled with his thoughts for several long minutes while Drago stood frozen still, waiting. Francis finally gave in. If he believed what he said to others, then he knew what he must do.

"Walk with me, Drago," Francis said without moving or lessening his resolve to protect himself and keep his attention on his assailant.

Drago did not immediately obey. He remained where he was, rubbing his useless arm to restore feeling to it. He had spent all this time hating this priest for being a weakling, and now his mind was reeling from his obvious error. He was embarrassed at having been handled with such ease but also relieved at having met his match. This man had done nothing to him and did not deserve harm at his hand. It was just a job. And according to Drago's code, the priest had had every right to kill him but hadn't. It had taken this particular moment for Drago to realize that doing this kind of dirty work was far from honorable and that perhaps he was not cut out for this life anymore. This thought shook him, hard.

Francis stepped back, turned, and slowly walked away from Jeff's loft. He did not look back, but he was nonetheless perfectly ready for a resumption of hostilities. He listened for any sign of movement from Drago.

Drago moved to follow, and Francis instinctively wrenched his body to the side, preparing for the worst. There was no need for evasion, however, as he saw Drago walking slowly with him. There was no obvious threat in his movement. They walked together for several minutes before Francis spoke.

Speaking in Italian, Francis began, "I will not ask who sent you or what your mission parameters were. I already have a good idea. Instead, I want to speak to you man to man. Can we do that?"

Drago nodded, feeling relieved but wary. *Who is this man*, he wondered? He should be calling the police.

"I do not blame you. Your behavior has been criminal to be sure, but you're just a pawn in a bigger game. I feel sorry for you."

Drago felt the priest's words pierce his psyche. His initial reaction was a surge of outrage. This priest felt sorry for him. Then suddenly, strangely, a calm descended, and Drago believed the priest. He was alarmed yet again at this realization. *The shocks keep coming*, he thought. This priest had alarmed him in so many ways since he had started this assignment. It was a new feeling for Drago. He was not often out of equilibrium. Until now, he had always felt competent in his skills and his emotional flatline. Now the priest had jarred him with what ... empathy? Thinking back, he had felt out of equilibrium ever since he had taken this assignment.

After first thinking the idea that had now occurred to him was crazy, Francis continued, "I want you to meet my friends. But first I need to hear from you that you have given up your assignment, and that you will harm no one. Can you make that commitment?"

"Yes," Drago said resignedly. He could not seem to say no to this man. There was something about him. The priest was much younger, but he seemed ageless by comparison and ... and something else.

It was quite late when Francis arrived back at the loft with Drago, but they found Jeff reading. Chloe and Rebecca had come to grab a glass of water and were conversing amiably.

When he and Drago entered the great room, the three turned and looked at the pair quizzically. Neither Chloe nor Rebecca looked surprised that Francis might leave alone and return with a stranger. Jeff, however, was clearly confused.

Francis introduced the stranger. "May I present Drago Milanovic, the man my superiors sent to punish me?"

Chloe leaped to her feet, recognizing Drago. "You brought him here after he put a knife to my throat?! Francis, have you lost your mind? He's dangerous!"

The other two gaped at this, also leaping to their feet fearfully.

"Please," said Francis. "Drago and I have reached an understanding. Have we not, Drago?"

Drago nodded meekly.

"Drago, this is Chloe, Rebecca, and Jeff," Francis said, gesturing to each in turn.

Drago nodded to each but remained silent. As crazy as this whole situation was, Francis expected Drago to make a dash for the door and leave this little group behind for good, but he didn't.

Francis motioned for Drago to sit at the dining room table. Francis sat down across from Drago, looked him directly in the eye, and said, "Drago, tell my friends about our agreement." Jeff, Rebecca, and Chloe remained standing three steps away.

In heavily accented English, Drago said, "We agreed that my assignment is over, and I would not hurt anyone. I give you my word." He looked everyone in the eye so each person understood that meant something to him.

Rebecca looked over at Francis. "Can we trust him?"

Francis replied, "Not yet, but perhaps someday."

Jeff looked nervous and unsure, and Chloe, showing equal reluctance, said, "If you think he can be trusted, I'll go along for now, but I am afraid. Why the about-face? What happened?"

"I know, Chloe. I'm not comfortable either, but I saw no other satisfactory way forward. It just felt right." Francis then turned to Drago and said, "Drago, it might help us if you tell us about yourself."

Drago was taken aback. He had tried to hurt the priest, yet here Drago sat, not being arrested and not dead as he should have been. And strangely, the priest obviously did not hate him. In fact, Drago felt something else, something unfamiliar coming from the priest. It felt something like compassion. It was like Francis was the only one in the room, so Drago melted. He could not help himself. He began his story, starting from when he was a young boy and not stopping until he was done. His eyes never left Francis' own. Drago was afraid to look away in case he broke the spell.

Drago told Francis about being born into a loving family, about the troubles in the former Yugoslavia, about losing his family, and about the part he had played in their deaths. He spoke in Italian, but Chloe translated quietly for Rebecca and Jeff. Drago even told Francis about becoming a child soldier and about the things he had done and the people he had maimed and killed. He told him about his pain, his fear, his self-hatred. He was completely drained when he finished. There had been no tears or outward expression of emotion, but Drago felt his emotions fray and tear as he told his tale.

There was a long pause after Drago finished. Rebecca, Chloe, and Jeff were mesmerized by the telling and were speechless at the end.

Francis was not speechless. "Drago," he said finally. "Your story is both terrible and beautiful. It is terrible because you had to experience those things but beautiful because you are now here with us. I have something for you. May I pray with you?"

Again, Drago nodded dumbly. He was at a loss to understand how badly and yet how well his assignment had gone. He had completely failed, and yet he had answered a call that had allowed him to tell his story for the first time.

Also, for the first time since he had lost his family, he felt he could be a bit vulnerable rather than completely inhibited. This was all so strange and yet intriguing. These people were not strangers, exactly, since he had been watching them for so long, but he still didn't know them. They should be afraid of him, and they were, but not enough to be normal. As a child, he had learned about

God, but he had only thought about Him sporadically since then. In his thoughts, God was to be feared, not embraced. It would seem the priest had different ideas.

Francis began. He looked Drago directly in the eye and did not waiver as he spoke. "Heavenly Father, we acknowledge you and ask you for your help. We are all imperfect and in need of your forgiveness and grace."

At this, Drago realized Father Francis, as he now thought of him, was including him, Drago, in a group that included himself.

Francis continued, "We all ask for your forgiveness for our shortcomings and that you restore our hearts to communion with you."

Drago could see Father Francis' prayer was affecting each member of the group. Chloe and Rebecca both had tears running down their cheeks, and Jeff, his eyes closed, was focusing intently on the words.

"We bring Drago Milanovic before you today and ask that you grant him the special blessing of your presence. Drago has suffered greatly in his life and needs you to intervene on his behalf. Drago has also made others suffer and requires your forgiveness. Lord Jesus, impart to Drago the understanding of the sacrifice you made for him."

At this, Drago realized his need and his guilt, felt the floodgates of his emotions release, and wept uncontrollably. Every breath came as a shudder. He felt the fearlessness of these people, and that broke him even further. There was no holding back his sorrow and shame, and it all flooded out. He was embarrassed and relieved, thankful and afraid, confused and joyful, and more than anything, sorrowful. *How had this happened to him? He was no longer strong and in control of his destiny. Who was he?*

After Drago's deluge of emotions subsided, Jeff rose and went to the kitchen to make tea.

Francis finally said, "Drago, you had better stay with us tonight. It's late and you may have some questions in the morning. Are we all in agreement on this?" Jeff, Chloe, and Rebecca reluctantly nodded their agreement, accepting Francis' evaluation of the risk.

Drago spoke the first coherent thing that came to his mind. "No. How could you invite me to stay, knowing what I came to do? How can you trust me?"

"I don't trust you one bit, but I'm willing to accept you based on your word," replied Francis.

Jeff acceded with action and said, "You can crash on the couch. I'll bring some bedding."

+ + +

Jeff's words incited Chloe to action too, despite herself. "I'll make up a bed for you," she said. Chloe found she had been powerfully impacted by what had happened. She had been weak in her faith since she had left home, and she had never experienced anything like this before. God's presence had filled all their hearts and touched them all, not just Drago.

She was in awe of Francis. She did not recognize the man he had become. He was filled with radical faith and did, from her point of view, radical things she had never seen from a priest.

By the time they had finished their tea, they were all drained of emotion. Drago was slumped over on the couch, and Chloe covered him up with a blanket. Each of the four looked at each other questioningly and quietly slipped off to bed, the girls making sure to lock their bedroom door behind them. They may have perhaps experienced a life-altering event, but that didn't mean they had to be careless.

+ + +

In the morning, Drago was gone. Francis was disappointed but hopeful they would see him again, but the other three were not so sure.

After breakfast, Chloe was the vocal one, wanting to go over the events of the night before. Jeff and Rebecca agreed.

Chloe launched the discussion. "Francis, tell me what happened last night. I don't understand."

"What we saw last night was God's intervention in a troubled man's life. God loves us all, whether we think we are good or bad. God will meet with any human being who acknowledges Him." Francis shrugged. "Obviously, Drago acknowledged God and was powerfully impacted by the encounter."

At this, Chloe burst into tears, dumbfounding the others. The others looked at each other, confused. Through her tears, she recounted how she had felt so worthless because of how she had lived her life. The fashion industry, she said, had led her to do things she was not proud of, so she saw herself as broken and dirty. Her emotions rushed out in a torrent as she told her story.

Rebecca rushed to her and drew Chloe into her arms, whispering to Chloe as they held one another. She then prayed a prayer remarkably similar to the one Francis had prayed with them last night. She asked God to show Chloe His love, convince her of His forgiveness, and cleanse her of her feelings of inadequacy and shame.

Chloe wept even harder as she realized the significance of Rebecca's words for her. She felt the release of the telling of her story. Knowing these people truly cared for her was rare. Just like Drago, she did not know what to expect next, but she was no longer afraid.

"Oh boy," said Jeff. "I'm not used to all this intensity, and it's freaking me out a bit." He raked his hand through his hair before shoving his hands in his pockets.

Rebecca, still with one arm around Chloe, looked at Francis and quietly said, "Francis, you seem to be a sparkplug in all our lives, and I thank you for allowing me to come with you on this journey."

Francis replied, "Rebecca, I think you are the sparkplug. You directed our path, and I just came along."

The front door buzzer sounded, and Jeff checked the video feed from the camera. "It's Drago."

At Francis' nod, Jeff buzzed Drago in and opened the door to the loft. As the once-mercenary walked into the living room, he said, "The Pope is dead. I've been ordered back to Rome."

CHAPTER 16

Rome

The Vatican's announcement addressing the death of the pope stated he had died peacefully in his sleep from cardiac arrest resulting from a previously unknown condition. The story appeared in every major media outlet around the world. A conclave of the College of Cardinals to select a new pontiff was launched in the same missive. The missive named the one hundred sixteen cardinals eligible to vote in the conclave. The main eligibility requirement was that they had to be younger than eighty when the conclave was called.

Conclave is a gathering of cardinals for the express purpose of selecting a supreme pontiff. It consists of a series of votes in an environment of radical secrecy. All conclave participants face excommunication from the Church if discovered to have broken confidentiality. Voting is held in successive rounds, with the results counted after each and communicated to the group. There can be many votes before a candidate reaches the required two-thirds majority. Theoretically, any name can appear on a ballot as long as the person is male and has been baptized into the Catholic

Church. However, since the year 1378, only a cardinal had ever been chosen.

Although a conclave was not considered a political process, Cardinal Carducci disagreed. He intended to be the next pope to ensure the trend toward more conservative policies continued and to ensure his personal power became absolute. He had begun his campaign years earlier without truly anticipating the death of the pope. Carducci had simply pursued influence among the brethren he felt would eventually consolidate into a voting block if and when the time came.

This latest conclave began with the first four votes revealing a persistent block of votes in favor of Cardinal Carducci, although eighty separate names appeared on the ballots. Carducci was furious more of his colleagues had not joined the block. After all he had done for them. He had preserved the power of the elite and furthered conservative principles that protected the Church from radical ideas.

His fatal flaw revealed itself in the discussion of his candidacy between votes. Some advocated strongly on his behalf. Others objected strongly because of the methods he had used in furthering his goals and objectives. Apparently, some of his tactics in more delicate situations had become notorious—much to his chagrin. Secrets he had thought safely buried came to light, and the voting trend swiftly moved away from him. It was then Carducci chose to intensify his campaign with threats and intimidation. That ended badly for him. His supporters vanished into the stampede to safety.

The fifth vote revealed Carducci's support had evaporated, and no strong contender had emerged to replace him. Each vote after the fifth produced no consistent candidates, and despair of a lengthy process set in. The eleventh vote produced a small consensus among cardinals from the west. The cardinals from Asia, Africa, and South America were still not oriented at all, but the men from Europe and North America had, with few exceptions, settled on one candidate. After two more votes and much discussion, the trend solidified and became unanimous.

The next pontiff was Pope Leo XIV, formerly Cardinal Alvin Massey from the United States.

Massey's selection sent fear through the Carducci voting block and Carducci himself. Massey had been a consistent critic of Carducci and his policies and would likely take it upon himself to act on his objections.

Why Massey had chosen "Pope Leo" was a mystery to all. It seemed to signal his intention to be a staunch conservative and preservationist. Pope Leo X had been the supreme pontiff when the rogue priest, Martin Luther, had in 1517 published his ninety-five theses that had set the Roman Catholic Church on its ear, launching the Reformation. Pope Leo X had not reacted gently or kindly to the challenge. It was unclear whether Pope Leo XIV would continue the previous Leo's pattern or reveal something else.

The new pope shunned the pomp and ceremony of a formal coronation, choosing instead a private investiture ceremony. To the shock of his new staff, he showed up unannounced at his new quarters, carrying his own luggage.

CHAPTER 17

Waiting

Drago's four new friends were shocked by his news. The world too was shocked by the passing of the pope, but his death created all sorts of collateral considerations, for Drago and for Francis. Drago said he was not going to immediately respond to the summons back to Rome. He knew the reason for the summons was not to congratulate him on a job well done but to bury him and his work so it would never be discovered by the new pope's administration, whoever that might be. He felt he had a week or so to drag his feet before the summons became more urgent.

Francis was well aware of the process for selecting the next pontiff, and he explained the conclave to the group in some detail. It was an historic event, but for him, it could either be a blessing or a curse. He did not think his departure from Rome was well-known, and at the same time, of those who did know, few would know the real reason. He might be well-known for his book and its popularity among everyday believers, but he was unsure of his standing with his fellow clergymen. As with many things in this twenty-first century world, he suspected there was a polarization of opinion: some positive, some negative, most ambivalent.

While they waited, the five built community. Drago especially needed guidance and support during his time of upheaval. Acknowledging God created space for a new awareness of self and a new belief system that was not just self-gratification. If God existed and had made a place for Drago, then nothing could remain the same.

Drago asked Francis, "What about what happened to me when I was young and the pain it caused me? How could a loving God allow that to happen?"

Francis carefully replied, "That is an age-old question human beings have been asking for thousands of years. In our Western culture, we're immersed in the idea that sex, as a symbol of love, comfort, and pleasure, is the best thing and pain and death, as symbols of discomfort, tragedy, and suffering, are the worst things. Yet an objective analysis of human existence reveals that pain and tragedy form a big part of every person's life. Just the fact that we only live seventy to ninety years is tragic, and the fact that portions of most people's lives involve excruciating physical and emotion pain makes a short lifespan worse. However, a human life can also include tremendous love, contentment, peace, and joy. Every person's life is unique and can be strongly influenced by choices and circumstances."

Francis paused when Drago nodded in understanding. He hoped he could give Drago the answer he was looking for. "What can be said of God's responsibility for the lives of human beings is that he is not opposed to pain, suffering, and death. He does not prohibit these things just because we wish it. The only rational conclusion is that pain, suffering, and death should not be viewed entirely negatively, and we should not spend our lives in a futile attempt to avoid them."

Drago opened his mouth to interrupt, but Francis continued quickly, aware of Drago's opposition. "As an example, in Western countries, there is a crisis: addiction to pain medications. The discussion, relating to the vast number of addictions, revolves around drug company conspiracies and their insensitivity to addictions to their products. The discussion rarely involves the root cause: an overwhelming desire to avoid pain. Avoiding physical pain in a reasonable manner is not wrong. The unfortunate element is that people use substances that help them avoid physical and emotional pain. Emotional pain may never end, particularly if we choose to do everything we can to avoid it. Taking pain medications for emotional pain is a recipe for disaster. It creates hell on earth for addicts."

After a quick breath, Francis continued so Drago had no opportunity to argue. "In your case, Drago, the trauma you experienced as a child has caused you excruciating long-term emotional pain. The fact that you purposefully turned off your emotions as a coping mechanism isn't surprising. If you had turned to drugs, you undoubtedly would have become addicted because while your pain continued to exist, you would have had to continue taking the drugs at continually increasing doses. Instead, you buried your emotions in your work. To be what you chose to become required you to suspend empathy for your fellow man. The suspension of empathy only exacerbated your suffering because, in your soul, you knew what you were doing was wrong, and you created an unassailable wall between you and the rest of humanity."

Francis paused here to gauge Drago's reaction so far. While he had crossed his arms, either in self-defence or self-comfort, Francis did not know which, Drago had a thoughtful expression on his face. Encouraged, Father Francis continued. "You were doing to others what had been done to you, but your conscience did not turn off with your emotions. Your decisions as a young man, because of pain and suffering, led you to a life of more pain and suffering. I'm sorry you went through this, Drago, but now that your spirit has been awakened, you can make different choices, and over time, you can reap contentment, peace, and joy instead. Your spiritual reformation will not occur miraculously. There is no such thing as magic. You must still seek help and do the work, but if you persist, you will reap rewards. God promises peace and joy, but that promise doesn't assume that pain and suffering are absent. If we study the life of Jesus, we can see the balance between pain and suffering and peace and joy in action, and that is instructive for us. Jesus suffered greatly yet projected peace. The bottom line is that we should not be living our lives to maximize comfort and pleasure while trying to avoid pain and suffering. That notion is countercultural in North America and Europe."

Chloe, Jeff, and Rebecca had entered the room and overheard Francis' explanation, and each had questions.

Chole asked, "Francis, doesn't God want us to be happy and fulfilled? I've been successful in my career. I've earned money and been given comfort and pleasure. Is that wrong?"

"No, Chloe," replied Francis. "That is not wrong in itself, but if that is the main driver of our lives, we miss some key elements of a relationship with God that involve struggles. As I said, purposeful attempts to avoid pain and suffering in our lives can leave us unfulfilled and unhappy. Also, our attempts to avoid the struggles can lead us to do things of which we cannot be proud. You must analyze your experiences to date and decide how you wish to live from this day forward."

Chloe was immediately pensive because although her life had been successful by the world's standards, was she really happy and contented? She thought not.

Rebecca asked, "In my Church, there was an emphasis on God providing health and wealth. How does that fit with your understanding of pain and suffering?"

Francis had a ready answer for this question too. "In my study of theology, I had one principle I always applied to my conclusions. If I reached a general conclusion that did not seem to apply to all human beings, I considered the conclusion to be false. So, if I were to separate certain scriptures from the whole, I might conclude that if we tried to be the best people we could be against an ideal, then God would bless us with safety, riches, and excellent health. But two things are wrong with this theology. First, it only works in rich countries with vast, diverse economies that reward people for their efforts. In most African economies, for example, there is insufficient breadth and scope to reward many, no matter how hard they may work and how good they are. If a principle doesn't work in Africa, to me, it must be false. The second error, which is somewhat insidious, is that God will reward us for the level of our performance against an ideal. God does not have an ideal standard to which we must judge ourselves or be judged by others. He does not require performance in return for his blessing. Trying to live up to an ideal standard is a trap because all standards are subjective, and we, or others, will change them over time. Further, we do not have perfect understanding of God, and His blessings may not even seem like blessings to us."

Rebecca replied, shifting uncomfortably in her chair, "I agree with you, and one other insidious feature of this theology is that if you weren't healthy and wealthy, people would think there was something wrong with you. They would ask sick people what sin they had in their lives that was disrupting God's blessing of health. That attitude would cause untold pain and suffering to those with illness or disabilities. It would also create an 'us' and 'them' distinction, which is terrible." After several minutes of silence, she said sadly, "Even a failed marriage could become a reason to be shunned."

Francis reached for his water glass, took a much-needed sip after all this discussion, and replied, "What you just described is an easy trap to fall into in rich countries where people don't have effective healthcare systems and don't experience scorching poverty. Even the poorest people in rich countries often enjoy a relatively high level of health and wealth when compared with the poorest people in the poorest countries, but it's not God driving this phenomenon, nor is it God creating the disparity."

Jeff had a burning question that he had struggled with for a long time. "Francis, how much of our relationship with God is circumstantial? It seems to me God deals with us as individuals, not as groups. In the Old Testament, God seemed to favor Israel. Is the institutional Church Israel, and does God only have relationships with people through the institutional Church? I see my question as a follow-up to the questions on blessing and pain and suffering. I also think it relates to Drago's life."

Francis sat quietly, thinking, realizing these four friends were reflecting the issues so many believers struggled with, and he was so grateful he could at least shed some light on the subject from his own research and experiences. He felt a keen responsibility to answer honestly and transparently.

"Jeff, your question indeed relates to all we've discussed this morning. In God's economy, He has a single denomination: one. As you know from reading my book, I've taken issue with many characteristics of the Roman Catholic Church. The Roman Catholic Church organized itself over the centuries, in many respects, to resemble the Old Testament nation of Israel. The Protestant denominations have followed the leader. My conclusion is that in doing so, they missed the concept that God sent Jesus to reduce nations into individuals. If we thoughtfully read the Old Testament, one glaring concept is the failure of the nation of Israel to consistently relate well to God. Many of the reasons for those failures now repeat in modern institutional Church organizations, both Catholic and Protestant, because the institutional character of these organizations, to be successful and achieve longevity, must teach that they are the only path to God. If instead, God is really interacting with individual human beings, then that should change our view of the world and our institutions. Forgive me Drago, but may I use you as an example?"

Drago nodded.

"If we look at Drago through the eyes of an institution, we wouldn't see him at all. He would be invisible in his suffering, as a sinner. He would not be a person our institutions would look to as a valuable asset, someone with whom they could build the institution."

Feeling better about the direction of the conversation now, Francis paused. But then he saw some confusion in the eyes of his friends, so he elaborated. "In the Gospel of John, Chapter 8, Jesus commented on this tendency in the Pharisees of his day when they brought a woman caught in adultery to him. The Pharisees brought the woman to Jesus so he would be trapped in a conundrum between sin and forgiveness. Would he free her or condemn her? They hoped he would be wrong either way. She had sinned, and according to the Pharisees' view of the world, she should be stoned to death. Instead of falling victim to the conundrum, Jesus treated everyone involved in the incident as a valuable individual. The Pharisees represented an institution, but Jesus saw each of them as individuals worthy of his attention and help. Jesus also saw the woman, not as a political pawn, but as a valuable human being worthy of life. He spoke of renewal and healing to the woman and suggested each Pharisee, free of sin, should cast the first stone. The Pharisees were individually offered an opportunity to evaluate their own standing with God. God seemed to respond to each of them and they quietly dispersed."

Rebecca and Chloe looked at each other as they processed Francis' words, and Jeff crossed his arms and raised his head, encouraging Francis to continue.

And so he did. "If we apply these principles to Drago, what is the result? According to the religious institutions of our day, Drago undoubtedly would be condemned for how he has lived his life. If we take the approach Jesus modeled, we see Drago as an incredible human being of substantial value and potential, who, through war and loss, was defined, trained, and used as a tool of war. Even after the war was over, his self-definition and vocation remained, and he traveled down the path of least resistance. However, God has intervened, and he is on a new road. We have all seen in Drago the miracle of rebirth. A process of redefinition and internal remodeling will happen over time, but the process has begun, and we must rejoice in that."

Francis turned to face Drago. "Welcome to a new life, Drago. As the woman caught in adultery was given a second chance, you have been given a second chance because you are valuable to God. You are also valuable to us." At Drago's almost imperceptible nod, he turned to the others and continued. "Drago cannot develop spiritually on his own. He needs familial relationships. We can all provide those, for his benefit and for our own."

At that, the other three went to Drago and each put a hand on his shoulder in turn, vowing to be there for him. Drago could find no words to respond, but his eyes were suspiciously misty.

+ + +

Later, after more discussion punctuated by a brief lunch, Rebecca asked, "Do you know Cardinal Massey, or should I say, Pope Leo, Francis?"

"Yes, Rebecca, very well. He is the man who facilitated my coming to America. His elevation to supreme pontiff is an answer to my prayers. I never thought it possible that an American cardinal could ever become pope, especially after all the controversy surrounding the American Church and the resignation of one of his American colleagues after allegations of sexual misconduct. I was afraid it would be another man, the man who sent Drago."

"What will you do, Francis?" asked Chloe, reverting to Italian out of habit.

"I don't know. I guess I'll wait. Cardinal Massey gave me a phone and said he would contact me. I have not heard from him since I left Rome, but perhaps I will now." Francis answered Chloe in Italian but then repeated himself so Jeff and Rebecca would understand.

"I think we should go for dinner and celebrate," said Jeff.

"What will we celebrate?" asked Drago.

"We have a lot to celebrate," said Rebecca and Chloe in unison. Everyone laughed at that.

+ + +

After the investiture, the new pope's life was a whirlwind of ceremonies and meetings. As Cardinal Massey, he had had all sorts of time for contemplation and study. His new life seemed brimming with things to do and people to see. His life was no longer his own. Apparently, people expected great things from him, and unfortunately, his election had caught him by surprise, so he was rather unprepared. Through no conscious planning, or even effort, his name had meteorically risen to the top of the balloting after Carducci's campaign had faltered and died.

It seemed his cardinal colleagues considered him a candidate of the masses, someone to unite the fractious leadership and steer the Church in a new direction. Pope Leo knew the direction he wanted to go, but he had no workable plan to bring the clergy and the people along with him. Following the example of our Lord, he decided he would start with a small cadre of good people and work from there.

His first task, though, was to quell the uprising Carducci was leading to bury him so deep in bureaucracy nothing meaningful could be done. Carducci had lost the election to become pope but had elected himself leader of the opposition. Pope Leo had heard from trusted sources that Carducci thought it inappropriate for the conclave to elect an American. Carducci's view was that at this important and tumultuous juncture, an Italian pope was required to steady the ship. He had told any who would listen that if an Italian could not be pope, then the pope would not be pope. In the position of Prefect of the Doctrine of the Congregation of the Faith, Carducci influenced a massive organization that could make the new pope's authority disappear into a maze of protocol and procedure.

Any ambition to change direction would require extraordinary patience and longevity. At seventy-six years of age, Pope Leo could not expect sufficient longevity to produce the change he felt was required. Longevity of change would require several generations, which meant younger, effective leadership willing to make meaningful reforms was required so the Catholic Church reflected the culture of the twenty-first century and returned to relevancy. Hopeless it was perhaps, but he would give it a shot. He would launch the Third Vatican Council.

He needed Father Francis Bauer at his side to have a chance. How could that be done? Pope Leo had chosen his name because his predecessor, Pope Leo X, had had to contend with Martin Luther, the reformer. Father Bauer was a Martin Luther, and the current Pope Leo wanted a Martin Luther on his team, not in opposition. Francis' book had launched an ideas reform, and now those ideas must be given wings.

He reached for his book of contacts and found the number.

+ + +

Chloe came across Drago in Jeff's living room and approached hesitantly with a question. Taking a seat on the couch opposite him, she asked, "Drago, what happened to you while you were telling us the story of your life? It seemed like you were speaking to us but were somewhere else at the same time."

"Well, I felt I was reliving much of my life while telling my story. I was telling you all the story, but at the same time, I was confessing my story to God. I was raised in the Orthodox Church and learned about the Heavenly Father and Jesus, but after my family was killed, I had no faith. Any faith I might have had as a child died with them. Then when Francis prayed, he either reintroduced me to the knowledge I must have carried within me, or he lent me his faith so I could acknowledge God myself. Before that moment, I had never told my story to anyone. I was proud of who I was and had nothing but disdain for those weaker than me. And yet when Francis prayed, I felt accepted by him and by God. That was the first time since I'd lost my family that I felt accepted for me instead of for my military skills."

Drago looked thoughtful and paused, so Chloe remained silent and waited until he was ready to continue. Moments later, he added, "At each event in my story, I again felt the feelings I felt at the time. I did terrible things in the army and then after, as a mercenary. I caused death and suffering. All those wrongs flooded me with guilt and shame. I knew they were wrong. But then I felt released. Well, released may not be the right word, but I felt cleaner and softer where I had always felt dirty and hard. It's hard to explain." Shaking his head, he looked at her and continued, "It appeared you had a similar experience as well?"

"Yes," said Chloe, sitting quietly with her hands between her knees. "I was raised a Catholic in a strict home. We went to Mass all the time. I felt as a child that I was living my life in the Church. I felt cramped and sheltered. As you did, I learned about God and Jesus and the Holy Spirit, but my experience as a child didn't make the learning tangible. When I left home, I also left the Church. I felt relieved not to be forced to conform. Deep down, I knew the truth, but I hadn't personally accepted it. I was part of a Catholic family, so I was Catholic, but I didn't have my own faith. My family had faith, so I went along with that."

Chloe stopped and sighed before continuing. "Then I heard your story, and I heard Francis pray. He prayed as if he knew Christ and Christ knew him and as if Jesus cared for him and he cared for Jesus. It all came crashing down on me. You know I'm a model. I too felt hardened and dirty from my life. I agreed to do things I felt were wrong to push my career forward. I used my body as a tool. Other people also used that tool. Like you, I felt something happen deep in me when Francis prayed. I was able to acknowledge that I was not the person I should want to be. I felt shame then, but the shame gave way to peace. At that moment, I desperately wanted God to be real to me."

Chloe rose and turned to go, but then turned back. "Drago, thank you for talking to me about this. Perhaps we are now travelers on the same road."

"Chloe, I should be the one thanking you. How could you not hate me for threatening you? I feel so bad about that. Would you be able to forgive me?"

"I will forgive you, but I can't trust you yet."

"I accept that," said Drago, though he hoped that would change in time.

CHAPTER 18

A Call

During the group's celebratory dinner, the cellphone that had never rung, rang. Francis was startled to attention. The four companions stared at him as he answered.

Not knowing what to say, he said simply, "Hello?"

"Francis, I had hoped you were still carrying the phone I gave you."

"Yes, Your Holiness, I have carried it always, as you requested."

"Francis, I need your help. I need a Martin Luther, and you seem to be the best candidate for the job. Further, I want my Martin Luther to be *on* the team, not *off* the team. Will you come? And call me Alvin."

"Your Holiness, I will, of course I will come. I am at your service, but I have one request."

"What is your request, Francis? And call me Alvin, please. It's a new day."

"Your Holiness, perhaps one day I will be able to call you by your given name. My request is that you assign a man named Drago Milanovic to me. Cardinal Carducci employs him at present. He is someone I was introduced to, indirectly, by the cardinal and now needs discipleship. I will explain further when we first meet."

ABOUT THE AUTHOR

As a lawyer and former pastor, Graham Baugh has worked for, professionally consulted with, and attended churches around the world for almost forty years, and like his protagonist, has a lively and wholesome faith even though he has been separated from institutional Christianity.

His experiences with faith, and the Church as an organization, have both inspired —*The Broken Cross*—and solidified for him the need for serious conversations about purpose and paradigm as it relates to Christian religion.

He currently lives in Calgary with his spouse, Melody. His children and their families live nearby.

Printed in Canada